ASH and BONES

Mike Thomas was born in Wales in 1971. For more than two decades he served in the police, working some of Cardiff's busiest neighbourhoods. He left the force in 2015 to write full-time.

Mike has previously had two novels published, was longlisted for the Wales Book of the Year and was on the list of Waterstones 'New Voices'. His second novel, *Ugly Bus*, is currently in development for a six-part series with the BBC.

He lives in the wilds of Portugal with his wife, children and a senile dog who enjoys eating furniture.

Also by Mike Thomas

Pocket Notebook
Ugly Bus

MIKE THOMAS

ASH and BONES

ZAFFRE

First published in Great Britain in 2016 by

ZAFFRE PUBLISHING
80–81 Wimpole St, London W1G 9RE
www.zaffrebooks.co.uk

A CIP catalogue record for this book is available from the British Library.

ISBN: 978-1-7857-6062-4

Also available as an ebook

1 3 5 7 9 10 8 6 4 2

Typeset by IDSUK (Data Connection) Ltd

Printed and bound by Clays Ltd, St Ives Plc

Zaffre Publishing is an imprint of Bonnier Zaffre,
a Bonnier Publishing company
www.bonnierzaffre.co.uk
www.bonnierpublishing.co.uk

For Ma 'n' Pa
And for Monk and our monkeys

Beyond this place of wrath and tears
  Looms but the Horror of the shade

Invictus, William Ernest Henley

Part 1

Clusterfuck

Ebute-Metta district,
Lagos, Nigeria

Dusk fell as the old yellow taxi rattled off the Third Mainland Bridge. From the rear seat, Chike watched the sun caress the ragged skyline of duplexes and dilapidated colonial buildings, its fading light turning the wooden shacks at the shoreline the colour of rust. Like the lagoon that fell away behind him, he was restless, and in a darkened mood.

He was thinking about the orphanage. And the papers.

And beyond that, food. Chike was hungry, the trip having taken longer than expected, the tailback on the bridge a good one today. A crash just south of Olususun, the overturned refuse lorry adding to the usual chaos as commuters fled the business district for their homes. His stomach griped, loud and bubbling, audible over the rumble of the taxi's engine. Once things were done he would get the driver to travel along Herbert Macauley Road. Pick up some pomo and sweet potato pottage from his favourite street vendor. Remember his childhood as he scooped it to his lips.

The thought made him glance out of the half-open window, down at the sprawling shanty town beneath the interchange. The smoke pyres, the shadowy figures hustling and bustling in the dying embers of daylight. Scavenging. Bartering. Arguing over scrap metal and broken transistor radios and soiled clothing.

Not for him, that life. Not anymore.

The taxi dropped down from the flyover, the driver humming to himself as they chugged through the traffic on Clinic Road, skirted left into Okobaba Street, then the crowded heart of Ebute-Metta. The roar of diesel engines. Music. Voices. People everywhere. The stench of the sawmill drifting on humid evening air. The September rains would be here soon. Chike could feel it in his bones.

He closed the taxi window. Another smell hit him, and he looked down at the boy sitting beside him. His filthy clothes. His deep black eyes darting about, terrified.

'All will be fine now,' Chike said, making sure he spoke in Yoruba. The boy had no grasp of Brokin, never mind English, and there was a simple, innocent air about him; Chike wondered how on earth the kid had survived for so long working and living at the dump.

The boy looked up at him, those eyes glittering in the darkness. Chike slipped his thick fingers around the boy's hand.

Squeezed.

A hand-painted sign, faded from Harmattan desert winds, hung lopsidedly from one pillar:

Baobab Tree House

Chike nodded to himself, pleased he'd found the place before the side streets – devoid of lighting – were swamped by the night; the useless taxi driver didn't possess a Sat Nav, and had relied on the directions Chike had memorised. He thrust a hundred-naira note into the driver's palm and asked him to wait. Was climbing out of the taxi when the orphanage gates swung open, hinges protesting.

He beckoned to the boy. Smiling. 'Wásúnmôdödé.'

Come.

The boy, silent, remained where he was sitting.

Chike glanced over a shoulder at the open gates. Saw the silhouette. The flare of a match in the twilight. Cupped hands lifting it to lips that gripped a cigarillo. The face of a white man, dark hair cropped and spiked. Eyes on Chike and the boy.

'Come,' *said Chike, taking the boy by the arm.*

The boy shook his head. 'Rárá. Rárá.'

No.

Chike pulled, harder this time. He was ravenous now. Sweating, in the heat. Wanted this over with. Wanted the finest street food his money could buy.

The boy, still protesting, flopped out of the taxi, dust puffing outwards where his knees hit the floor. Chike eased him up, placed a meaty arm around his bony shoulders, guided him through the open gates and into a small courtyard. The boy whimpered as the gates squealed closed electronically.

From one murky corner, the white man watched them over the glow of his cigarillo.

'So you found us.'

The pastor was an overweight man in an expensive-looking suit, the coffee-coloured skin of his neck straining at the collar of his shirt. His face was bulbous and slick with sweat, despite the air conditioning in the office, which Chike sensed had been turned up to maximum, and which was now making him shiver. Behind the pastor sat a woman who was of similar build, her pendulous breasts resting on the edge of a desk. She peered at a sheaf of papers, hair curled and greying and shimmering under the fluorescent light affixed to the ceiling. Music played from somewhere, faint yet melodic; Chike recognised it from his youth, from Sunday mornings spent in the village chapel.

He tried not to look at the miniature spare tyre beneath the pastor's chin as they spoke, using English so the boy would not be spooked further. 'I am sorry we are so late, but the taxi dri—'

'You are here and that is good,' the pastor smiled, cutting him off. He looked down at the boy, huddled against the arm of Chike's tatty shirt. 'So who is this fine young man?'

Chike gave the boy a gentle nudge. 'This is Bepeh. He is twelve.'

'Bepeh,' said the pastor, extending a hand. In Yoruba: 'Very pleased to meet you, Bepeh.'

The boy lowered his head, hands staying at his sides.

The pastor chuckled, and the fat woman at the desk chuckled, so Chike chuckled too.

'He'll be fine,' said the pastor, switching back to English. 'We have so many like this when they first come to us. But all will be well. What is your relationship with the boy?'

Chike stopped chuckling. 'I am his . . . uncle?' He hadn't thought of this.

The pastor sighed. 'And does Bepeh have another name?'

'Another name?'

'A family name. You are his uncle, yes?'

'Oh, yes. His parents, they are both gone, pastor. The virus.'

'The virus.'

'Yes. It was terrible. Very bad. Very bad for the boy. His heart is broken. My own heart, it is cracked and I fear it will never mend.'

'A tragedy, I am sure,' said the pastor. 'And what of his papers?'

Chike had been dreading this moment. 'He . . . he has none, I am afraid.'

The pastor swapped glances with the woman at the desk. 'Do not worry. We will make sure everything runs smoothly.'

After a moment the woman pushed the chair backwards, the linoleum floor squeaking, and eased her tubby backside off the seat. Walked over to the boy, a soft smile on her mouth, in her eyes. Raised a hand to his face, and as he drew away gently brushed her fingertips along his jaw line.

'Bepeh,' she said in Yoruba, squatting down to look him in the eyes. 'My boy. You must come with me now.' Her fingers worked their way into the knots of his hair. 'You shall eat, and bathe, and sleep in a fine bed, yes?'

The boy's chest rose and fell, his eyes downcast. A minute passed, then he looked up at the woman, then at Chike. Back to the woman. Slowly, he laid his head on her shoulder, collapsing into her embrace.

Chike watched as she led him through a door, and out of sight.

The sticky night air was a welcome relief from the icy temperature of the office. Chike heard jùjú drumming and hip-hop beats, smelled the street vendors' foods. His stomach lurched. From his elevated position atop the orphanage steps he could just make out the driver's feet sticking out of the taxi window. The man had fallen asleep in his seat.

'You have done a great and useful thing,' said the pastor.

Chike paused. Turned to him. 'I just hope it helps in some way.'

The pastor placed a hand on Chike's upper arm. 'It always helps.'

Chike nodded. Waited.

'And so,' said the pastor, exhaling. He reached into a jacket pocket. Withdrew an envelope.

Handed it to Chike.

Chike took it, checked the contents. Stared at the pastor.

'I was told it would be one hundred and fifty thousand naira.'

The pastor smiled patiently. 'It is one hundred thousand.'

'I would get more for selling a cow at the cattle market,' Chike barked, tapping the envelope with the nails of his free hand.

'If you want to try your luck at Olewonashana, then do so,' said the pastor. 'But the slaughter slabs are not for the faint of heart.'

Chike shook his head. 'The deal is for one hundred and fifty.'

'One hundred and fifty with papers,' the pastor smiled. 'He has no papers. This makes things difficult for us.'

'So give me one twenty.'

The pastor looked out into the darkness of the courtyard, impassive. 'You can always discuss it with my business associate, if you believe it will help your cause.'

Chike followed his gaze. Saw the red dot in the gloom. The glow of the cigarillo in the shadows. The white man.

Thought about Baobab Tree House. What he'd heard. The rumours.

He looked at the envelope he held in his hands.

Felt the hollowness in his stomach. Soon to be filled, thankfully, with food.

Chike looked up at the pastor. 'One hundred is fine.'

The pastor grinned, lips wet and shiny. 'God smiles on you, my child.'

'For this,' Chike said, 'I doubt he's smiling on either of us.'

1

Light on.

Garratt held the phone for a moment, blinking at it, his face illuminated in the darkness by the glow from the tiny screen.

Finally.

'Good news?' asked Masters.

He looked up and smirked. 'Somebody's home.'

Masters slapped him on the upper arm. 'Then let's go.'

Barclay, a disembodied voice from the gloom to his left: 'Fuckin' right. Let's do him.'

He gave another nod, grinning now despite the tiredness. Eyed the text message again. Shoved the phone into his pocket, plunging them into grey half-light. Stretched, the five hours not going away easily, his bones clicking and popping in wrists and elbows and knees. His mouth dirty with stale air. A knot in the pit of his belly at the thought of more hours stretching ahead if this went right.

Through the one-way glass of the window: Butetown. The estate was washed in muted orange: a hive of concrete walkways and dank, moss-swamped alleys, of drab maisonettes, of council money pissed away on regeneration after regeneration for people who, as far as he was concerned, deserved none of it. Graffiti on shop shutters, shatterproof bus stop glass shattered and glittering in gutters. The tired rectangular monolith of Loudoun House. Beyond its glassy flanks, the Millennium Stadium's spires scraped the early-morning sky.

'Don't forget the Big Red Key,' he said.

'Yeah,' Masters grunted with the effort, his shoulders working as he hoisted it to his chest. 'Game faces on.'

Barclay pushed himself up from the wooden bench, his gangly shape appearing next to Masters. 'Fuckin' right,' he repeated. 'Let's do him.'

Garratt looked from Masters to Barclay, their faces slick from the trapped-in-a-tin-can heat, their eyes wide and bright from the adrenaline. 'Hard and fast, remember?' he urged.

'Hard and fast,' they replied in unison.

His fist slammed down on the handle and he kicked open the transit van doors. Cool September breeze pinched his cheeks and just for a second, standing there on the metal lip of the doorway, he revelled in it, glad to be out of there at last, to be doing something.

He felt a nudge in his back, heard Barclay in his ear: 'Get a fuckin' move on, Bob.'

His trainers scuffed on tarmac as he jumped down. Sprinted, his fists punching air, eyes quick-panning back and forth: no shapes lurking in doorways, no curtains twitching. Above the thump of his own heart he heard Masters and Barclay behind him, their breaths ragged, their heavy footfalls slapping on concrete cobbles as they made it to the pavement.

The Hodges Square maisonettes hunkered ahead of them, a complex of pebbledash and drab orange brickwork, of fenced-off weeds masquerading as gardens. There was a light on in one ground-floor window. It had taken them ten seconds, tops, to cross the courtyard from the back of the van to the front door.

'Just shitty R 'n' B,' Barclay said, ear placed to white UPVC.

'I'll cover the back,' Garratt said, nodding to the alleyway.

Masters and Barclay swapped glances.

He shrugged. 'You'll be fine. Remember the layout. Kitchen's on this side . . .'

'Yeah,' Masters said. 'Damn back-to-front flats.'

He gestured to the Big Red Key in Masters' hands. 'So do it.'

He bolted into the alleyway, was halfway down when he heard the bang.

Wakey wakey, everyone.

The rear garden was as shitty as he'd expected: overgrown, uneven lawn liberally peppered with debris and split bin bags. A solitary car tyre. Wood fencing, rotten and faded. A pathetic six-slab patio swamped with nettle and bindweed.

He snuck across it. Edged nearer the French doors.

Waited. Listened. Heard raised yet muffled voices. A gamble, going it alone like this. Always was. But it always worked. He smiled as he pictured it: front door fucked, Masters and Barclay barrelling in there, Leon King shitting himself, pleading, trying to run for it, making for the back of the maisonette, bursting through the French doors.

Straight into his arms. *Sweet.*

And then he heard the noise. Another bang, the timbre different to when they put the door in. Louder. Duller.

He swallowed. Reached for his mobile phone, his fingertips brushing the casing as he weighed up the odds. Call it in, just in case the wheel had come off inside? Or wait it out for a few minutes, let Masters and Barclay do their thing, then take the glory?

He peered through the French doors, could only see a few feet into the darkened room. 'Come on, guys,' he breathed. 'Come o—'

A third bang. Like a firework.

Like a gunshot.

There was a scream from inside the maisonette.

He pulled the phone from his pocket, fingers heavy and fumbling. Saw movement, a figure advancing towards the French doors. Towards him. He backed away, couldn't see if it was Masters, if it was Barclay. He jabbed at the keypad, speed-dialled Hooper.

'You got him?' Hooper's voice in his ear.

'I think we might have a problem,' he breathed, turning away. Eyes wide, searching for some place to hide. For cover. For an exit. So he could think. Take stock. Work out what just happened.

There was a hiss of static down the line, Hooper's voice crackling: 'What sort of prob—'

Then: a ringing in his skull. A metallic stink in his nostrils.

His only thought: *I'm in trouble here.*

He pictured his wife. His daughter.

Saw the open French doors. The pistol muzzle, smoking.

Felt the patio stone, cold and hard against his cheek.

2

He felt the pillow, hot and uncomfortable against his cheek.

MacReady shifted onto his back. The quilt, twisted and heavy with his night sweats; he pushed it down and away from his neck, his chest, relished the cool morning air that settled around his torso. The plantation shutters leaked bright light into the lounge and he squinted, looking around.

He'd never had – needed – a so-called Man Cave, but the room was slowly morphing into one. Settee for a bed. Used cups and half-read books and items of his clothing. DVDs and empty takeaway cartons and a ten-year-old washbag, pitiful with its fudged bar of soap and lone stick of deodorant, perched on a shelf above a television he'd forgotten to turn off before falling asleep the night before. Twenty-four-hour BBC News on the screen, sound muted, tickertape scrolling its breaking story about yet another murder in the city. It was just gone six thirty in the morning; he'd set the alarm on his phone for six forty-five, knowing as he'd swiped and tapped the screen he would wake before it sounded.

He rubbed at his eyes and stretched. Heard his wife move about upstairs, Megan's light footsteps padding from bathroom to bedroom and back again: her routine, the one he used to look forward to when he came off night shifts, where he'd lie in their bed, tired eyes watching her slink from room to room, getting ready for a day where he'd sleep while she worked.

MacReady closed his eyes.

Thought: *when did it come to this?*

Opened his eyes. Glanced around the lounge again.

Said: '*How* did it come to this, Will?'

He knew the answer, though. He recalled the previous night. Trying again, both of them. Just as they had been for months. Couple of glasses of white, a nice meal, an effort to paper over cracks. An exercise in denial. The tension there and growing more unbearable as the evening wore on. He'd known what was coming. What she wanted. Where the drink would lead. So they'd fumbled around and he'd gone with it and then he couldn't and she'd cooed and whispered in his ear and said and done the right things. But it hadn't been enough. And he'd rolled away, ashamed. And nothing she'd said had made it better. And then the conversation had once again turned to doctors, to more costly treatment, to adoption, even to sperm donors, and at that point – seeing how far she was willing to go, her desperation for a family – he'd gone numb, tuned her out. Slipped out of their bed and walked away, feeling her eyes on him as he went.

Returned to the lounge – his room, now – and lay there, unable to sleep, hating himself. Hating how he couldn't perform at home. Worrying if it would be the same in the morning at work with a crowd of new, demanding faces.

His first day on CID.

MacReady heard Megan's footsteps on the stairs. Spun onto his side. Pulled the quilt up to his chin. Closed his eyes as the lounge door opened. Slowed his breathing.

Heard Megan's slow breaths from the doorway. Wondered what she was thinking. Wondered if she would speak. If she would try again to make it better. Or if she had finally had enough.

Then the door closed quietly and she was gone.

You gutless coward. Pretending to be asleep just so you didn't have to face her.

MacReady opened his eyes.

On the tickertape: breaking news.

The murder victim.

It was a police officer.

MacReady threw back the quilt. Checked his mobile. Saw the text:

We need you in work immediately.

'Shit', he croaked, and climbed off the settee.

So this was the Bob Garratt he'd heard so much about.

Seven years' service and a high flyer. Already a stripey on the divisional Volume Crime Team, where they were putting in doors across the capital on an almost daily basis. Already being groomed for greater things. Garratt was job pissed and mad for it, even if it was locking someone up for an eighth of 'nabis and bald tyres on their motor. *Proactive*, or so it went, the copper's euphemism: a busy boy who got results whereby the ends justified the means. Where the bosses turned a blind eye as long as he brought in the bodies. And if there were no bodies, then at least two dozen boiler burglary TICs sucked up by an already-over-the-wall lag in exchange for a bag of burn during a prison visit. As long as Detective Sergeant Robert Garratt cleared up those pesky crime figures. As long as he met those precious Home Office targets.

It was the first time MacReady had met Garratt, and Garratt was dead.

The flap of the CSI tent wafted lazily on the morning breeze, and MacReady kept catching glimpses of Garratt: on his back, head tilted towards MacReady, his fingers clamped around a mobile phone. There was a half-centimetre hole in the skin above his right eye. The right side of his grey face was frozen in a confused expression; the lower portion of the other side was dis-tended and deformed around the cheek and jaw, an ugly sight, the bullet doing its worst as it rattled around inside.

Harrison clucked his tongue. Said, 'What a bloody mess, mun.' Comical in his sandals and bright white socks, a fifty-something Valleys couldn't-give-a-fuck who stank of fag ash and fried food.

MacReady said nothing. Nodded and checked his watch. It was nine thirty, the sun hanging low and bright, the NPAS chop-per a buzzing silhouette on the horizon. Ambo and fire trucks with wheels on pavements. Police vans blocking police cars blocking civvy vehicles on their hardstands. MOPs gawking from windows, from the cordon tape, camera phones aloft. The *meeja* with their satellite trucks and microphones, their hungry eyes and vicious mouths. Frustrated firearms crews with nothing to aim their Hecklers at. Top brass everywhere, more pips and shoulder spaghetti than he'd ever seen in one place before. They milled around in their uniforms, clueless, pointless, sucking on fresh air for the first time in an age.

'Inside?' MacReady asked.

'Same.' Harrison wiped at his lips with thumb and forefinger. His breakfast rushed, coffee and sandwiches wolfed down after the phone calls to get them into work soonest, the remnants in the jowly corners of his mouth. He'd moaned about it all the way over here; it was the first time they'd met and he was already getting on MacReady's nerves.

Techies drifted in and out of the garden, all suitcases, boxes, booties and coveralls. One of them dusted for latents on the glass of the French doors. A row of crawling uniforms PolSA searched the wild lawn, a line of rubberised soles and upturned arseholes in long, knotted grass. A German Shepherd barked and snapped, going batshit crazy. Its handler wrestled with a lead of frayed rope and linked metal, cursing under her breath. MacReady knew her from old, and nodded an acknowledgement.

'Cadaver trained.' Harrison tilted his head at the dog. 'Can smell Garratt.'

'Right,' said MacReady, and watched a man duck under police tape; it took a moment to recognise him from other scenes, when MacReady had been in uniform and freezing on a rainswept cordon. The Home Office pathologist. Bespectacled, reed thin. An old smoothy, sixty-something and blasé to the point of ignorance. MacReady couldn't recall his name but had already learned not to care. 'Garratt's people?'

'You can interview one of them.'

'Are they in any fit state?'

Harrison shrugged. *Job to do.*

A gust of wind and the tent flap fell closed. MacReady said a silent farewell to Garratt and followed Harrison up the alleyway.

More techies were in the process of opening up a Forensic Response Vehicle in the courtyard: a mobile smorgasbord of evidence bags and tents and babygros, of drawers and cupboards full of potions and powders MacReady couldn't begin to understand. Across the tarmac Garratt's men huddled together at the side of their decrepit surveillance van, a clutch of pale faces, their low voices drowned by the generator belching at the back of the FRV. Like everybody on scene their shock was yet to give way to raw fury. One of them rubbed at his eyes, chest hitching, struggling to keep it in. His colleagues placed reassuring hands on his shoulders. MacReady saw the bright red enforcer ram on the concrete between the man's feet.

Trumpton had placed screens around the maisonette entrance. For prying eyes, MacReady knew, but it blocked their way. Harrison shoved one aside, created a gap for them to slip through.

'They're there for a reason,' one of the water fairies pouted. 'For God's sake.'

Harrison moved it another foot or so. Smiled. Humourless. Said: 'God created police officers so firefighters could have heroes too.'

MacReady gnawed at his bottom lip.

The maisonette's front door was ruined, a mess of buckled UPVC, the handle hanging by a lone screw, the hallway beyond littered with pieces of white plastic. A uniform stood at the open doorway, crime scene log gripped in one gloved hand. Thin-lipped, angry at the loss of one of his own.

Harrison paused in front of the plod. 'DI in there?'

'Who's asking?'

Harrison bristled. 'I'm asking.'

MacReady between them. 'We're all on the same side here, guys.'

'Fucking woollies,' muttered Harrison.

'DC Warren Harrison, DC Will MacReady,' said MacReady.

'*Trainee* Detective Constable MacReady,' Harrison said.

The uniform sniffed. Scribbled on the log. Waited a beat, just because. 'Fine.'

Harrison ignored him. To MacReady: 'After you, boy.'

The kitchen was poky and grim, the muted sunlight from a small window bolstered marginally by a foot-long strip light flickering above an Ikea pine table. Cheap wood-effect cupboards lined the far wall with a filthy four-burner range cooker sat beneath them. The sink festered with food-stained dishes, its water the colour of ash, the air around MacReady and Harrison thick with grease and cannabis and the bitter tang of iron.

To MacReady's left, another door leading to the rest of the maisonette. Through it he could see more CSI working the lounge: a chorus of digital camera clicks, video arc lights throwing shapes onto walls, clear plastic bags tagged and filled with stolen electrical equipment, with paperwork, with DVDs and CD cases and a typically tiny lump of personal blow.

Towels and gauze pads were spread across the linoleum floor, left behind by the paramedics. Sopping and red and not enough to soak up the blood swiped and streaked everywhere – crimson dots and impact spatter speckled worktops, cupboard doors, the shabby net curtain diffusing light at the window.

Harrison belched. 'Should've skipped the sausage sandwich this morning.'

Food again. Always seemed to be food with Harrison. Mac-Ready glanced at him, found him staring at the table. Looked. Saw forensic numerical markers next to a pub ashtray with its thick, half-smoked doobie and new paint job.

'Lots of blood there,' MacReady said.

A voice from the lounge doorway: 'One shot took his finger and thumb off.'

MacReady turned, saw the figure in a black trench coat, tie loose, top button undone. Buzzcut brushing the frame of the lounge doorway. Olive-skinned face bloated, as if he was hung over, or just exhausted before the day had even begun.

MacReady looked back at the ashtray. 'Leon King?'

The man's eyes narrowed. 'Unless one of Garratt's people has lost a coupla pinkies and not noticed it yet.'

'Jesus.'

'That bastard won't help us, son.' The man turned to Harrison. 'You rounded up the witnesses yet, Wazza?'

'Just about to,' Harrison said. 'Showing the newbie around first. This is Will MacReady. Our new beck and call boy. Willy, this is Detective Inspector Danny Fletcher.'

MacReady proffered a hand.

Fletcher eyed him as he shook. 'Want to be CID, right? Solve all dem big crimes and get your name in the papers?'

'Just want to learn, sir,' MacReady replied. He smiled as he said it, but felt unnerved by Fletcher's dead eyes on him, and the rough hand that pumped away at his.

'Well, your first lesson,' Fletcher said, and dropped MacReady's hand, 'is that you're trampling through here and contaminating my fucking crime scene. So be gone, both of you.'

Harrison hesitated. 'Anything?'

Fletcher exhaled. 'Shooter fired from here,' pointing out from the doorway, 'when the Volume Crime boys came in to lift King. Two shots. One through King's hand, one into his chest. Then he gave it toes and bumped into that idiot in the garden. Put one in his swede before legging it into the jungle.'

MacReady closed his eyes. Pictured Garratt. 'I don't understand.'

'You don't understand because you don't know anything,' Harrison grunted.

'Why no ARV, though? Why no support?' MacReady turned to Fletcher.

'Thought he was untouchable,' said Fletcher. 'Cobbling together these low-level jobs all over Cardiff.'

Harrison shook his head. 'Glory boy.'

'Everybody's luck runs out in the end,' Fletcher said quietly.

MacReady stared at the streaks on the floor. 'What about King?'

Harrison nudged him with an elbow. 'You SIO now? What's with all the questions?'

'Armed guard while they work on him at hospital,' said Fletcher. 'Sewing his bits back on so he can hold his reefers properly. Garratt's lot tried to stem the blood flow,' he gestured to the towels, 'to keep him with us.'

'Least they got something right this morning,' Harrison said.

'So he could tell us about the gunman?' MacReady asked. 'If he wakes up, that is.'

Fletcher nodded. 'You should be a detective.' To Harrison: 'You done with the tourist trip?'

'We're done,' said Harrison.

'I'm very happy for you,' said Fletcher. 'Because Major Crime are on their way to stand around making us all feel unimportant. So please piss off and do some work.'

3

Harrison and MacReady took DC David Masters, the officer they'd seen crying outside the maisonette. *He hid in the hallway after the first shot so saw fuck all, really.*

The easier job, then. MacReady knew: less likelihood of him taking a duff statement that could cause problems further down the line. The three of them plotted up in a small office next to the parade room at Cardiff Bay. Chipped desk, two swivel chairs, frosted window of safety wire glass affording the fuzzy vista of overgrown bushes and council recycling bins. On the sill, an unplugged beige telephone that looked like a late-nineties relic. Myriad forms scattered on the floor. A grimy desktop computer terminal for MacReady to type on.

'I could write this thing myself,' Masters complained. His hands folded and unfolded a Neighbourhood PACT leaflet. He looked forlorn in his paper zoot suit; Major Crime had ordered CSI to seize his clothes for forensics.

MacReady nodded. 'But you're a significant witness. We don't want to miss anything.'

Masters' head recoiled. He looked at Harrison, back to MacReady. 'You cheeky little . . . I've been banging statements

out for over twenty years. Don't sit there in your cheap poly-
ester suit giving it large, all right?'

'That's not what I meant.'

'So what did you mean?'

MacReady studied Masters: dog-tired. Awake for over twenty-
six hours. Face pallid, jaw a rash of silver bristles, pale blue eyes
watery and cracked with red. 'I can't begin to comprehend what
you've just gone through,' he said. 'And I know you could do a
proper job here, but . . . what with your DS . . . well, we thought
we could do some of the heavy lifting for you.'

After a moment Masters sank into the chair. Sighed. Waved a
hand in the air.

Whatever.

Exhausted Masters may have been, MacReady and Harrison
still took their time with the man. Couple of open questions to
warm him up, then just listened to Masters' first account. No notes.
Limited prodding. Just worked through the PEACE Model for
interviews and let him get it out. MacReady nodded as Masters
went off on tangents, rambling and shaking his head before reeling
himself back in. He sensed Masters needed to do it.

What they got: Leon King had been on the radar of various
authorities – and *known to police* – since he was eleven years of
age, his mother struggling to control him after his old man fucked
off. From there it was the same old same old. Damage, antisocial
behaviour, thefts from vehicles, smirking in and out of custody
suites, the cautions and reprimands stacking up and then the final
warning he paid no heed to. By the time his fifteenth birthday

rolled around he'd graduated to street robberies and his mother to a cocktail of antidepressants, rendering her unfit to attend custody suites to act as appropriate adult to her son.

When he went over the wall for the first time, she cut all ties with him. When he came out: credit card fraud after more robberies, creeper burglaries, handling. It was the distraction burglaries that gripped everyone's shit, though. Naively trusting pensioners were King's prime targets and he was stealing to fund a coke habit that would make a supermodel blush. King had been ripping apart OAP complexes for the better part of a year and a half, until the wheel came off for him six weeks ago. The son of a frail eighty-two-year-old lady came home to find his dear old mum *discussing a new gas meter* with King. Son freaked. King upped the ante by bludgeoning him with a cosh, then – as was the depressing norm nowadays – bludgeoned him some more. Then he ran – not forgetting to leave a healthy amount of dabs and DNA behind to ID him – after scooping up the screaming octogenarian's handbag while her boy leaked onto the lounge carpet.

Whispers afterwards. King flopping at different houses and bedsits, using different cars. People protecting him, assisting him. Bar a fleeting glimpse in a city centre all-you-can-eatery two weeks earlier – where he was immediately on his toes, leaving an overweight PCSO dry heaving after the effort of a half-mile foot chase – it was as if King had emigrated.

'He's a piece of work,' said MacReady.

Masters screwed up his face. 'You think?'

'So how did you locate him?' asked Harrison. He'd slipped low in his chair, had hoisted one sandalled foot up to a knee.

'Crimestoppers, would you believe.'

'Anon?'

Masters was nodding. 'Female caller reporting DV. Said she worked with King's girlfriend. No idea where. Just said that King's other half had come into work covered in bruises, clearly roughed up, and was refusing to make a formal complaint about it. Refusing to speak about it at all. So the friend called, and it came down the pipe to us.'

MacReady leaned back in his chair. 'She gave you King.'

Another nod from Masters. 'We made contact. She gave us the Hodges Square address he was dossing in.'

'Any idea who the caller was?'

'Nope. No trace on the mobile number. Unregistered pay as you go.'

'Any idea who the girlfriend is?'

'None whatsoever. Didn't even give it a second thought, to be honest. We just wanted King.'

'Did you feed any of this back to the Intel Officers?'

'Bob wanted us to run with it. Keep it in-house. We were planning on farming out the intel after King was in the bin.'

'So nobody else knew?' MacReady's voice was almost incredulous. Harrison glanced at him and narrowed his eyes.

Masters threw the leaflet onto the desktop. 'Look, you had to know Garratt to understand what made him work. He was one of those hundred-miles-an-hour guys, y'know? Hated villains.

Despised them. Anything to lock them up. Anything to put them away. And sometimes he'd . . . keep things fluid.'

'Take risks to get a result, you mean.'

Masters glared at MacReady. Looked to the floor. 'Yeah.'

Harrison finished picking at a loose thread on his sock. Stood, wandered over to the door and rested his backside against it. 'So what happened at the maisonette?'

'The usual, at first. Bob was all smiles and winks. Hooper drove us in to Butetown, parked the surveillance van next to the old Paddle Steamer building, then got out and walked to the unmarked car on Hannah Street. For comms.'

MacReady checked his notebook. 'Thought you didn't use radios for this raid?'

'When I say comms I mean mobile phones,' Masters said. 'Bob was paranoid about radio encryption failing. These sorts of jobs, the . . . easy ones, we just kept to our own phones. Just in case.'

'So nobody knew you were down there and you had no job radios to call for backup.'

Masters eyed him. 'Hindsight's a wonderful thing, isn't it?'

'And then you waited,' Harrison said.

'Five hours. Maybe six. Three of us in the back of the van. Waiting for King to come back to the maisonette. We knew he'd probably be out and about. He still kept his hand in with the robberies. Y'know, waiting for pissed punters to come out of the city centre clubs. Easier to turn them over when they can't walk in a straight line.'

'When did he arrive home?'

'About quarter to six this morning. Hooper clocked him from the unmarked car. Saw the light go on in the kitchen. Sent Bob a text.'

'And?'

'We went in. Bob took the rear. Me and Pete, we did the door and went in front.'

MacReady glanced at his notebook again. Pete. DC Peter Barclay. The Major Crime DS already statementing him in a room down the corridor.

'Was King alone?'

'We go into the kitchen shouting and bawling like usual. Leon was standing near the table, white as a sheet. Had his hands up, begging us. We laughed at him. Can you believe it? Laughed at him shitting himself. Then we realised he wasn't shitting himself about us being there.'

MacReady urged him on with a nod.

'King was looking towards the door that leads into the lounge,' said Masters, swallowing. 'Really pleading. Crying, y'know? So Pete looks and his mouth kind of hangs open and I take a look and there it is. Poking through a gap in the doorway.'

'A pistol.'

'Silver muzzle. I couldn't . . . I couldn't understand it. It didn't compute, you know? After all these years, my first firearm. And then the wheel came off.'

'The shots.'

Masters, head hanging on his shoulders. Hunched over. 'King went down. Like somebody cut his legs from underneath him. His fucking hand, it just . . . exploded. The bullet . . .'

'Thumb and forefinger,' grunted Harrison. 'We know.'

'All I can remember,' Masters said, talking at the carpet. 'All I can remember is diving back into the hallway and looking into the kitchen and seeing King's sovereign ring spinning on the filthy lino. Spinning and spinning like it was never going to stop. Right next to Pete's head. He was under the table. Curled up and screaming, like a frigging toddler. And that's when I knew I had to get the fuck out of Dodge.'

MacReady let out a breath. 'Fight or flight syndrome.'

'Yeah,' Masters said. He looked up. 'Something like that.'

'Did you see anything else?'

'Nope. Heard another shot. Then a third. By this point I was halfway across the estate and looking for Hooper in the unmarked car. When I got to him he was green, you know? Bob had just called him, panicking. Hooper said there was a loud bang on the line, and then dead air . . .'

Masters' feet worked the swivel chair, eyes on something far away.

MacReady instinctively patted him on the arm.

'We'll get him for you.'

Masters stared at MacReady's hand, then up into his face.

'Not before Complaints do my legs over this,' he grimaced.

MacReady didn't know what to say, so said nothing. He looked at Harrison, saw him nod a *get on with it, then*, open the door and slip out of the room. Time for a smoke.

MacReady swivelled to the terminal. Logged in. Began typing.

'Twenty-one pages? That why it took you so long?'

Harrison swigged from a mug of coffee and finished clicking through the MG11s MacReady had uploaded to the Niche system. There were pastry flakes on his tie and meat juice glistened on his cheek – the remnants of a lunch MacReady had missed. Harrison's gut hung over the waistband of his trousers, and he'd unbuckled his belt to ease some of the pressure.

MacReady looked around the Major Incident Room. Banks of computer terminals and LCD screens. At least a dozen support staff at the keyboards. Telephones – landline and mobile – chirruping. Suits and epaulettes and sour faces everywhere. The room buzzing. At one end, a large whiteboard. Next to it, a flat-screen television bigger than the one he had at home. He'd never been to the MIR before and nobody on the team had bothered to show him where it was this morning. After statementing Masters and adding the MG11s to the online case file he'd taken the stairs to the SMT's lair on the third floor – *the flight deck*, as it was known by the boots on the ground – and proceeded to get hopelessly lost. After half an hour wandering around Cardiff Bay Police Station's samey-same corridors he'd knocked on the cleaner's door for directions.

He nodded, choosing to omit the real reason for his lateness. 'Wanted to do it right.'

Harrison looked up at him from the desk, eyebrow arched. 'Didn't you just.'

'So did Peter Barclay come up with anything?'

'Apart from moaning about going home to change his underwear? Nothing.'

'Did Major Crime ask him about the shooter?'

'Oh no,' said Harrison, shaking his head. 'They didn't think it was relevant. You muppet.'

'Sorry. I just . . .'

'You just what, Willy? Haven't you been told to watch and learn? It's your first day on the team, for fuck's sake. You're a trainee. You're here for *experience*. So stop acting as if you're going to crack the case in an hour like them pretend cops on the telly. It'll piss people off.'

'Piss you off, you mean.'

Harrison stared at him. 'What you do doesn't matter to me, boy.'

'Well it matters to me,' MacReady said. 'I'm just keen to muck in –'

'Well you can muck in with the Sarge when she's back from her latest *women's empowerment* jolly up at HQ. You're cooking my swede already. Go and make yourself busy with some HOLMES indexing or something.'

More menial work. MacReady felt heat in his cheeks. Watched as Harrison logged out of Niche and walked off. Heard the profanities muttered into his mug. Harrison sidled up to the DI. Danny Fletcher listened as Harrison mouthed into his ear, then glanced across at MacReady. Held his gaze for a moment before turning back to the uniformed superintendent he'd been talking to.

With nothing to do, MacReady walked over to the whiteboard to distract himself from the rumble of his empty stomach.

Studied the neat jags of marker pen. Saw what they had at the moment: one cop murdered. One shit in intensive care, sucking on a ventilator. Somebody walking the city with a pistol they were unafraid to use. And nobody in the bin for any of it.

'He's a softy, really.'

MacReady turned to the voice, found Fletcher standing next to him, eyes on the whiteboard.

'Harrison, I mean,' said Fletcher, then faced MacReady. 'It might surprise you, but you could learn a lot from him. Warren's got the years in, got most of the T-shirts.'

'He's been a little . . . off.'

'Old sweat,' Fletcher smiled. 'Doesn't like change. You should have seen how upset he was when PACE was brought in and he couldn't handcuff scrotes to the radiator anymore.'

MacReady checked across the room: Harrison, in a huddle of suits, laughing along at some joke, *yukyukyuk*ing and glancing at MacReady and Fletcher. 'I was wondering if it was because of . . . y'know.'

A patient sigh from Fletcher. 'Your family? Ah, you can't choose them and all that.'

'Harrison was involved, though, back in the day.'

The DI waved it away. 'Good work with the statement. Plenty of meat there.'

MacReady hitched his eyebrows by way of a thank you.

'You can shoot off whenever you're ready, Will,' Fletcher said, and checked his watch; MacReady saw it was nudging 4 p.m.

'I'll wait a while, maybe tag along to the presser,' he replied, and looked at the images Blu-Tacked to the board. Bob Garratt's warrant card photograph. Leon King's mugshot. 'They're both smiling. It seems so weird.'

'The dead and the dying,' Fletcher said quietly.

MacReady nodded. Turned to the DI again.

Fletcher had walked away.

4

Smartphones and microphones recording. Banks of cameras in hands and on tripods, the strobes and flashes throwing flickering shadows against walls, the arc lights throwing out heat into a room that needed none. The small conference room full, too many people, hacks and HQ media handlers and pips and suits, jostling for space in front of a hastily erected trestle table littered with recording equipment. Behind the table: the force crest, enlarged and screen-printed on cardboard, the maxim *Keeping Our Community Safe* splashed across it at intervals.

Safe. MacReady pictured the maisonette. A twisted, unrecognisable face staring at nothing from the patio. Rivers of blood on linoleum floor.

He watched from the side of the room, a press conference virgin, the air seemingly alive with tension and urgent questions, journos half off seats and hands raised, school kids trying to get teach's attention. The Chief Constable down from her ivory tower and seated behind the table; it was the first time he'd seen the woman in the flesh. It was exciting to be present, even if he was playing no part in it.

'Can't believe how many are here,' he whispered.

Harrison beside him, sweat beading his nose. 'Copper gets killed, the public gets interested. Even now.'

'Even now?'

'After Hillsborough, Tomlinson, Plebfuckingate and the rest? Some of them feel for us, most couldn't give a toss. A few will even be glad another scuffer is dead.'

''Twas ever thus,' MacReady said.

Harrison curled his lip, looked sideways at him. 'Like you'd know anything about that, Mister Four Years In.'

'It's long enough to know how the MOPs think about us.'

'The great unwashed think what they're told to think by this lot.' Harrison leaned against the wall, tipped his head at the small crowd of journalists. 'And this lot are all about fucking us over given half the chance.'

'The anti-police media narrative,' MacReady said. 'We really don't help ourselves a lot of the time, though.'

Harrison screwed up his face. 'Whatever. Just don't talk to 'em is best.'

'What about partnership working?'

'Christ, buzzword bollocks. Didn't the DI tell you to go home?'

He turned away from MacReady. *End of conversation.*

MacReady shoved hands into pockets. Flanking the Chief at the trestle table: uniform rankers, Major Crime, the press liaison officer. The DI at one end, blinking at the smartphone camera flashes, a weariness about Fletcher already as a Chief Superintendent repeated the same phrase: 'We can't comment on that at this moment in time.'

That's because we know four-fifths of nothing at this moment in time, MacReady thought. He followed the voice asking the questions. A woman, directly opposite him, on the edge of the throng of journalists, pushing for more answers, ignoring the glares from her colleagues, the rasps to *sit down and give some other twat a chance, love.*

Mid-to-late twenties, like him. Petite. Brunette. A stray lock of hair hooked over her right eye. Hands wringing as she spoke. Booted foot tapping. Wired.

'We can't comment on that at –'

'At this time,' the woman cut him off. 'Yes thank you, Chief Superintendent.'

MacReady watched as she lowered herself to her seat, tapped at the screen of her tablet, fingers working quickly, the *tictictic* of her nails audible even over the hubbub. He found himself thinking things he shouldn't but couldn't look away. Then the woman paused. Sensing something. Turned to look directly at MacReady. Before he could avert his eyes she caught him staring.

The woman smiled, lips parting slightly, a glimpse of bright white teeth between purple lipstick. A small nod, then fingers pushing that strand of hair behind one ear.

MacReady felt the room grow warmer. Felt heat creep up his neck and to his cheeks.

Felt his mobile vibrate against his hand.

He returned the nod, slunk out of the room and answered the call, mildly irritated at the interruption.

Listened to the voice on the other end of the line.

Closed his eyes, his stomach knotting.

Said: 'Keep him calm. I'm on my way.'

The response car was parked across the driveway, blues still flashing on its roof.

Shadowy figures behind net curtains in the windows of neighbouring houses. A woman in a nearby garden, bent over with secateurs clipping at a hedge, feigning lack of interest. At the front of the next house a grizzled and thickset sixty-something busy rolling up a hosepipe, his corded arms working, freshly washed Merc gleaming behind him, suds and water running down the neat path towards MacReady's battered motor.

MacReady clambered out of the driver's seat, ducked his head at the car washer. The sun starting to dip now, the air cooler already.

'Sorry,' he said, and not for the first time.

The man stared, jaw clenched. 'He only gets away with it because you're a policeman.'

'It's nothing to do with th—'

'It's everything to do with it,' the man said. 'And we're all sick of it. Listen to them in there. This is a respectable street. Quiet. Used to be, anyway.'

MacReady heard it. The profanity. The smashing, yelling. The same old same old.

He made his way through the gap in the garden wall; the entrance gates had been sold for scrap a year earlier, just before being reported as stolen. The lawn a pathetic clump of browning grass in the centre of a cracked mud patch. Children's toys scattered and abandoned and broken: pushbikes, the frame of a swing, a scooter with its rear wheel missing. The house and garden the antithesis of its well-ordered neighbours, the entire place reeking of neglect, of occupants too busy punching lumps out of each other in drink, their kids starting to ape them, to fight amongst themselves, to fight the other residents, their lives already shaping up to emulate their father's.

MacReady pushed open the front door and walked into chaos.

'Oh, here he is.'

MacReady's brother, in the centre of the lounge, a sweat-ball wrapped in a faded blue tracksuit. Bouncing on heels and adrenaline, tensed for a rumble with the two uniforms who circled him warily, their boots crunching on splintered crockery and glass. MacReady didn't recognise either cop but they clearly knew him, and his links to this house. Behind them, in the doorway to the kitchen, his brother's girlfriend Kirsty and their children. Breathless, teary, Kirsty's cardigan ripped at the collar. Their youngest crying into her shoulder as she shushed him. Her eyes on MacReady.

'We thought it best to . . .' said one of the uniforms. He placed a hand to the side of his mouth, thumb and pinky extended into a hand-phone. 'Y'know.'

'Sure,' MacReady said. 'Leave it with me.'

'Chickenshit coppers,' his brother spat, walking behind the uniforms as they left the room. 'Too scared to deal with me yourselves, yeah?'

'What are you doing, Stuart?' MacReady asked.

His brother spun to face him. Eyes wild, face slick. 'What are you fuckin' doing, baby bro? Why your boydem's ringing you every time I has a falling out with my missus?'

A voice from the doorway. 'Take him away, Will. I don't want him here.'

'Shut the fuck up, Kirst,' his brother shouted over MacReady's shoulder.

'You shut up,' she shouted back. 'You and me are fucking finished, let me tell you.'

MacReady kept his eyes on his brother, heard the children burst into fresh sobs. He didn't want to look at them. Three kids, three beautiful kids that his brother seemed to care so little about. Clueless, Stuart. Not realising how others would give everything to have what he had.

'You can't keep doing this, Stu. You're going to get me into trouble.' MacReady kept his palms raised as he spoke. Kept his voice calm. 'I can't come up here every time –'

'Then don't.'

'The neighbours are going to complain to my bosses.'

His brother shrugged. Less surly now. Sulky, almost.

'If I lose my job then I'll have no money to give you,' MacReady said. 'And where does that leave you and Kirsty and the kids?'

'I'll work.'

'You've never worked, Stu. Not a single day.'

'I've worked.'

'Selling scrap you've lifted from skips isn't a job.'

A sneer. 'Beats being a filthy copper.'

'A copper that pays half your rent every month.'

'You're just like Ma with the old guilt trips.'

MacReady waved a hand at the broken mugs and ashtrays. 'And you're just like Dad.'

His brother stiffened. Cocked his head. Stepped closer, teeth clenched. 'You ever compare me to him again and I'll knock you the fuck out, bro.'

His brother's hot breaths on MacReady's face. His shoulders hunched, fists balled.

'Back off, Stu,' MacReady said. 'I'm looking out for you here.'

'And I looked out for you, baby brother,' his brother said, voice a rasp. 'I took the beatings for you, 'member? When he was on the sauce, when he didn't get his dinner on time, when Ma left. Took the hidings when he needed to blame someone for his shitty life, yeah?'

His girlfriend's voice again: 'Leave him alone, Stu.'

'He can't do that to you anymore,' MacReady said. 'The police made sure of it.'

'I would have sorted it one way or another,' said his brother, forehead almost touching MacReady's. 'Just your lot got to him first once he did old Ma. So less of the guilt trips, all right?'

He pushed his forehead into MacReady's. Just enough to nudge MacReady's head back a ways. Just enough to remind him that he was bigger, and stronger, and had no issues with pounding on his kid brother if the mood took him, just as he'd done throughout their childhood, usually moments after their old man had given Stuart a beating.

MacReady studied him for a moment, fighting the urge to just walk, to change his mobile number, to advise Ops Room that uniform were never to call him again if his older brother had another little DV incident with Kirsty. Just let them get on with it. Let them kill each other if necessary. Wouldn't be the first MacReady family member to go over the wall for murder.

He glanced at the children. Saw the fear there. The hands, clutching their mother's clothing. Remembered what it was like as a child, in the flat in Edinburgh's High Riggs, hiding behind the settee while his father paced and prowled and lashed out.

'Grab some gear,' MacReady said quietly. 'You can crash with me again.'

'I'm not going anyw—'

'*Christ*, Stuart,' MacReady said. 'Just a few nights, all right? So everyone can calm down.' He leaned in to his brother. Said quietly: 'So the kids don't have to see any more of this.'

His brother eyed him.

'So they don't have to deal with what we had to, yeah?' MacReady pleaded.

A few seconds of silence. Then: 'I'll be back soon as,' his brother said, not looking at his girlfriend.

'I might not let you in,' she replied.

MacReady looked at her, eyes pleading.

'All right,' she said. 'No rush though.'

His brother filled a carrier bag, left the house without a goodbye to Kirsty or the children. MacReady nodded a thanks and followed him out to the car.

'Meg's not going to be happy with me turning up again,' his brother offered from the passenger seat. Calm now, the switch flipped, as if none of the last half-hour had happened.

MacReady started the engine. Noticed the fuel gauge touching empty. Thought about the ten quid and change he had in his wallet. Not enough. Not by a long stretch.

'She'll be fine,' MacReady said, although on this he was less than sure.

'Sweet,' his brother said. 'We stopping off on the way, like? You can shout me a few cans for this evening, to calm me nerves after that nonsense. I'm totally skint, bro.'

5

'Late one again,' Megan said, voice low and quiet. 'Pub?'

MacReady stood behind her. Kissed the top of her head and breathed in the scent of shampoo. Held his breath, waiting for her to recoil. Mindful of the lager fumes, the drinks he'd shared with Stuart during a stop-off to sort him out, to talk things through. Just a couple of pints each to take the edge off. His last tenner, pissed away into the pub's urinals before they left.

Megan had cleaned up his things while he'd been at work. Or while he'd been necking pints with his brother. The lounge was back to normal and he wasn't sure what to make of her actions, what it meant. What her reaction would be – tersely polite then an earful in private, most likely – when she realised he'd brought Stuart home with him again.

She looked up at him from the settee, down at another one of those magazines held in her hands. She shrugged and gave a weak smile, sliding the mag under a cushion. On the coffee table, next to her heels where she'd raised her feet to stretch out, MacReady spied more leaflets and pamphlets. More paperwork and forms to fill in. Just like work. And it felt like work, now. He placed a hand on Megan's shoulder, felt a stab of guilt about the previous night, about feigning sleep this morning, when she tilted her head to nuzzle her cheek against his fingers.

'Just some things to sort out,' he said eventually, letting his hand fall away to his side. He turned to his brother hovering in the gloom of the hallway with carrier bag in hand, shrugging at MacReady as if unsure what to do.

'Alrigh', Meg?' Stuart called.

Megan stiffened. Just for a fraction of a second, MacReady noticed, and he winced.

'Ah, Meg,' he said, and cleared his throat. 'Stuart's going to crash here for a couple of nights. If that's OK with you, obviously . . .'

Stuart stepped into the lounge, fingers curling and uncurling the carrier bag at his midriff. 'Yeah, up to you, Meg, y'know? No bother to me if it's a bit short notice, like. Just me and Kirst, we had a rumble again and you know what it's like when she does my fuc—'

'It's just a few nights, Meg,' MacReady interrupted, and gestured for Stuart to shut up. His brother shrugged again, retreated a few paces into the hallway, giving a roll of the eyes and a yawn.

Megan exhaled slowly and shifted her feet off the table. Sat upright, hugging her knees, face downcast and partially hidden beneath a curtain of dark hair. Her body language saying all: she was clearly unhappy that Stuart was there.

MacReady felt his stomach muscles tighten. Braced himself for it. There'd always been tension between the two of them, a little heat bubbling just beneath the surface; he knew Megan disliked Stuart's lifestyle, the way he treated Kirsty, and just about managed to keep a lid on it whenever they were in each other's company.

Instead: 'Are your kids OK though, Stuart?' she asked, and looked up to study MacReady's brother, her own face unreadable.

'Uh, yeah,' he replied, not looking at her. 'Yeah, they're fine.'

She glanced at MacReady, a strange expression forming; he couldn't work out if it was barely suppressed anger or, more worryingly, disappointment. Resignation, perhaps.

'That's good,' she said softly, shifting her gaze back to Mac-Ready's brother. Stared at him for a moment, eyes lingering on the fidgeting form half in and half out of the hallway, Stuart seemingly fearful to fully commit to the lounge. 'You're their father. Never forget that.'

'I never would,' came the reply.

'Take the spare bedroom then. You're more than welcome here any time.' A patient smile from Megan. Another glance at MacReady. Sadness in her eyes, now. 'Stay as . . . long as it takes.'

'Thank you,' Stuart said. A final twist of the carrier bag. 'I'll give you guys a bit of room to, y'know . . .' He didn't finish the sentence. Shrugged for a third time. Scooted past MacReady, disappeared through the hall doorway and up the stairs.

'I'm sorry for bringing him here,' MacReady said quietly. 'I'll take him with me first thing. Early turn tomorrow.'

Megan shook her head. She seemed preoccupied again. Was biting at her bottom lip, eyes unblinking, looking through Mac-Ready. 'Leave him be, Will,' she said eventually. 'He'll just sleep all day like he always does.'

MacReady blinked several times. It was an odd reaction from her. He had nowhere to take Stuart, certainly not the MIR, or the CID office. Harrison and the other old sweats would have a field day. And if he dropped him back to Kirsty, MacReady would be back there refereeing within the hour. But Megan's response had thrown him a little.

'Fancy a brew?' he asked, shutting the hall door on his brother.

'You're not at work now,' said Megan, eyeing the door Mac-Ready had just closed. She seemed distant, all of a sudden, as if she'd drifted off a little. 'Tea would be nice, though. If you're making.'

In the kitchen, kettle bubbling, he yanked off his tie, leaned against the worktop, letting the day fall away from him. Glanced at the dirty plate, the cutlery next to the sink. Her dinner, eaten before he was home. Eaten alone. He sometimes wondered if throwing some crockery about and beating each other up would ease the pressure a little. Release some of that relationship steam. It was constant now. Suffocating. His thoughts careened from the King investigation, to Garratt's murder, to the pro formas lying on the table next to his wife.

To the magazine she'd held in her hands. To all the things he had no answer for.

He placed a mug of tea next to her, took a seat on the opposite settee. The television in the corner was off.

'See the news?' he asked, thinking of the maisonette.

She gestured at the empty black TV screen. Raised an eyebrow.

MacReady nodded to himself. *Too busy with her own work then cleaning up after me.* He sank back into the settee. Pinched the bridge of his nose, closed his eyes for a moment. 'I know. Sorry.'

She retrieved the magazine from beneath the cushion, flipped back to the page she'd folded over. Eyes flicking back and forth as she read, asked, 'So how was it? Your first day?'

He looked at the television. It wasn't her thing, sitting and watching rolling news or catching up on events via social media. She wouldn't know about the shooting, and he didn't want to inflict it on her. Besides, he didn't have the energy to go through it all again.

'All good,' he lied. 'Made a lot of tea.'

'Coppers and their tea,' Megan sighed from behind her magazine. Said: 'We have another appointment with the agency.'

He looked heavenwards. 'OK.'

'Tuesday morning.'

'OK.'

Megan flopped the mag onto her lap, caught his pained expression. Her brow furrowed, that thin horizontal crease appearing in the centre of her forehead like it always did when she was frustrated. 'Are you sure it's OK, Will?'

'Of course –'

'Because I'm starting to think otherwise,' she said, an edge to her voice, and he sensed she was trying to quash the annoyance she felt. 'I don't want you being a nodding dog just to please me. I need to know if you're OK to move on with this. It's supposed to be a joint decision. It's something we really need to talk about.'

'We've discussed it, Meg.'

'No, *I've* talked about it, you've sat there looking miserable, wishing you could be anywhere else but here. Work, most likely.'

MacReady shifted forward, hands dangling between his knees. 'I'm doing all I can. I'm working every hour I can for a reason. The IVF treatments cleaned us out, and this adoption . . . none of it is cheap, Meg.'

'Neither is your brother's rent,' she said pointedly, her patience finally gone, her eyes glassy with sudden tears, her expression already one of regret at what she'd just said. She looked down at the magazine, away from him.

MacReady could see the photograph of the mother and baby on the cover, smiling at each other. Soft focus. Warm tones. So fucking perfect, with an undoubtedly perfect daddy whose balls didn't fire blanks lurking somewhere out of camera shot.

Silence in the room bar the creak and shuffle from the upstairs box bedroom, Stuart moving about, probably folding into a drawer the one spare pair of underpants he'd stuffed into his carrier, thinking he was making a special effort now he was a guest. Stuart, blissfully unaware of all that he was blessed with, and the two people sitting beneath him who would give anything to be in his shoes. In five minutes or so, MacReady knew, his brother would be back downstairs and asking if there were any beers in the fridge, having decided that he'd given them enough time to discuss whatever they needed to discuss.

Megan lifted her head up from the magazine, stared at the ceiling, at the noise.

'I'm really sorry, Meg,' MacReady said, and hooked a thumb upwards. 'I didn't know what else to do with him.'

She dropped her eyes down to him. 'How far would you go, Will?'

He squinted at her. 'I don't understand.'

A tremor in her voice now. She seemed nervous, almost. 'It's a simple question. This is not working. *We* are not working. So what would you do to get what we want?'

A beat. *Because I am not working properly.* Then: 'Whatever it takes to make you happy.'

She nodded to herself. Swallowed, throat clicking.

'What are you thinking?' he asked.

'I'm thinking: so would I,' she said, and got up from the chair.

Without looking at him again she left the room. MacReady heard her footsteps on the stairs, across the landing. Heard their bedroom door close.

For a long while he just sat there, watching the steam from her mug dance in the air.

6

Beck was talking.

And talking.

MacReady liked her. A lot, which helped, given that Fletcher had designated her MacReady's unofficial mentor upon her return from her course at the Dream Factory of HQ. Six weeks since Garratt, since Harrison lost interest in pretty much anything MacReady said or did, but Beck had been there for him every which way. Marginalised from the Garratt inquiry herself – tasked with keeping the team's other seemingly endless number of robbery/rape/infanticide/you name it cases ticking over – she'd taken some of her precious time to explain the mechanics of a murder investigation. Fast-track actions. The minutiae of the MIR. HOLMES2 and SPOC enquiries, workflow management, graphical indexing. Even making tea for the team. One fewer round of drinks for him to prepare each shift.

Coming to work was now only slightly less painful than staying at home.

For this reason alone, he tried to keep up with Beck's regular monologues. Nervous energy, he'd noticed. Flicking her fore-

and index fingers together. Fidgeting in her seat. Nails bitten and ragged. A regular chatterbox anyway, but more pronounced when she became excited. Even during house-to-house for the Garratt investigation, when he'd stood silently at her side, his Detective Sergeant had talked at Butetown homeowners for ten minutes straight. Couple had even closed the door on her.

The procedural stuff: fine, and not a little helpful. Some of the gossip, fine also. He especially enjoyed her disclosures about their Detective Inspector. Danny Fletcher, once in drink – and he drank a lot, MacReady frequently noting the puffy face, the bleary eyes of a morning – was fond of exposing what Beck referred to as a *prime specimen . . . if I was that way inclined.*

This afternoon she'd finally lost him as she turned the CID car on to Lloyd George Avenue: a woman's role in modern policing was not a subject he had much of an opinion about, other than *you take the wage, you take the bollocks.* He said nothing of the sort, though. As much as he liked Beck, and suspected she felt likewise, in the current climate of bullying or routinely grassing up colleagues for a careless word he thought it better to glaze over and watch the world go by.

'So that's why it's *Charlie*,' Beck continued, 'instead of Charlotte. Always used it, even before the police.'

A blur of apartment blocks in MacReady's eyes. 'Right.'

'More chance of an interview when they think you're a guy. Especially in this job with its macho nonsense. It's difficult for women, Will.'

'Sure.' MacReady thought about the hated *Positive Discrimination.* How he'd been passed over for this trainee CID post on five occasions. How all the slots went to female officers, or BME plods.

The Avenue bled into Bute Place; beyond that, the regenerated glitz of Cardiff Bay. Gone, the whores and pimps, the gambling dens and sailors' dives, the notoriety, the birthplace of Shirley fucking Bassey. A whole new hub of glorious homogeneity bolted on to the ragged fringes of the old Tiger Bay: chain bars and chain restaurants and chain fast food outlets. Comedy club. Boutique shops and tourists dining on Turkish Cop Shish over the water, the steady drum of rain on windows as they ate a depressing reminder of where they actually were.

And the old Graving Docks. Now the *Millennium Waterfront*.

The reason for Beck's oral fifth gear.

MacReady drifted away. Closed his eyes, knowing Beck wouldn't notice. Thought about Garratt again. About the tension in the MIR. About the lack of progress eating away at them all. Nothing from the community. Nothing from forensics, including the nine-millie bullet recovered from Garratt's ruined skull. The pressure from above, ACCs and DCCs dropping in, even the pointless Police and Crime Commissioner full of piss and vinegar until he caught sight of the crime scene shots of Garratt's bullet-swollen face and had to leave the room. Pep talks and business speak, of no use to anyone, just arse-covering bosses cluttering the room day after day. He wished he was back there, doing something. Anything. He liked Beck, but this was her gig. Shunted aside, again. Handed over for someone else to look after.

Irritated, he opened his eyes. Sensed something was wrong. Couldn't put his finger on it for a moment. Realised: all he could hear was the diesel engine. Beck had stopped talking.

MacReady turned to her as the car eased onto New George Street. She was looking at him. Smiling. Fingers playing with a hank of bobbed blonde hair, other hand guiding the CID motor past the Mermaid Quay complex. 'Am I making your ears bleed?'

He cocked an eyebrow. 'I could listen to you all day long, Sarge.'

She dropped down a gear. Swung left into Stuart Place, through the gap between Woods Brasserie and the Spice Merchant. 'You don't really have much choice. Nobody else wants to play with you. Or fill in those stupid forms for your development profile . . .'

'It's a cruel world.'

'You're not wrong there, Trainee Detective Constable,' Beck said. Then: 'Bloody hacks . . .'

MacReady looked forward. Exhaled. Checked his watch. Fifteen forty-four hours. Made the calculations: Ops Room received the three nines call at fifteen twenty-two; uniform blarted up six minutes later. Confirmed the initial reports: a body in the water next to the most overpriced gastropub in the Bay area. Just sixteen minutes, and the cobbled walkway behind the Pilotage Building already crawling with media.

'Thought our transmissions were encrypted,' MacReady said. 'Isn't that what the force spent two million quid on a few years back?'

Beck cursed, the car almost clipping the wing mirror of a satellite truck. 'Social media. Every time. Journos would be lost without Twitter.'

'The great Echo Chamber.'

'Aren't you on it?'

'Tried it for a bit. Meh, you know? I'd rather watch a good film.'

'I'm surprised. You seem to enjoy talking to yourself while being ignored by everyone.' Beck winked at him and chuckled, slowed the car to a crawl. Stopped at the bollards in front of Landsea House. 'You're here for the fresh air, OK? It's just a suicide, is all.'

MacReady sighed. 'I know the drill. Watch and learn how the real police deal with a bloated floater.'

Beck killed the engine, yanked up the handbrake. Reached for the door handle.

'Stop your whining, William,' she said, eyeing the scrum of reporters. 'Beats being the tea boy, doesn't it?'

She was out of the car. MacReady watched her at the cordon, police tape fluttering at her midriff as her mouth moved.

In the face of a uniform, and talking.

MacReady gave it half an hour, listened to the Airwave set bleep and fuzz, to Ops Room giving out emergency call after emergency call to uniform across the city. Pub rucks, domestics, shoplifters fighting security over two cans of Lynx deodorant, thefts of and from vehicles, Facebook death threats and lost three-year-olds. Your typical Sunday afternoon fodder, and never ending.

Grey sky darkened further, the crowd of onlookers and media swelling in number. When the SST arrived in their shiny new carrier and started shipping kitbags through the bollards he climbed out of the car.

Wind buffeted the exposed Graving Docks. Drizzle in the air, tickling his face. MacReady buttoned up his jacket, made his way across the cobbles until Stuart Place petered out. The water in the lock dark wavelets, whipping themselves into small, foam-topped peaks. The lock walls dark green with algae and engine oil, a lone cormorant atop a pontoon, pecking at floating fag ends.

Children pressed faces up to glass inside the Techniquest building, watching. Behind them the science exhibits arced and glowed and went ignored. West across the lock, dominating the dull skyline: the metal sweep of St David's Hotel's sail-topped roof. Beyond were the wetlands, the enclaves of high-spec apartment complexes, thrown up a decade ago and still struggling to sell in the downturn.

The air was chilly, the water would be colder still. MacReady neared the outer cordon, spotted the three officers stretching on wetsuits. Kitbags and pieces of equipment on the ground. Specialist Search Team. Drafted in from HQ to retrieve the corpse from a waterlogged concavity in the dock wall.

Slipping on a pair of fins and an oxygen tank was, as far as MacReady was concerned, only to be enjoyed in thirty-degree waters. The Maldives, perhaps. Somewhere in the Caribbean, a cool lager awaiting you after the resort dive. Not that he could afford either. But those lunatics: swimming the freezing temperatures of Cardiff Bay or dredging some effluent-filled brook next to a sewage works. He thought of the last – and only, until now – time he'd seen them at work. Another suicide, few years ago, a flooded and disused quarry on his patch in the north of the city. Some fucked-up, bankrupted businessman drove his Chelsea Tractor into the water, lay undiscovered for weeks. Body came apart at the seams as they recovered it, one of the divers surfacing with a rotten arm in his hands and vomit clogging his respirator.

Then again, MacReady doubted the SST officers would want to swap places with any of Garratt's team at the moment. Masters, Barclay and Hooper: suspended. The Rubber Heelers of Professional Standards already pressing hard and digging deep.

At least the divers would be out of the shit in an hour or so.

Beck was talking to a woman whose back was turned to MacReady. Slight frame. Hair dark. He could see her booted foot beating a rhythm on the cobbles.

He remembered the press conference.

Beck and the woman turned to him as he crouched under the cordon tape. MacReady found himself thinking things he shouldn't, again. He stared at the journalist.

'Will, this is Klaudia Solak,' Beck said.

'Journo,' MacReady replied.

Beck nodded. 'S'right. Don't tell her anything.'

Solak laughed; throaty, impish. 'Hi again, Will.' Gloved hand, brushing at that strand of hair. Eyes on him.

MacReady's mouth twitched a smile. 'Meetcha. Properly, I mean.'

Beck's eyes narrowed. 'You've met?'

'At the Garratt presser,' Solak nodded. 'Ships passing in the night kind of thing.'

MacReady chuckled. 'You seemed quite keen to get what you wanted that day, I must say.'

'I always get what I want,' Solak smiled.

'I mean it,' said Beck, playfully pushing MacReady away. 'Don't tell her anything.'

'Spoilsport.' Solak gave a fake pout. 'So what have we got?' she asked Beck. Still looking at MacReady.

'*I've* got more work, it appears.'

'Helpful, Charlie. Come on, can you give us a little more information?'

Beck smiled. 'More than you've got already? We got a call, we attended, you were here before us. I'm sure you've already spoken to –'

'The witness?' Solak nodded. Turned and pointed at a despondent-looking man sitting on a bench, flanked by a couple of uniforms. A little boy skipped in circles in front of the trio. 'He says it looked like a body. So is it?'

'We don't know yet.'

'Tell me later?'

'No.'

'Drinks at Henry's? Catch up. You can give me the latest gossip on the Bob Garratt thing.'

'Not my baby. And anyway, two words: Filkin Report.'

'You could do with some *late-night carousing*.'

Beck sighed. 'Ring me.'

Solak glanced at MacReady. 'What about you?'

He swallowed. 'Me?'

'You'll be there?'

'Leave the new kid alone,' Beck said, pulling at MacReady's arm. 'He doesn't know how you operate, girl.'

A giggle from Solak. 'Bye, Will.'

Beck dragged him away. Pushed through a clump of techies and suits, into the inner cordon, the sterile area. Plods, paramedics, harbour staff. Hustle and bustle. More screens erected by the fire service, shielding the scene from the main road, from the residents standing on balconies of the Harbour Point flats. Solak gave him a little wave. Raised her collar against the chill.

'She's gorgeous,' blurted MacReady.

'Isn't she?'

He smiled. 'So . . . you and her?'

'I wish it were so, Will. Fancied her since we were in school together. Failed miserably to get her on side.' Gentle thump on his arm. 'Not that it's any of your business.'

'Henry's is on my way home, you know.'

'I'm sure it is. And I'm sure you'd enjoy flirting with Klaudia. But not as much as she'd enjoy flirting with you just to loosen your tongue about Garratt. So, in a word, no.'

MacReady threw a look over his shoulder: Solak deep in conversation with her cameraman, a handsome, bleached-blond beanpole, unlit cig bouncing in the corner of his stubbled mouth. Busy busy, both of them. Preparing for the money shot.

'Go talk to the witness,' Beck urged.

'But the body . . .'

'What are you going to do, reanimate it? Go do some work for me. You can come and have a sniff in a bit, if it keeps you happy.'

She was gone into the crowd, fingers flicking together. Collaring a techie, the ambo crew, the fire head honcho. Group huddle at the wall overlooking the water, talking them through it.

Talking.

MacReady walked over to the witness, a jeans and tracky top picture of misery bookended by two uniforms who loafed against the scum-dirty sandstone of the lock wall. The officers were grinning beneath their lids; in front of them a three-year-old boy, wrapped tight against the chill and with a mop of blond hair, ran in circles on the cobblestones. MacReady could swear the kid was burbling *fuck, fuck, fuck* as he went.

'Lucas, no,' the witness sighed.

MacReady recognised the uniforms now he was up close. Davidson and Lee. Response officers from his old station. The Chuckle Brothers. A pair of jokers, or so they thought.

A wolf-whistle from Davidson. 'Who's a pretty boy, then?'

Lee: 'Oh, it's *you*, Willy.'

The witness looked up at MacReady and he cringed inwardly. 'Guys,' he nodded at the officers.

Davidson: 'Sorry, Mac. Didn't recognise you out of the cloth.'

A snort from Lee.

MacReady offered a patient smile, turned to the man and introduced himself. 'Are you OK to talk, Mister . . .?'

'Cornelius.' The man nodded. Glanced at the child. 'Simon Cornelius. But not in front of my boy, right? I'm in enough trouble as it is.'

MacReady looked at Davidson and Lee. Palms upturned. *Anyone?*

After a few minutes cajoling both Davidson and Cornelius's son to go for a wander *to see the fishies* Cornelius began talking. Divorced after cheating on his wife, this Sunday afternoon was his designated visiting time with Lucas, the only four hours he got each week and something he'd fought long and hard to get from an understandably miffed ex. MacReady nodded along to Cornelius's monologue of marital woe, saying nothing, musing how having a child might not be the panacea he and Megan hoped it would be, that perhaps their relationship had deteriorated to the point of no return. That everything they'd been through, were planning on going through – the IVF, the adoption – might ultimately be for naught.

MacReady shook it away and his thoughts drifted, annoyingly, to Klaudia Solak as the man wittered on, saying a lot but not giving MacReady very much at all. Cornelius – yet another MOP who seemed desperate to tell their life story to a complete stranger – had been arguing with his new girlfriend on the phone while Lucas threw stones into the water. Calling for his daddy to come look. Pointing out through the railings, at the mouth of the dry dock. When Cornelius ended the call and went to his son, he saw what Lucas was looking at: a shiny, dark brown mass bobbing on the surface of the grubby water.

'Thought it was a plastic sack at first,' Cornelius said. He swallowed, a look of distress passing across his pasty, unshaven face. 'Then the sun cut through the clouds and it was all bright down there for a second and it was well obvious what I was looking at. Before I knew it I was, like, what the fuck, y'know? Out loud an' all. And anyway Lucas heard me.'

MacReady checked across the dock at Davidson. He was bent over at the waist, laughing as the kid skittered around his legs, dropping F-bombs every couple of steps.

'My ex is going to murder me,' Cornelius moaned.

'I truly hope not,' MacReady said.

'There's none of us left to investigate if she does,' Lee offered.

And that was it. Nothing to take from it at all, other than *man finds floating body*. MacReady thanked Cornelius for his time anyway, gave him the old *we'll be in touch* and watched as he plodded across to Lucas. The pair of them wandered off towards the sodden waterfront eateries at Mermaid Quay, the father with his son and, seemingly, the weight of the world on his shoulders.

'You two old sweats slumming it on a cordon?' MacReady turned to ask the uniforms. 'Where's the probationer?'

'*Student officer*, William,' said Lee. 'Couple of months away from response and you've already forgotten the PC lingo? Tsk, tsk.'

Davidson, mock-disgusted: 'Diversity course for you, cuntstable.'

'Yeah, yeah,' MacReady said. 'Any gossip? I'm missing the banter.'

'Can't say,' sniffed Davidson.

'We don't speak to the Colouring-in Department unless we have to,' winked Lee.

Davidson, studying him: 'You've definitely gone to the dark side. Get you, in your CID threads.'

'Lemme guess: Primark?' Lee asked.

Davidson shook his head. 'No, no. This is William MacReady we're talking about. He'd have pushed the boat out. Marks and Spencer, definite.'

MacReady rolled his eyes. 'Muppets.'

Lee lifted his lid, scratched at a forehead pale from shift work. 'So are the glorified statement-takers teaching you anything?'

MacReady shoved hands into pockets, thought about a little embellishment. Knew they'd see through it. He shrugged. 'I can make a shit-hot cup of tea, now.'

'Must be like being a probationer again.'

'*Student officer.*'

'Least you've managed not to get shot,' Davidson yawned.

Lee *tch*ed out the corner of his mouth. 'That fucking Garratt. Cost me sixteen quid out of my pay packet.'

Bob Garratt's wife. His daughter, still a toddler. Sitting in Fletcher's office off the MIR last week, backs to the audience they didn't know they had. MacReady had watched, they'd all watched through the glass: FLO wobbling in with a tray of tea, the DI, haggard, uncomfortable, hand clawed as it dropped to the woman's shaking shoulder. The blinds Fletcher drew weren't enough to mute the wretched sounds from within.

He blinked it away. 'You could always drop out of the death benefit scheme.'

'Fuck that,' Lee said. 'When I peg it I want this cunt,' he nodded at Davidson, 'to feel the pain in his wallet.'

Sniggers. Elbows.

Garratt in the CSI tent, jaw fixed with rigor, neck tendons stretched, already frozen, a froth of leaked cranial fluid and blood against grey skin, against grey stone, his wife beating at her chest, wailing, bereft, damned, his daughter with her sallow skin and scared, wide, innocent eyes not knowing, not understanding and the blinds drawn shut . . .

'Pricks,' MacReady muttered, but they weren't listening to him anyway.

A surge of bodies. Divers descending a rusted ladder into the black water. Uniforms with hands out, hands up, warding off the onlookers, the reporters. Solak amongst them, the beanpole with his camera at her heel.

'Here we go,' said Lee.

Beck, gripping the wall, shoes submerged in a rain puddle, coat flapping against her calf. Staring into the lock.

MacReady hung back, next to the screens, in the dim shadow of the fire service hoist. Heard snorts of air from respirators, the lap of water against rock. Then nothing.

Silence for a long while. Davidson whistling to himself while Lee stared out to the horizon; MacReady decided he didn't miss uniform work at all.

Then: splashes at the surface. Shouts carried away on wind.

Beck, arms waving, pointing, organising.

Trumpton swung their rig over the lock. Hook and chain clanked, the rescue sling lowered out of sight.

'Like fishing for mackerel,' Lee said from behind him.

MacReady didn't bother to turn around.

'All this fuss,' said Davidson, looking about, 'for a suicide.'

The rig juddered, fire staff working the winch beneath a barrage of camera flashes.

A forensic recovery bag at the wall, a diver following it up, hands on its bulk. CSI technicians easing it over, onto the quayside, onto a tarpaulin. Filthy water dripped and ran. The crowd became still.

Beck. Talking at the techies. Talking with the diver. MacReady saw her swallow. Nod. Rock on her feet, as if the wind were strong enough to blow her small frame into the depths.

'Christ,' winced Davidson. 'That's nasty.'

Then Beck was walking towards MacReady, walking towards him to talk about the recovery, about what was in the bag, what they'd found, but MacReady didn't need her to tell him anything and her offer to have a sniff was pointless because, even from where he was standing, he could smell the thing already.

Murtala Muhammed International Airport, Lagos, Nigeria

Aleksandar outed the cigarillo under his heel.

Held smoke in his lungs, watched warm evening rain fall on the roofs of taxis and minivans. Watched people scurry past, rushing into the building, out of the deluge and into the madness. Around him the chaos of bodies and bags and PA announcements that he could barely understand. Above him a steady drum of water on the concrete overpass. Yet more people up there: more vehicles, more voices and horns sounding. Beneath it all the faint and wheezy whine of an aircraft engine.

He exhaled, blue smoke billowing into the downpour and across the small public garden; the empty pool with its quartet of concrete dolphins, frozen mid-jump, glistened with rain in the fading light. Aleksandar allowed a smile. Turned. Studied the drab bunker of the international terminal, its jolly, faded adverts, its signs and directions and warnings that he paid no heed to.

He pushed his face to the glass. Eyes narrowed. Searching the crowds.

The children. Gathered around the pastor. Another man, a man Aleksandar did not know, standing before them with hand out, his eyes needy.

Aleksandar sighed, the smile dying, and pushed his way into the place he hated most.

The man withdrew his hand upon seeing him.

Aleksandar grabbed it anyway. Bent and squeezed, hard enough for the man's knuckles to crack. For him to squeal, the sound lost under the cacophony of a hundred different conversations, of arguments, of luggage trolley wheels on tiles, of airport security messages.

'If I see you again I will kill you,' he said. 'Pička.'

The man understood, English speaker or not. His fearful face backed away, disappearing into a morass of indifferent travellers, fingers limp and twisted and held to his scrawny chest.

Aleksandar heard the pastor's syrupy voice: reassuring the children, no doubt, in that strange patois of his. He turned, saw the pastor's fleshy arms gathering the group of boys and girls in an embrace of sweat and sticky clothing.

Ten pairs of young eyes on Aleksandar.

Bepeh's wide eyes, so black and bottomless and wonderful.

Like Tihomir's eyes. His baby brother. Gone so long now, those Srpska bastards.

'I could have dealt with it, Aleks,' said the pastor in English.

'They have to learn, these chancers,' Aleksandar replied. 'Bullying people for dash?'

The pastor held his gaze. 'Judgement. From the likes of you.'

Aleksandar chuckled at the hypocrisy. Wiped at his brow. So hot in here. Hotter than outside: this pathetic, filthy country with its pathetic, filthy airport. The noise and the stink and the confusion, with little or no air conditioning to alleviate the irritation he felt every time he came here.

No efficiency. No . . . organisation.

He glanced at Bepeh. Felt a stab of guilt. Snapping the man's fingers in front of the boy was a mistake. A risk, after all the hard work. After earning Bepeh's trust in order to see things through. It had been necessary to win his confidence at first, a job, but in just two weeks Aleksandar had grown fond of the boy. A mistake, he knew. Dangerous, even. Tihomir's ghost doing its work. But the boy had warmed to him like no other. It had thrown him, and caused him to lose sleep. Last night had been the worst; miserable and spun through with dreams of his brother, calling out from the blood and twisted corrugated metal of Markale marketplace.

Aleksandar kneeled in front of Bepeh. Ruffled his hair and smiled.

The boy smiled back. Those eyes.

Tihomir.

'The documents?' he asked the pastor, not looking at the man; his swollen belly and slick skin made Aleksandar feel unwell.

'Here,' said the pastor. In his hand, a pouch containing all they would need. Passports. Visas. Medical cards. Immunisation records. All clean. Authentic. 'God speed.'

Aleksandar looked down at the pastor's extended hand. Ignored it. As he shepherded the children away, all but Bepeh cried and called for the fat man they'd left behind.

*   *   *

VIP treatment at the check-in desk.

Sick children. Orphans. Going to a better place by private charter flight. Going to a better life, one devoid of illness, of solitude, of misery. They'd paid extra money for the priority lounge, and Aleksandar was in touching distance of cool AC on his skin.

He handed over the travel pouch to a bored-looking clerk; a benevolent smile appeared as the man realised what he thought he was dealing with. Keystrokes on the battered laptop sitting in front of him. Forefinger plunging one key at a time. The screen reflected in his frameless spectacles.

In English: 'Portugal, yes?'

Aleksandar nodded solemnly.

The man eyed them over the countertop: ten children. Boys, mostly. Fake football tops and Hello Kitty sweaters, the typos and poor stitching glaringly obvious. He hesitated, tapping Aleksandar's passport against one hand.

Tap, tap, tap.

Tap, tap, tap.

Then: 'Why go there?'

Aleksandar's chest tightened. 'Special treatment they cannot receive here, unfortunately. And they will be meeting the stars of football!'

The man blinked. Leaned over the counter. Spoke his gibberish at the children. Laughed when they jumped and sang, feet bouncing, shouting Ronaldo Ronaldo Ronaldo . . .

The man handed the pouch to Aleksandar. Waved him away. Wished them well.

Aleksandar turned to the children. Settled on Bepeh, grinning at him, those eyes so wide. 'Ronaldo,' he nodded. 'Ronaldo and Bepeh, yes?'

Bepeh giggled. Placed his small hand in Aleksandar's.

They walked towards the departure lounge, Aleksandar's heart aching.

7

'*Charlie.*'

Beck paused. Stood up, waved at the computer screen. 'Look but don't touch.'

MacReady cupped his chin in his hand. Watched her drift through the noise of the MIR to Fletcher's office door. She hung there for a moment, nails *rat-tat-tat*ing at the doorframe, talking quietly with the DI. Fletcher glanced over her shoulder at him as they spoke.

MacReady turned back to the screen: the NSPIS crime report for one of Beck's cases. One of her many cases. She'd been explaining it to him, unnecessarily he thought, because it seemed pretty straightforward. Knifepoint robbery of a fresher five days ago. Yet another pissed-up student, first time away from home, four in the morning and wandering the wrong part of town *looking for some munch*. iPhone, wallet, gone. Knife not used, but his nose broken, even after he'd handed over the goodies. His statement: useless. Descriptions: teens in sports clothing, *might have been black, some were definitely white, like . . .* His parents: irate phone calls to the brass, demanding justice, and things done *now*, and people jailed, even though their boy was so drunk he couldn't remember his own name when response found him lying in a gutter with piss on his jeans and crying for his mother. MacReady knew Beck had better – more important – things to be getting on with. He'd said nothing. It was keeping him occupied, which he supposed was the plan. Not as occupied, he knew, as some of the team. The Task Management suite for the Garratt case on HOLMES2: he'd sneaked a look at it when he came in this morning. Harrison alone had over thirty actions of varying priorities on his workload, the majority yet to be viewed.

Not enough people to go round. And here he was, doing nothing.

'Get your coat, you've pulled.'

Beck, at his side again. He glanced up. 'Don't tell me: we've run out of teabags.'

'Such cynicism.'

'All right. Milk?'

'Ops Room just called the DI. Somebody screwed the maisonette overnight.'

MacReady sat upright. 'Leon King's place?'

'Get you, so perky all of a sudden.'

'I thought Estates secured it for us last week after the scene was released?'

'Scrote's flat, rammed with boys' toys?'

He nodded. 'Rich pickings. Quite fancy a new PlayStation myself, actually.'

'Typical manchild,' said Beck. 'So we'll go take a look-see. *Then* you can pick up some teabags.'

* * *

'Got to board it up again. This going to take long?'

The civvy from HQ's Estates Department: short and griz-zled, overalls flecked with sawdust, with paint. Nub of pencil behind one ear. Talking to MacReady, grey and wiry eyebrows furrowed. Hand placed to his forehead, shielding his anxious, sunken eyes from low morning sun.

Beck was crouched, studying the splintered chipboard that had been prised away from the French doors. The doors, forced open at the lock. 'We'll see,' she said, those fingers going again.

The civvy ignored her. Still at MacReady: 'Got five more jobs and it's not even lunchtime. And it's just me. Bloody budget cuts, lost all my staff. Up to my eyeballs, I am . . .'

Beneath MacReady's shoes, a pale pink circle on patio stone. A reminder of what was lying here weeks ago, still visible even after the fire service wash-down. He stepped away from it. Pictured Garratt. The search officers fingertipping the garden. The dog handler, her animal yapping and straining at its lead. Going berserk.

Beck straightened. Snapped on latex gloves and stepped towards the civvy. 'I've got four street robberies, a rape, a string of serious assaults, yesterday a body washed up in the Bay, and now this. And there's just me and the tea boy, here.' She threw a pair of gloves at MacReady. 'So please stop talking.'

The civvy squinted at her. Turned to MacReady. 'Thought you were in charge?'

Beck cocked her head. 'Because he has a penis?'

A scowl from the man in woodchipped overalls. He trudged over to the garden fence, rifled in a pocket. Brought out Rizlas and baccy, began rolling a smoke, muttering to an amused-looking uniform about the job going down the shitter.

MacReady exhaled. 'Think you won the pissing contest, Sarge.'

'These old sweats always defer to the male officer. It's annoying.'

'I'm sure you enjoy putting them right.'

An angelic smile: 'Put your gloves on, there's a dear.'

Musty inside the maisonette. The faint smell of damp, of blood, of fingerprinting chemicals. Sunlight through the French doors, falling as a bright, skewed oblong on dirty red carpet worn to its underlay. In one corner a square of cracked concrete floor, the carpet missing completely. Sagging furniture, tired and stained. The lounge spartan, no pictures, books, ornaments, but with the *de rigueur* jumbo flat screen, the Sky+ box, the games consoles, the piles of Blu-rays, DVDs and CDs. The important stuff, MacReady thought. He'd been inside so many houses, houses where you'd wipe your feet on the way out, houses with three-year-old kids running around in shit-filled nappies, with feeble parents drinking Spar lager for brekkie, Argos catalogues the only reading material, the cupboards and fridge bare. But they all had their tellies, their Xboxes, their *twenny Benny Hedgehogs*, their overflowing ashtrays and slack-jawed expressions. When he first started in the job he hadn't been able to understand it, had tried to empathise, to encourage. Within a year of the same faces, the same families, the same excuses, he'd stopped giving a shit.

'Landlord been contacted?' he asked.

Beck, poking at the tower of CD cases. 'Harrison's been digging. Can't trace one.'

'So we don't know who owns this place?'

'Nope.'

'So . . .'

'So what?'

'So . . . re-securing it comes out of the force budget?'

Beck eyed him. 'Yes. But that's not what you really wanted to ask, is it?'

'The landlord,' MacReady shrugged. 'We need to trace him or her, find out –'

'Find out who's renting it, put the arm on them, maybe it'll lead us to the person who shot Bob Garratt?'

He said nothing.

'You're not the OIC on the shooting, Will,' Beck said, standing. 'And this is what it is. Straightforward burglary, probably by a junkie looking for anything they can rip and sell for their next fix. Don't get carried away, all right?'

'I could be helping out. More.'

'You are.' Beck's voice softened, and she smiled at him. 'You're helping *me*, OK? And believe me, I need all the help I can get at the moment. Everyone else has been seconded to Garratt and the crap doesn't stop coming just because a cop's been murdered. Crime goes on, y'know?'

MacReady puffed out his cheeks. 'So what are we looking for?'

Beck surveyed the lounge. 'Anything that's been moved, or disturbed. You know the drill. CSI would've been careful not to move anything, and anything they did move would have been returned to its rightful place. Just keep an eye out for . . . anything odd or out of its rightful place.'

'I'll take the kitchen,' MacReady said.

'You'll like it in there,' Beck smirked. 'There's a kettle.'

He rolled his eyes. Pushed through the lounge door.

No wash-down by the fire service in the kitchen. The room in stasis since the scene was released and the boards went up. The linoleum floor crusted with dried blood. The splatters of brown on the worktop, the cupboards. The sink with its putrid water, half-moons of festering dishes rising from scum. Bluebottles zuzzing and tapping at the window, circling the unlit strip light above the table. MacReady imagined Peter Barclay curled beneath it, screaming.

The room was filthy. He stood in the centre, ignoring the flies alighting on his head, his shoulders. Filthy, but . . . oddly untouched. This was a burglary, after all. Yet there were no drawers pulled out, no cupboard doors ajar, none of the classic signs of somebody speeding through the place, frantically yanking things open, yanking things apart. Not caring about the damage. Not caring about the mess. Just that tunnel vision, that urgency, that getting what they wanted, what they needed, and nothing and nobody would stand in their way.

They'd stolen none of the audio-visual equipment in the lounge. Not the games consoles or Freeview box or Sky system. They'd even left King's stereo sitting on the kitchen worktop, and a cheap-looking iPod dock on a shelf.

It was all too clean. It didn't make sense.

MacReady cocked his head. Squinted at the windowsill. At the limp pot plant with its mantle of dead bluebottles. At the washing-up liquid bottle next to the sink. At the small food recycling bin next to the microwave. Shifted his eyes to the tea makings: the cream containers holding sugar, teabags, coffee.

All these things, moved, turned over. Plant soil dusting the sill. Rotted onion peelings lumped at the base of the bin. The sugar spilt, the container upended and emptied.

'Sarge,' MacReady called.

Beck in the doorway, rubbing at her nose with the back of latex hand. 'Anything?'

'No,' said MacReady. 'And that's what's strange.'

'Strange how?'

MacReady turned to her. 'Is anything disturbed in the lounge? The bedroom? Y'know, drawers pulled out, mattresses turned over?'

'Nothing,' she said.

'What about the CD cases? The DVDs?'

'Well they've been opened. You going to tell me what's on your mind, Sherlock?'

MacReady stared at the sugar container.

'They were looking for something small,' he said. 'When the techies bagged everything, what did they recover that was small?'

Harrison's bulk leaning against the doorframe, breathing noisily. Heavy-lidded eyes on a packet of Tesco sandwiches, mouth working the ham and cheese. One ankle hooked behind the other, thick red socks encased in sandals.

'Thanks, Warren,' MacReady said to him.

A shrug from Harrison. Thick shoulders juddering. 'Don't thank me. Been told to keep an eye on you while you play detective.' Another bite of brunch. 'Beck's busy making phone calls about that floater, so I got the shitty end of the stick.'

'Yeah, well.' MacReady nodded, gave a half-smile. 'Thanks anyway.'

The property store at Cardiff Bay. A basement room off the underground car park, racks of deep shelving fixed to the building's mammoth concrete support struts. A gloomy cavern of brown paper sacks, of sealed plastic evidence bags, of lost property tubs filled with key fobs and mobile phones. Row upon row, shelf upon shelf, each bundle and pile and tag and defendant name telling its own story: a machete used to hack at staff inside a bookies; oxyacetylene kit for burning and cutting coin boxes out of telephone kiosks; tube fashioned out of rolled-up Sellotape and used by a female druggie to secrete heroin inside her vagina. Knives, pills, hub caps. Nine-ounce bars of cannabis resin, hydroponic equipment, underwear and bra from another rape victim.

An archive of awful crimes, of human stupidity and depravity. Waiting for court cases. Waiting for destruction orders. Waiting for a civvy to come down and do an audit then bollock the OIC for ticking the wrong box on a property form.

MacReady sat amongst it all, cross-legged on the floor. Surrounded by evidence bags filled with items taken from Leon

King's maisonette. The usual stolen gear: car stereos, mobiles, laptops, a handful of video cameras. A CS canister, couple of coshes, seemingly King's weapons of choice when out on the rob. The remains of the blunt he'd been smoking when Garratt's men burst in. Clothing, mostly. Seized for DNA analysis, to see if anything from the shooter had transferred. King's blood-soaked tracky top. The bottoms, bright red, then dark brown at the rear where King had soiled himself. MacReady could smell it through the plastic.

'What exactly are you looking for?' asked Harrison, nose whistling as he breathed.

MacReady placed the tracksuit bottoms to one side. 'I'll know when I see it,' he said, and rooted through a paper sack.

'I can barely contain my excitement,' said Harrison. The sandwiches were gone; he looked forlornly at the empty packaging.

Inside the paper sack: smaller, sealed plastic bags. What he was looking for. MacReady fished them out. Sorted through them, holding them out in front of him. One filled with small blims of 'nabis, King's personal. Another, coiled SCART leads and phone chargers. A third, a selection of XXX-rated porn DVDs with their imaginative titles.

At the bottom of the sack, what he was looking for.

'Gotcha,' he said.

Harrison stifled a yawn. 'You finished fucking about with grown-up stuff now?'

'I'm done,' MacReady said.

'Can't believe the DI let you in here.'

'Didn't take long, did I?'

'It pains me to ask, but what have you found that's making you look like you've got a boner? Other than those wankfilms, of course.'

'These,' said MacReady, hoisting a larger plastic bag from the floor as he stood, 'are camcorders. I saw them being bagged up by the techies at the Garratt shooting.'

'I know, mun. I've been through it all myself.'

'And these,' MacReady raised the bag he'd just found at the bottom of the sack: half a dozen small black plastic squares, 'are memory cards.'

Harrison looked from one bag to the other.

'Cocky little fucker,' he muttered, and shifted backwards to let a smiling MacReady out of the property store.

'So they *were* looking for something tiny.'

Beck, at his side, telephone calls finished, post mortem for the body in the Graving Docks arranged for tomorrow. Juggling, organising, clearly wishing she could split herself in three. She nudged MacReady's elbow with hers. 'Clever clogs.'

'Aw, shucks,' he said.

On the desk: the camcorders. Samsung, Panasonic, Hitachi. Stolen. Probably untraceable. Next to them, the memory cards, a neat line, Beck having arranged them so.

'Nice work,' said Fletcher. The DI in his chair, his back to the slate water of the bay and blue October sky. He glared at Harrison as he spoke. Harrison's neck coloured, eyes on the window, pretending to study something in the distance. 'But why?' Fletcher threw a hand at the SDHC cards. 'Why screw the maisonette for these?'

'We don't know if they were looking for them, specifically,' said Harrison.

'Warren, go make the tea.' Fletcher, jabbing a finger. 'You should have been all over this, not cuffing it like some lazy fucking uniform carrier.'

A tic in Harrison's eye, the colour creeping into his cheeks. MacReady looked at the floor, felt Beck do likewise. Silence for a few seconds. The sound of Fletcher's office door opening and closing.

'Right,' said Fletcher. A clap of the hands. 'These things charged?'

MacReady: 'I gave them a blast for half an hour.'

'Should be enough.' He waved a hand. *Get on with it.*

Latex gloves for the second time that morning. MacReady handled the camcorders, Beck the memory cards. Turning them on, turning them over. Opening slots, examining ports and holes in the casings. Scratching at heads. MacReady, embarrassment creeping up on him.

'These are antiques,' Beck eventually said.

Fletcher glanced at the door as Harrison rattled in with the tea. 'Meaning?'

'They're analogue. Obsolete. They use videotape.'

'Not memory cards.' Fletcher pinched the bridge of his nose. 'What about smartphones? Could we . . .?'

Beck shook her head. 'They're not micro or mini cards.'

'I'm sorry,' said MacReady. 'I should have checked.'

'One of the computer terminals out there?' asked Fletcher. He gestured at the MIR.

'Our kit is older than these,' Beck said, looking at the camcorders.

Fletcher sighed. 'A laptop, then? Surely one of us has a laptop with an SD slot?'

Harrison, smirking. 'Stolen memory cards? Good luck getting anybody to let you stick one into their own gear.' He set the tray on Fletcher's desk.

Fletcher stared at Harrison, jaw working. Yanked the phone from his desk, held it to his ear as he jabbed buttons, slurped at his tea. 'Jimmy,' he said into the receiver. 'Just the man. You still got that card reader in your office?' A beat. 'Sounds about right. No worries. Yeah, up to our tits in it.'

Fletcher ended the call.

Beck: 'Who was that?'

'Local intel office upstairs,' Fletcher said. He picked up a pen, pushed at a memory card with its nib. 'The LIO has a gadget that can read these things. But, as per, theirs is kaput.' He smiled at Beck: 'So it looks like you're going on a jolly.'

'Sir?'

'Headquarters. I want those cards downloaded to disc by TSU.'

'Today? I've got –'

'We've all *got*, Charlie,' said Fletcher. He swivelled his chair to the window. 'I'll ring to let them know you're on your way. And take clever clogs with you.'

8

Couple of years since MacReady had been to HQ. Diversity course, compulsory, where he spent three days arguing with holier-than-thou civilian trainers. Grinding his teeth as they patronised, generalised. Ducked and dived when he challenged them. When he questioned the need for three days off shift, when there were only four of them as it was. Four cops to cover twelve square miles and thirty thousand-plus MOPs.

Lunch had been nice, though. Always was, up at the Dream Factory. Those senior ranks did like their perks. Prawn sarnies and endless coffee as they created flow charts, exchanged buzz-words, held meetings about how to hold an efficient meeting.

At the entrance Beck waited for the ANPR to recognise the job motor's plate; after a few seconds there was an audible beep from the camera and the electronic gates shifted skywards.

'Welcome to the Kremlin,' she muttered, and accelerated through the gap.

MacReady brushed a thumb over the memory cards through the plastic evidence bag. Hoped the trip would be worthwhile. Beck was annoyed. Irritated with him, with having to play chaperone when she had a million other things to deal with. He'd never known her so quiet for so long. He sat, saying nothing, the redbrick façade of the main headquarters building drifting by. To its right, the shiny new Scientific Support wing, a legacy of the last chief. His only legacy, the rest of tenure time spent bullying and demoralising the entire workforce over targets and government milestones and reducing stop-and-search figures while maintaining low knife-attack rates.

Into the guts, the engine rooms behind HQ's frontage. Out of public view, a drab and depressing jumble of huts and sixties concrete brutalism, of poorly signed Portakabins and prefab Terrapins. Potholed and pathetic car parks with no room to turn a Smart car, old office furniture piled against barbed wire fencing. Generators belching beside leaking downpipes. The Technical Support Unit right amongst the grime and puddles of water, a flat roofed bunker cowering at the base of the main radio mast.

'Bit shabby,' MacReady said.

Beck opened her door. 'Unlike the work they do.'

The camcorders and memory cards. A little jab there from his Sergeant, and it stung a little. He followed her into the TSU building.

Low ceiling, half-light. Racks of DVD players, hard disc drives, flickering LEDs, cables and wiring. Desks littered with paperwork, radio equipment, electrical tools, a mug emblazoned with *A monkey could do this job but I was here first*. A mess, but MacReady guessed there was some kind of organisation here, even if he couldn't see it.

The lone occupant peered up from a workbench. 'Coffee?' she asked, a smile beneath her trendy spectacles. The room was hot, sweltering, but she wore a gilet over her coveralls.

MacReady was about to ask for two sugars.

'Flying visit,' Beck said.

'Shame,' the woman said. 'We have the best Poundland can offer.'

'Did my DI –?'

The woman pointed to a corner of the room: two chairs, a table, a small box hooked up to a desktop computer via USB. 'Rigged it myself,' she said. 'Will read anything. Play anything. Burn images, too.'

'Thanks.' Beck nodded at her, but the woman was face down and back at the internals of a couple of Airwave handhelds she'd prised open. To MacReady: 'All yours.'

Other people's lives on the cards. Birthdays, holidays, domestic mundanity. Pets and kids and visiting elderly relatives. Stolen memories, the faces in the videos and stills long since paid their insurance money after the dwelling burglaries and thefts from vehicles. MacReady sat next to Beck, gloved up again, swapping the cards in the reader, clicking at the mouse, working through the files. Watching people he didn't know do all the things he might never do with Megan: recording their child's first steps. Their first words. Their first day at school. He thought of the adoption appointment: painful in the extreme. Taking on somebody else's child had been his idea all along – an escape from IVF prodding and poking and tests and endless payments, from the constant disappointment in his wife's eyes – and she'd gone with it, shown willing for so long, but this time Megan had been businesslike bordering on curt, almost as if she didn't care. As if none of it mattered anymore. MacReady had squirmed in his seat, the agency man on the other side of the desk all warm gestures and soft words, ring on his wedding finger, photograph of his wife and three children screaming their smiles.

MacReady pushed another SD card into the reader. 'Wish I had a coffee.'

'Tough titty.' Beck urged him on with a flick of her fingers. Dropped her eyes to the mobile phone on her lap. Checked the time. Exhaled, her breath blowing at her fringe.

MacReady clicked on the mouse.

Beck leaned forward. 'Hold on. Isn't that –?'

'Yeah,' said MacReady. Heart picking up the pace.

The maisonette. Leon King's place on the screen in front of them. The camera being whipped around, the picture shaky, flashes of lounge wall, threadbare carpet. Somebody using it for the first time. No time or date on the recording. Zoom in, zoom out, zoom in again. Voices, laughter. A face filling the screen, eyes narrowed, looking down the lens.

MacReady paused the MPEG. A nostril, pale skin, acne welts. 'Nice close-up.'

'King,' said Beck, face lit by the computer screen. 'Let it run.'

A click on the mouse. MacReady watched. Listened to King's voice, the street patois, *I'll give youse twenny dollar for it, bra, tha's much money, much money for dis ting.* He sounded drunk. Stoned, maybe.

The camera spun around.

Two faces. One black, one white. Wannabe gangstas, the patterns shaved in hair, in eyebrows, the posturing, the fingers cocked into gun shapes, the crooked teeth and junkie sweats and five-fashion-seasons-ago Helly Hansen tops. Haggling with King for more money for the camera they'd brought to him after screwing a van at a motorway service station while the owner bought smokes and flirted with the female staff.

MacReady paused the video again. 'Recognise them?'

'No,' Beck said. Fidgeting. Rocking. 'Play it. We might see something.'

'It's nearly finished,' MacReady said, pointing at the slider: almost all the way across the bottom of the screen. 'And we don't need to see anything else.'

'Why not?'

He grinned. Pointed at the white male.

'Because I know who he is and where he is.'

9

'This guy on the left is Dane Sillitoe.'

MacReady stood before the widescreen TV in the MIR. Beck at his side, face set and serious. The recording they'd burned onto DVD at HQ now paused. The faces of the two males filling the screen with wild eyes and yellow-toothed grins.

MacReady's finger hovered in front of the frozen features of the white male.

His audience: a dozen more frozen faces, watching him intently. The DCI, the Detective Superintendent, the rest of the Major Crime wallahs. Typists, indexers, the office manager. Harrison, staring from under knotted eyebrows.

Fletcher, nodding slowly, silently, eyes narrowed as they flicked from MacReady to the image fuzzing on the widescreen. He leaned to one side, the DCI whispering in his ear.

'I've never come across this Sillitoe,' said Fletcher, nodding as the DCI's mouth moved at the side of his head. 'You sure it's him, Will?'

'He's from the north of the city,' said MacReady. 'Used to deal with him a fair bit when I was stationed there on response.'

'For?'

'Juvenile crap. Minor damage. Drinking, bit of drugs and public order. Pain in the arse rich kid who went off the rails, really.'

Harrison: 'Looks like he moved on to bigger things if he's mixed up with King.'

Beck shook her head. 'For a while, maybe. But not anymore.'

'No offence, Sarge, but you couldn't possibly know that.'

'This recording,' MacReady dipped his head towards the TV, 'there's no time and date on it, but it's definitely not recent. Sillitoe looks like he's still on the gear in it. I'd say it's at least twelve months old. Probably older.'

'We've checked PNC and he's got nothing for the last fourteen months. And anyway . . .' Beck looked at MacReady.

'He's been breaking good and gone legit,' MacReady said. 'Few months ago, I pulled him on a routine traffic stop/check. Ran a red in a stretch limo. Suitable advice about his driving and all that, but we had a little chat. He's been clean for a year or so. Working for his old man, driving limousines and private ambulances.'

Beck: 'Hence the lack of recents.'

Harrison chuckled. 'Another scrote that's *cleaned up, man.* What a load of bollocks. He needs to come in.'

MacReady shrugged. Glanced about the room. At the faces staring at him. At the DCI muttering to Fletcher again. Didn't know what to do so shoved hands in pockets and waited.

'Nice,' Fletcher said to him eventually. 'Very nice, Will. I suppose you know where we can pick up this Dane Sillitoe character?'

MacReady nodded. 'His father's place is over by the steel-works. I'd go there if I was after him.'

'Well you are after him,' Fletcher said. He leaned his head towards Harrison, spoke without looking at him: 'Wazza, go with him. Pick up Sillitoe.'

'Cheers for that, boss,' muttered Harrison, squinting at the widescreen.

Fletcher broke up the gathering, clapping his hands, shoo-ing people to their desks and terminals. The DCI and Detective Super shuffled to one corner, deep in discussion.

'I mean it, Will,' said Fletcher, taking hold of MacReady's arm. 'Great work.'

'Local knowledge and all that, sir,' MacReady said. 'Isn't that why they roped us in on it?'

'This is all very bromance and backslappy,' said Beck, study-ing the TV. 'But what about the other guy in that picture?'

Fletcher looked at MacReady. At Beck. Was met with shrugs.

Car keys arced through the air towards MacReady. Hit his chest. He snatched a hand at them, stopped them falling to the floor, ignored the sharp pain in his pectoral and squeezed at the keys, angry.

'You're driving,' grunted Harrison. To Fletcher: 'And the lanky black kid is Jermaine Tate, aka Easyman, just in case you were wondering. Only just worked it out, but it's definitely him.' He glared at MacReady. 'Local knowledge and all that.'

Fletcher sighed. 'Fine. Deal with Sillitoe. Charlie and I will look for Tate.'

A laugh from Harrison. 'Best of luck. Nobody's seen that muppet for a long old time. It's like he's dropped off the face of the earth.'

Rover Way: a bleak and busy concrete two-lane skirting the eastern flank of the capital. Wild fields and rutted grassland. Social housing redbricks overlooking mudflats. The river, brown and languid, drifting into the waters of the Severn and onwards to the sea. Industrial units, slag heaps, the traveller site with its satellite dishes and feral dogs and burned-out stolen vehicles littering the shore behind. The area looked tired and dirty, as if the powers that be had once thrown a bit of money at it before deciding they couldn't really be bothered anymore.

MacReady dropped the CID car into second, matched pace with the line of HGVs rumbling towards the old docks in front of them. Beyond the wagons, in a haze of dust and late-afternoon sunlight, the colossal outline of the steelworks. Chimneys belched. The smell of sulphur in the air, in the car.

'Fucking gypos,' Harrison barked.

Three skinny nags on the roadside embankment. Loose, heads down, munching at grass. Oblivious to the passing traffic. Not long before they wandered into the road. Not long before the multiple three nines to police. MacReady shuddered as he thought of the countless incidents he used to attend when in uniform, shooing travellers' horses into fields, wasting hours rounding them up from dual carriageways and private estates. The visits to their owners, who'd deny all knowledge, refuse their details, or pretend they were the other Colin O'Flaherty and *no sir, dat's me brudder ya talkin' about and no ya can't speak to 'im he's gone back to da mudderland.* And whenever he'd put the arm on them they'd bleat about being the victim of ethnic abuse and threaten to make complaints to his Inspector.

MacReady didn't miss it one bit.

He was missing Beck's constant chatter, though. Cursing the travellers was the first thing Harrison had said since they had left the MIR. 'So how are we going to play this?' he asked.

Harrison continued staring out the window. 'You seem to be flavour of the month with the boss. You can do the talking.'

'And that's it?'

'I'll be there if needed.'

'Thanks for that.'

'Just think of it as good for your detective school report. All those boxes to tick . . .'

MacReady ignored him. Turned off Rover Way at a mini roundabout, snaked through the rows of parked cars outside a rental place. The industrial estate fanned out before them: corrugated warehouses, spiked fencing, MOPs trundling along in flatbeds with necks craned, searching for scrap metal dealers, for reclamation sites, for a quiet side road to fly tip the white goods bulging from the backs of their trucks.

He'd checked his old incident reports for the stop/check he'd done on Sillitoe before leaving the MIR, had Googled the father's company for the location. 'Here it is,' he said, pointing at a blue fence to their left.

'"Viper Travel"?' Harrison screwed his face up as he read the sign.

'VIP and Emergency Response.'

Harrison said nothing as MacReady drove onto the site.

Sillitoe Senior was clearly doing well for himself. Half a dozen stretch limousines lined the wall overlooking the shore. Four Mercedes Sprinter vans, blacked up and blacked out, *Private Ambulance* in white on their bonnets, neatly parked in a cluster near a row of storage containers. A workshop to one side, the roller doors open, another limo being worked on by overalled grease monkeys, a concrete ramp sloping down to an underground car park. In the exterior car park where MacReady stared out of the CID car window: ten staff spaces filled with expensive German motors and executive 4x4s.

'I'm in the wrong job,' he said. Eyes on them now, the mechanics stopping to scrutinise their car, cock their heads at the telltale sound of plod's diesel engine sputtering as MacReady swung it around the car park and slid into a space near the roadside fence.

'Could've told you that when you joined the department,' said Harrison. He opened the car door. 'You think this kid is in work today?'

'I rang before we left. Asked for Dane. He came to the phone.'

'Well done you.'

The reception area was cramped but immaculate. Potted yucca, three low seats, a table with a selection of magazines and free newspapers. Locked door leading into the bowels of the business. Local radio whispering from hidden speakers, the latest disposable TV talent show quartet emoting to a lush backing track while their nascent career inched inexorably towards headlining Butlins.

'Good afternoon.'

MacReady guessed the woman at the hatch was late forties, early fifties, but looked good for it. The smartest receptionist he'd seen: business suit nipped and tucked in all the right places to show off her slim frame, hair chopped and feathered and achingly trendy. Reading glasses perched on top of the dyed copper spikes. Smile warm and welcoming.

He showed his warrant card and the smile thinned.

'Afternoon.' He flashed teeth anyway. 'We'd like to have a word with Dane Sillitoe, please.'

'Can I ask what it's about?'

Harrison: 'Of course you can.'

Her face hardened. 'What is it about?'

'We can't tell you,' said Harrison.

'Well then I can't let you in.' A shrug. 'So piss off.'

'How easily the mask slips,' said Harrison. 'Dragged up and all that.'

Behind her, heads had turned. Staff members looking up from their desks, their laptops, sensing the shift in atmosphere at the public counter.

MacReady threw Harrison a look. 'Madam,' he said, turning to the woman, 'we'd rather talk to Dane in private, if that's OK. It's rather . . . sensitive.'

'That may be the case,' she said. 'But you're in my business premises asking to speak to my son.'

Not a receptionist, then. MacReady nodded. 'Mrs Sillitoe, we –'

'Just let them through, Jan.'

The voice came from behind her. MacReady dropped his head to one side, saw a flash of spiked black hair as a male disappeared into a glassed cubicle wedged into the corner of the room. A hand pulled closed the vertical blinds.

Mrs Sillitoe's chest rose and fell in a sigh. She closed her eyes for a moment. 'The master has spoken,' she muttered, polished nail pressing a button on the counter.

The door buzzed; MacReady pushed through it. Harrison yawned as he followed. In the open-plan office the staff pretended to work, typing nothing, talking on phones to nobody.

'In here,' the male called from the cubicle. Loud, clear, commanding.

'Thanks,' MacReady said to Mrs Sillitoe.

She blinked slowly, sat down at a desk, said nothing. Mouth pinched as she watched them tramp across the carpet towards what MacReady assumed was her husband's inner sanctum.

He was surprised to find Dane Sillitoe in the cubicle. Lounging on a chair on the other side of his father's desk. Suited up. A charcoal effort, shoes gleaming, one ankle hooked over a knee and jiggling. His mouth worked gum. His eyes, narrow. Old habits around the filth.

'Looking good, Dane,' MacReady said.

Sillitoe winked, looked from Harrison to MacReady. 'Not so bad yourself, officer. Where's the funny hat?'

'Long gone, thankfully.'

'We've both gone up in the world, then.'

A snort from Harrison. 'It might not last.'

Directed at them both, MacReady knew. And a nudge from the old sweat, too.

'Dane,' MacReady said. 'We need to talk to you ab—'

'Gentlemen,' the father said. A faint smile. He rose, proffered a hand. A thick watch on the wrist. 'Scott Sillitoe.'

MacReady shook. Felt smooth skin. Smelled aftershave, woody and overpowering. The father's grasp tight and lingering. A little too tight, perhaps. Sillitoe Senior's gaze on him. Studying MacReady. MacReady did likewise, saw Dane in twenty-five years' time: face fleshier, slight paunch, flecks of grey at the temples. Father and son shared the same whiff of arrogance.

'Pleasure,' said MacReady.

'All mine,' said the father, sitting. 'Now close the door, please.'

There was something in the tone of voice; a man used to his own way, to people immediately doing what was asked of them. MacReady watched as Harrison waited a second or two, then pushed it closed ever so slowly, as if it was oh-so-much effort. There was a heavy, expensive *thunk*. Harrison leaned against the door, hands in pockets, expressionless.

'Was it you lot that rang?' Dane Sillitoe asked. Chewing the gum.

'Of course it was,' MacReady said.

'Old tricks,' said Dane.

MacReady nodded. 'Wasted journey otherwise. You know what it's like.'

'Not anymore. Business man now.' Dane gave a smug smile. 'Earning more coin in a couple of days than you plods do in a frigging month, yeah?'

'Like we haven't heard that one before,' MacReady shrugged. 'But well done you for getting the jibe in.'

'Prolly because it's true. Yours is a mug's game –'

'He's out of all that rubbish now,' Scott Sillitoe interrupted. 'And we're extremely busy. So can we hurry this along?'

'Jermaine Tate,' MacReady said. 'Also known as Easyman. Remember him?'

Gum paused between Sillitoe's teeth. A flicker of something across his face. Gone in an instant. 'What about him?'

'You were running with him about a couple of years back.'

'Like I said, not anymore.'

'We have you on a video recording with him. On a memory card. Found it in a maisonette in Butetown a couple of weeks ago. You heard about what happened down there?'

Scott Sillitoe: 'Is this the shooting?' His fingers steepled beneath his chin. His eyes flicking from MacReady to his son. A faint look of displeasure on his face.

MacReady nodded. He was staring at Dane Sillitoe. 'The recording was made in that maisonette, Dane. You've been in there. You know the guy who was dossing there. Leon King? Ring a bell?'

'That was a long time back,' Sillitoe said. His shiny shoe jiggled furiously. 'I was fucked up a lot then. It's different now . . .'

'Well I'll tell you what's really fucked up, Dane,' MacReady said. 'We have a dead police officer. Leon King was also shot but we can't ask why because he's in a coma. And despite your swanky suit and swagger you're currently our best bet at working out who did it. So you're coming in with us.'

Sillitoe paled. The shoe went still. He looked to his father. Up at MacReady. Swallowed. 'I haven't shot anyone. I didn't know Leon had been shot. I haven't . . . I don't even remember . . .'

Scott Sillitoe stood. Leaned onto his desk, knuckles down. Spoke quietly. 'What the hell have you gotten yourself into, Dane?'

'It's nothing to do with me.'

'You're under arrest, Dane,' MacReady said.

'What the fuck for?'

'Handling stolen goods, for a start,' MacReady said. He pulled cuffs from his jacket pocket. 'After that, who knows?'

'What the hell have you brought into my business?' Scott Sillitoe roared.

A face at the narrow window in the door. Spiked copper hair. Glasses wedged on top. Mrs Sillitoe's frown beneath.

Harrison opened the door a crack. Shook his head at her.

'I can't let you in,' he smiled. 'So piss off.'

This time Harrison did the talking.

Picking up Sillitoe, the donkey work, done. The nuanced detective work handed over to the seasoned vets. MacReady stared at the digital numbers on the recording device, still bristling at the Major Crime DCI's decision that Harrison should take the lead during interview. Harder to take was the fact Harrison moaned about having to do it. About not getting home on time again, about earache from his wife, *and if it wasn't for the fuckin' ovies I'd be out the door.*

Dane Sillitoe's brief: Malcolm Gill. The Sillitoe family solicitor. Toothpick-thin, bespectacled, gauzy thatch of white hair. Never looked at anybody when he spoke. Ruddy face in notes on the interview room desk, pen in hand, scribbling.

Said: 'My client's already answered that question, officer.'

And Sillitoe had. He knew nothing about Garratt. Could provide dates and times when he was ferrying clients or introducing them to the delights of the city's casinos, and he was working when it happened. The arrogance, gone. But he was lucid and convincing and MacReady believed him. It was clear Harrison did, too.

Harrison sniffed. Different tack. 'Tell us about Jermaine Tate.'

'Easyman?' Sillitoe asked. 'What d'you want to know?' Tilting his chair backwards on two legs. Rocking. Chewing again. As if he didn't know what they were talking about. Fucking disclosure and poxy defence briefs.

'We need to speak to him too.'

'I can tell you he had nothing to do with this dead copper.'

'That's very helpful. Where is he?'

'Psshh.' Sillitoe shrugged. 'He's, y'know, long gone, brother.'

'We don't want to be doing fifteen dawn raids on his LKAs. So where?'

'Abroad.' Another shrug. Chair rocking. It was annoying MacReady. The room so hot, too. He wanted to kick the other legs from under Sillitoe's chair. Keep the fucker still. He was trying for cocky, but there was something underneath. Nerves, maybe.

Harrison, irritated: '*Where?*'

Gill looked up. A hard stare at Harrison. Dropped his face back to his notes.

'Europe,' said Sillitoe. 'Er . . . Portugal, think it was. Not seen him for time, man. He's doing all right, last I heard. Got a wife and couple of kiddies, apparently.'

'Apparently?'

'Well yeah. Spoke to him the other week, didn't I?' Sillitoe licked at his bottom lip, blinking quickly.

'I don't know, Dane. Did you?'

'Yeah . . . Yeah, I did.'

'Sure about that?'

Sillitoe dropped the chair down onto four legs. A quick look from Harrison to MacReady, back to Harrison. A smirk. 'Positive.'

Harrison bailed Sillitoe.

Unconditional. Four weeks. Argued that it was enough time to turn up Jermaine Tate. Enough time to eliminate Sillitoe from the inquiry altogether, most likely. Like Harrison, MacReady was certain Dane knew nothing about Garratt, but wasn't convinced about other aspects of the interview. He'd ensured he got Tate's mobile number before Sillitoe left the custody suite.

'Well, it's my call,' said Harrison. 'I've run it by Fletcher and he's pushed it further up the pipe and it's nods all day long. Bail. Bish bosh, job done, I go home for my tea.'

They were in the small kitchenette off the main custody booking-in area. A civilian jailer feigned deafness in one corner, eyes not taking in anything on the newspaper page he held in front of him.

'We could have charged him,' MacReady said.

'Handling a stolen memory card that costs a fiver? You're having a laugh, boy. Get the civvies at the hub to spend hours prepping a file only for the CPS to drop it? Or get him a conditional discharge at Mags? That's uniform-level rubbish.'

MacReady shook his head. 'Something's not right.'

'Oh Christ, here we go.'

'Sillitoe's lying. About Tate.'

'Scrote doesn't tell the truth and whole truth to the police, shock horror.'

'I could tell. I don't think he knows where Tate is. He's lying about Portugal. He looked more nervous when we asked him about Easyman than he did with any of the questions about Garratt.'

Harrison rubbed at his temples, looked to the floor. Up at the jailer. Back to MacReady. 'I'm going home now. I have had enough of you today. Goodbye.'

He checked his pack of smokes, gathered his coat, walked out of the kitchenette.

MacReady called after him. 'I'll try Tate's number now, then.'

'You do that,' Harrison's voice came back at him. 'Fuckin' golden boy.'

* * *

Tension.

The lack of it. When he arrived home – on time for once – he'd sensed something was off. Something was different. Missing.

It had taken him a little while to realise what was wrong: everything was all right.

Megan, in the kitchen. Preparing food for them both, bottle of white already on the go. Singing along to the music playing on the radio. Breathy, barely audible, like she always did when she was happy. Like she hadn't done for so long. She'd looked up at him as he walked in. Smiled, the spoon to her lips, tasting food as she cooked. She'd stepped over to him. Placed hands on his shoulders, stared into his eyes. Leaned forward, placed a soft kiss on his lips.

'Thank you,' he'd said, genuinely surprised.

He'd been thrown, had recalled the night weeks before when it had all gone so terribly wrong, that night before Garratt was shot dead: meal, drinks, an attempt at a roll around on their bedroom floor swiftly followed by embarrassment and guilt. But MacReady had gone with it again tonight. Had enjoyed it. Hadn't questioned it. So tired of all the questions at home and in work. They'd eaten, and made small talk, and laughed together for the first time in an age, and the evening had drifted on and he'd drifted with it, content to sit and just be.

MacReady lay next to a sleeping Megan in the dark heart of the night. The quilt rumpled, still warm from their lovemaking. From their first time in months. One arm draped over his eyes. Thinking. Thinking about the sudden change in Megan. Trying to make sense of everything. The mess of the Bob Garratt case.

The whereabouts of Jermaine Tate. The contact number Dane Sillitoe had given him: dead air. Sillitoe and his lies. The constant enmity with Harrison. That tomorrow would be another day spent marginalised in the MIR. Making tea. Menial tasks. Pushed to the fringes.

Most of all he was thinking about the magazines. The adoption paperwork. Megan's collection of forms and notices, her calendar marked with appointments and meetings with agencies and doctors. All the things she'd been doing – just for him. Adoption, when what she desperately wanted was a child of her own.

He hadn't seen any of them this evening. Had checked the recycling bin before bed. Had found most of them curled inside. Unwanted. Discarded. He'd walked up the stairs, relieved it was over. Relieved she'd made the decision not to go along with what he'd forced upon her. They'd talk about it tomorrow. Talk when she was ready.

MacReady yawned, rolled over to Megan. Curled an arm around her midriff. Pulled her tight against him. Felt her soft skin against his. Felt her fold into his embrace.

Fell asleep.

10

The University Hospital of Wales. The UHW. *The Heath* to the locals. A sprawling mass situated off the main arterial road that cut through the city from east to west. Over a hundred buildings on the site. Seventies architecture mixed with post-modern style: all steel tubes and glass and metal walkways and canopies, an enormous hamster cage. A maze of roads and miniature roundabouts that were marginally less confusing than the layout of the main hospital interior.

MacReady never enjoyed visiting because every time he did he got lost.

It was morning, and busy. The car parks with their exorbitant fees jammed with visitors' vehicles. Beck eventually found a slot near A and E, dumped the CID car next to a rubbish skip beneath the helipad. Placed the vehicle's log book on the dashboard, force emblem visible to deter ticket-happy Parking Nazis.

'Should keep the pavement wasps away,' she said.

MacReady had slept fitfully. Had dreamed about Megan, and fresh starts. About the inquiry. He was first in to the MIR, had tried the mobile number again, hoping for Tate to answer. Static in his ear. He'd cursed Sillitoe once more. Fired off emails and made phone calls, too early for any of the agencies to be open yet: the Identity and Passport Service, the Department for Work and Pensions, Special Branch at Cardiff Wales Airport. Checked the electoral register on the force mapping system. All for Jermaine Tate. Anything to trace him. His movements. His whereabouts. He didn't believe Sillitoe was being straight about Portugal, but if he was MacReady wanted to know when Tate left the country. If and when he'd returned. Where he was picking up his dole money.

He'd left contact details. Stressed the urgency in getting a reply. Something to do. Something to help. Anything.

Beck led the way along the hospital concourse, low heels clicking on glossy floor.

'Seen a PM?' she asked him.

MacReady was checking his mobile. Willing some early bird at the DWP to ring him, to tell him Easyman was collecting his benefits in a post office just around the corner from a police station. He blinked. 'On video, at training school. Never in the flesh, so to speak. But I've dealt with enough sudden deaths to know what to expect.'

'Really?' A hint of a smile.

There was warmth in his cheeks. 'I'll just see how it goes. Should be an experience.'

Her hand towards his. 'Fiver says you hurl.'

He didn't have five pounds in his wallet. Shook anyway. Saw the grin. 'You know something I don't, Sarge?'

'Already had a chat with the pathologist. I think the word we're looking for is *fruity*.'

The mortuary was tucked behind Accident and Emergency. *Convenient*, MacReady thought. So many drug users and pub brawlers gone quickly from one to the other. So many grieving relatives sitting in the waiting room, sobbing. In just over four years he'd seen it all: boy racers who'd walked away from RTCs but died of massive internal injuries an hour later; student girls who'd taken their first 'E' during fresher week before collapsing on a dance floor and being brought in DOA; first-time parents who'd left their infant unattended in a car on a hot summer's day, boiling it to death in ten minutes.

People never learned.

A cheerful chap in a pale blue gown, the pathology technician handed them gowns of their own. Cast sideways glances at Beck. Ushered them into a brightly lit room.

MacReady recoiled at the smell. It filled the room, cloying and pungent. Claustrophobic, almost. He swallowed. Placed a hand under his nose.

Beck: 'Very fruity.'

A dark lump on the stainless-steel dissection table. Meat and flesh and the powder white of jagged bones. Blackened and swollen. The Home Office forensic pathologist bent over it. *Barnard*, thought MacReady, remembering the name now, picturing the old smoothy lifting crime scene tape. *Gordon Barnard. He was at the Garratt shooting.*

The cheery technician stood attentively to one side, exhibit bags and labels on a desk. In the corner a photographer was busy adjusting settings on her digital camera.

'Detective Sergeant.' Barnard looked up, his raised eyebrows strips of steel wool curled around the bar of his bifocals. The faintest of smiles beneath a surgical mask. His voice calm, unhurried: a man chatting to a friend over a fine meal. 'Missed you at the Graving Docks the other day. A shame. Always a pleasure to see you.'

Beck winked. 'Likewise, Prof.'

'You're rather late.'

'Hospital parking,' she shrugged.

'Quite,' Barnard said. 'But we had to start without you, I'm afraid.'

He waved a gloved hand. Gristle on the compound bone-cutter he held.

The putrid stench thick in the air, in his nostrils. MacReady stared at the lump. Couldn't work it out. Turned to Beck. Found her eyeing the redhead holding the camera. He thought of Bob Garratt. Wondered if Barnard had done the post mortem. Pictured Fletcher and Major Crime in here, making the same small talk, eyeing the same redhead. Garratt just so much meat and bone to be opened and weighed and measured.

'So what have you got for me?' Beck asked

Barnard returned to the mound of decomposed flesh. 'Well I hope you're not busy at the moment.'

'I'm always busy.'

Barnard glanced upwards. 'This poor . . . *thing* has been in the water for some time. But even at this early stage I can tell you it's clearly not a suicide.'

MacReady, still staring, saw Beck's shoulders slump out the corner of his eye. Heard the sigh.

A pause. Then: 'Isn't that just wonderful,' she muttered.

'Sorry,' Barnard said. He poked at the lump, latex finger on green-black flesh. 'But you're looking at a torso. Decapitated. Limbs amputated. Eviscerated. Rather difficult to do this to yourself, no?'

MacReady's head swam. Finally made sense of what he was staring at. The curve of ribs. The marbled nub of a shoulder. The powdered, shrunken remains of the genitals. He turned to Beck, to the smiling technician, to the redhead leaning against one wall. Back to Barnard. 'Hollowed out?'

'This here,' Barnard nodded, reaching into a bowl in the meat, 'is the stomach cavity.' His hand disappeared.

Beck was shaking her head.

'It's in a very poor state,' Barnard said. His eyebrows shifted upwards. 'And there's much work to be done. But I'd say what you have here is the torso of a young adult male.'

The pathologist's mask shifted. His lips pursed. Thinking. Studying the lump.

'Or,' he said, 'possibly a teenage boy.'

MacReady turned down Beck's offer of a coffee in the hospital cafeteria.

Left her shaking her head as he scurried out. Found a toilet in the corridor. Locked the cubicle door. Dropped to his knees. Brought up his breakfast. The smell of decayed flesh still on his clothes, his skin. He retched until he was dry-heaving, until there was nothing left.

'Christ,' he drooled into the toilet bowl. Reached for tissues, wiped at his mouth. He'd lasted the distance while Barnard sliced and sawed, but any sense of achievement was sullied by losing the bet. A fiver he couldn't afford to part with. And the knowledge Beck would likely tell everyone in the MIR that he'd puked like a proby at their first sudden death.

In the corridor he hesitated. Looked at the cafeteria doors, pictured Beck waiting for him, hand out. Told-you-so smile. Couldn't face it.

He headed for the lifts.

A low hum to the Adult Critical Care Unit. Hushed, the soft sound of medical equipment working, of bleeps and flat shoes whispering on polished tiles. The tang of disinfectant cloaking the hallway leading to the nurses' desk.

MacReady showed his warrant card. 'Leon King?'

The nurse glanced up from a computer screen. Pointed.

'Thanks,' he smiled.

'Hands first,' she said. Moved her finger to the dispenser on one wall. 'Please.'

He rubbed the alcohol gel into his hands, his clothes. Over his face. The nurse studied him, eyebrow raised. He didn't care, just wanted the stink off him.

'How is he?'

Two ARV officers in the bed area. One sitting. Other leaning against a wall. MP5s, sidearms, body armour. Old *FHM* magazines and empty vending machine cups on a table next to them. They looked bored, frustrated at having to babysit.

'He's great company,' the one in the chair muttered. He yawned, placing hands to his mouth as he leaned back. Muscled upper arms, the swirl of a tattoo poking from beneath his black tee. 'Real chatty, like.'

MacReady glanced across the room. Leon King, flat and pale under sheets and blankets, wired and tubed to ventilators, surrounded by monitors and pumps and filters and a clutch of people whose faces were drawn and angry. It was odd to see him at last. Until now he'd been just a name, a blurred close-up on video, a photo tacked to the whiteboard, a ghost hovering in the MIR.

'Family?'

The second firearms officer nodded. 'Yup.'

One of them, a woman, turned towards the sound of their voices. Glared. Clutching the bandaged hand of King. MacReady pictured the blood on the maisonette floor, the table. Ducked his head at the woman.

Fuck off, she mouthed. Turned away.

'Wouldn't bother,' said the muscled officer. 'They're anti.'

'Clearly,' said MacReady. He wanted King to wake. To talk. Willed him to open his gummed eyes right there and then. 'Anything from him? From the family?'

The gun plods swapped glances. The officer leaning on the wall straightened. 'You serious?'

'Don't you lot talk to each other?' asked the officer in the chair. 'There's suits in here every day, asking the same SFQs, when it's obvious that fucker,' he hooked a thumb at King, 'is never going to wake up.'

'Bollocks to him anyway,' said the other officer. 'One less scrote.'

'He's somebody's son,' said MacReady. He felt hot. Infuriated. His collar tight. 'And we need him alive. We need him to tell us what happened. Don't you get it?'

Another exchange of glances. Faces looking their way from King's bedside.

Somebody's son. MacReady looked at the woman who'd cursed at him. King's mother, no doubt. He thought of Megan. Of what they'd been through of late. Of last night, the sudden turnaround, the change. Her decision not to go ahead with the adoption.

Better not to have something at all than love it then lose it, he reasoned.

He made as if to speak to the ARV gorillas. Felt his phone vibrate in his jacket. Dug it out of the pocket, saw Beck's name on the screen.

Her voice in his ear: 'You'd better not be where I think you are, numbnuts.'

11

Bob Garratt's funeral only served to compound the sense of inertia. It was an acute reminder of who they had lost, and what little progress had been made in the investigation. MacReady had hovered on the fringes, chewing at the insides of his lips, mouthing platitudes to anybody who he thought might be related to Garratt. He'd chatted quietly to the pencil-thin crematorium manager, a nervous man who constantly fingered limp strands of hair that fell over his eyes. They'd sung and bowed heads and listened to the eulogy, shut out the sobs from his wife, his child. It was over in twenty minutes, and they had trooped out of the crematorium chapel and into the rain, and that was that.

The gloom followed them back to the MIR. No hustle, no bustle. Telephones silent. Screensavers swooping on LCD screens. The whiteboard a morass of names and locations and question marks. So many questions marks.

One face in the middle of it all: Jermaine 'Easyman' Tate. His most recent custody photo, his PNC ID and CRO number underneath. His last known address, his contacts and associates and family. All of it over a year old. All of it prior to his trip to Europe.

Tate was now the man they were looking for.

From the maisonette: a microscopic drop of blood on a skirting board. Analysed for Tate's DNA, and Easyman's name pinged up as a match at the Forensic Science Service lab. The result had come in as they were leaving the MIR. No time to do anything other than shelve the information for an hour or so. The Major Crime Detective Super had affixed Tate's mugshot to the board and waved staff out of the office and to the line of police cars waiting to take them to the crematorium.

MacReady knew – they all knew – that the blood could be old, could have spurted from a vein while Tate injected gear a long time ago. No way to tell if it dropped there during the burglary, or after Garratt's shooting, or at any other time beforehand. CSI at the Garratt scene might have missed it on a sweep. But along with the video recording, it placed him at the maisonette at some point. And it was all they had. But that was enough, for now.

All they had to do was find him.

More results had appeared in MacReady's email inbox during the funeral.

Negative from Job Centres citywide and beyond. Nothing on the electoral register. No bank or building society accounts. No arrests for fourteen months. Not in prison, in a hostel, in the Hilton snorting coke off the nipples of five-quid-an-hour Eastern European whores. The drinkers and vagrants who sank meth and cheap cider on the embankments of the River Taff in sun and pissing-down rain: none of them knew Tate. His family: anti-police, knew nothing, hadn't seen him, didn't care and *if you comes round 'ere again I'll set me fuckin' dog on you, bra.*

MacReady scooped up what he had, trotted over to the DI's office.

Fletcher studied the sheaf of papers, face in hands. 'I'll let the Super know.' He didn't look up. 'Thanks for checking anyway.'

Anyway. Like he knew it would be pointless. MacReady batted it away. 'I'm still waiting on Special Branch.'

'Your contact?'

'Tim Randall.'

Fletcher closed his eyes. 'Ring him again,' he said, then looked at MacReady. He slumped back in his chair; rain tapped the window behind, thick rivulets of water running on glass. 'Now. And keep ringing him.'

'Something I should know?'

'His old man was an ACC back in the day. Timothy rode on it. Let's say I . . . *arranged* for him to leave my team a few years back. Got fed up with him walking around corridors with files under his arm and pretending to be busy. You need to keep haranguing him, because he's still riding on daddy's rep.'

'Don't you just love nepotism?'

'Not really, no.'

MacReady picked up a phone in the MIR, dialled the SB extension. Was about to hang up when the call was answered. He recognised the voice as Randall's.

''Lo?' A tone. Irritation at the interruption. Behind the grunt: a television. Female voice: . . . *that's right, plummeting property prices have made the Costa Blanca a buyer's market.* MacReady shook his head, pictured Tim Randall's typical day: sitting in the Special Branch office at the airport, feet up and flicking through daytime TV as he munched on snacks. Occasionally, MacReady knew, Randall would wander out into the passenger area to puff up his chest and flirt with the catering assistants in the departure lounge restaurant.

He brought Randall up to speed, impressed upon him the urgency of the enquiries he'd emailed about Jermaine Tate, and hung up. He suspected that Randall had been pretending to scribble everything down during the call.

With Beck out of the MIR working the bloater and Harrison avoiding him, MacReady had nothing to do and nobody to do it with. He stretched, thought about making a brew. Thought about slipping out of the room to ring Megan.

The telephone rang.

Switchboard: 'Call for DC Will MacReady.'

It was Randall. 'Got some stuff for you.'

'Fuck me, that was quick.'

Randall yawned. 'Came through yesterday lunchtime, actually, but I forgot about it to be honest. Been a bit hectic here . . .'

MacReady stifled a scream. 'Go on.'

'Jermaine Tate, lemme see,' Randall said. Paper rustling. Did that *tch-tch-tch* thing down the line that MacReady hated. 'Yep, here we go. Records show he flew from Cardiff International to Lisbon in March of last year. KLM to Amsterdam, Amsterdam to –'

'To Lisbon,' MacReady said. 'So he did go abroad.'

'Looks that way.'

'Alone?'

'Looks that way, too.'

Sillitoe. He'd been straight up about Tate leaving the country. MacReady glanced at his emails, all the negatives from agencies. It explained why they had no record of him.

'Owe you one, Tim,' MacReady said, thinking he owed him nothing. That he could have been working with this since yesterday. He went to put the phone down.

'You want the rest of it or not?' Randall asked.

'There's more?'

'Sure is. Return flight was three days later. Lisbon to Amsterdam to Cardiff, alone.'

MacReady stared at the emails.

No record of Tate whatsoever.

'He came back,' he breathed.

MacReady was on his feet and walking towards Fletcher's office; the phone lay on the desk, Randall talking to no one.

Twitching blinds. Fag-smoking baby mommas watching from doorsteps, all tattoos and muffin tops and the sallow skin of KFC diets. Kids astride stolen, battered pushbikes, wheeling around the car, a circle of hooded, vacant eyes in hoodies. Satellite dishes dripped rain, dripped Jeremy Kyle and shopping channels and endless daytime reruns into homes where floors remained uncarpeted and teens were schooled by first-person shooters.

MacReady thought of his brother. 'Shall I keep an eye on the motor?'

The kids, still orbiting the CID car. Nine, ten years old at most. Fearless. Noisily clearing throats, gobbing on the road. Fletcher crawled the car into the cul-de-sac, killed the engine. Shook his head at MacReady.

'Rather have you with me. Car can be fixed easily. Me, not so much.'

MacReady checked through the windscreen. Boxy homes, the metal mesh of council house curtains, hardstands glittering with broken glass beneath vandalised cars. Saint Mellons. Sounded lovely. Wasn't in the slightest. A mass of new-development toy houses lumped around cul-de-sacs and twisting tarmac. Uniform unfortunate enough to work this remote eastern outpost referred to it – with faux *Kairdiff* accent – as *The Mellon*.

The house they were visiting: streaked and mottled with mildew. Front garden a badly paved resting place for car parts, a sprung sofa, a rotary washing line *sans* line. The rusted hulk of a Ford Granada wedged against a low breezeblock wall, windows long gone, tyres flat and bald and overgrown with weeds. Chained to the front door: a squat, muscular dog, silently watching them as they approached, black eyes tapered, one fang already erupting from the drool of its mouth.

'Junior officer first,' said Fletcher.

MacReady paused at the gate. A low growl from the dog, strutting towards them, the chain rattling on concrete. 'Boss, I'm not sure –'

'Joking,' said Fletcher. Riffled through the file he carried. Dug out his mobile. 'I'll get them to come out and secure it. I might be the old friendly black face for the Tates to see, but I very much doubt that thing cares about skin colour.'

MacReady listened to his DI put a call into the house, argue with Jermaine Tate's mother. The dog – a bulky, brindle Staff – strained at its chain, a rumble in its throat; MacReady pictured the police dog at the Garratt shooting again.

'Coming out now,' said Fletcher, ending the call. To the Staff: 'Nice doggie.'

MacReady turned to Fletcher. 'Thanks for letting me tag along.'

The DI waved it away. 'You did all the desk work off your own back. Thought you'd like to see it through. Besides, I suspect it might not be a warm welcome. I got uniform to come here, ask some questions about Tate. It didn't end well.'

'I heard.'

'So now we know he came back . . . thought we'd do a proper job.'

'A proper job.' MacReady hitched his eyebrows.

'You're not a woodentop anymore. No need to take offence.'

'None taken.'

The front door opened. A shriek, coarse and deafening: '*Caesar, in.*'

A woman glared at them from the door. Overweight, large breasts, larger thighs shrink-wrapped in Lycra leggings. Bulbous eyes sunk into the flesh of her dark skin, hair braided into cornrows. The Staff now at her feet, her hands working the chain free, baggy forearms juddering as she hauled the dog into the house.

'Stand there playin' with your bollocks and giving these twats,' a thick knuckle thrust at staring, smiling neighbours, 'more stuff to gossip about? You want to come in you come in now, righ'?' Back turned on them, she waddled inside.

'She seems lovely,' said MacReady.

'Charming,' said Fletcher. A fixed smile as he opened the gate. 'And I bet it's less than five minutes before she calls me an Uncle Tom.'

'Or a coconut,' MacReady chuckled.

Fletcher glanced at him. 'Less of it.'

'No offence.'

'None taken, honky.'

Jermaine Tate's mother said nothing of the sort.

She said nothing at all for a while. The television blared; no offer to lower the volume let alone turn it off as Fletcher explained why they were there. She watched them from the frayed settee, thick legs crossed at the knee, slipper hanging from her raised foot. Calloused skin on the heel. One hand draped over an ashtray on a side table, cigarette burning between fingers, TV remote control next to the ashtray. Other hand curled around her right eye, trying for nonchalant yet failing to hide bruising that was yet to fade completely.

'We know he came back into the country, Marie. So where is he?'

Fletcher, working her. Patient. Battling to be heard over the flat screen. Over the whining and scrabble of claws coming from the other side of the kitchen door.

She looked to the window: her husband – Jermaine's step-father – framed there, a scrawny silhouette leaning against the sill, arms folded. The animosity coming off him in waves.

She puffed on the ciggie, turned back to Fletcher. 'Not seen him. We told the other coppers. Not seen him. Not seen him for a time.'

Her voice, robotic almost. Things were well off, MacReady knew. An atmosphere there, air thick with stale fag smoke and spilt lager fumes and tension. The living room: drab, decorated a decade ago, paintwork chipped and scraped to plaster. The door to the hallway cracked and buckled, fist-sized holes pocking yellowing gloss. Behind them, at a dining table, a pretty young woman sitting with a mug of tea in one hand. Sipping, listening. Something about the tightness in her face doing nothing to dispel MacReady's concerns that all was not right in this house. Jermaine Tate's sister, no doubt. The resemblance was there.

Fletcher shook his head, his frustration clear. He turned away, rubbed at his eyes and hooked a thumb at the television. 'Any chance we could mute this thing?'

MacReady squatted to his haunches in front of Jermaine Tate's mother as she lifted the remote and turned off the TV. 'Please, Mrs Tate, if you –'

'It's Brissett,' said her husband. His jaw clenched and unclenched, his head lowered and looking up at them through thin, furrowed eyebrows. 'She don't use that name no more.'

'Shut up, Nathan.' Marie Brissett outed her cigarette, agitated. Blew smoke at MacReady. Lit another Lambert and Butler, eyed Fletcher and MacReady over the glowing tip, speaking as if by rote, as if the words were scripted and even she was bored of trotting them out to the law. 'You can keep astin' and astin' and you'll get the same answer. We ain't seen him, we don't know where he is, and if you lot keep coming round here we're going to get a lawyer and sue you for harassment.'

Her hand fell away from her eye as she spoke. The bruises. Pale, threaded with broken blood vessels, scabbed cuts on the bridge of her nose, around the eyebrow. MacReady turned to Nathan Brissett. Saw the scram marks and swollen furrows on his neck, matching bruises on his arms, his tightened jaw.

His and hers.

The doorway with its fist-holes.

The young woman at the table, rigid, fearful. Eyes flitting from her mother to Nathan Brissett. Lips parted, as if she wanted to say something.

MacReady placed a hand on Marie Brissett's leg; she flinched. 'Is there anything you want to tell us, Marie? Not just about Jermaine. Is there anything at all going on at home? We have specially trained officers you can talk t—'

Brissett: 'Get your fuckin' hands off my wife, boy.'

A clatter as the girl sprang from the table, chair banging against a wall, and rushed towards Brissett with hands raised.

'No,' she cried. 'Don't. Please.'

'Mind your business, Soraya,' Brissett growled.

Fletcher met him halfway across the living room. 'Easy now, Nathan.'

Eyeball to eyeball. Brissett pushed his forehead against Fletcher's. 'You fuckin' sell-out.'

'No selling out here, Nathan. Just working.'

'Please, Nathan,' the girl pleaded, tugging at her stepfather's sleeve. 'Please don't wind them up. *Please*.'

Brissett ignored her. 'Working, cha,' he spat at Fletcher. 'You a performing monkey, bruv. Dance for your masters, yeah?'

Fletcher stepped away. Looked from Brissett to the girl. Turned to MacReady. 'We're done here.'

'Fuckin' right you cunts are.' Brissett, pacing the room. 'You come back, the dog is on you.'

MacReady stood. The business card he'd left next to Marie Brissett's thigh disappeared into the palm of her hand. He held her gaze. Nodded. Saw her swallow.

'We'll see ourselves out,' he muttered.

Their hooded boy-bikers chaperoned them out of the cul-de-sac.

'She's lying,' said Fletcher. A small bump already forming on his forehead from the clash of heads. He yanked the CID car into second gear, accelerated. Angry.

'Or scared,' MacReady said. 'Think Brissett's an abuser. Marie's face . . .'

'I saw it. And the girl, too. Soraya? Copped a look on our way out. Neck nicely swollen and purple.'

MacReady shook his head. 'I don't get it, though. Even if Brissett's putting hands on them, surely they'd want to tell us where Jermaine is if they knew?'

'More going on there than meets the eye,' Fletcher said. 'Submit the DV forms anyway. Least your arse is covered when one of them wants to stop the arguments via a six-inch carving knife.'

* * *

A point-to-point call on his PR from Beck: she needed a ride.

MacReady dropped Fletcher at the station on James Street, the DI muttering about grabbing some munch before another pointless *progress meeting* with an increasingly nervous brass, who were desperately scrabbling around for something – anything – positive to feed the ever-present media. He stalked off, pressing at the skin above his eyes as he cursed Nathan Brissett.

Grey skies and congestion all the way back into the Civic Centre. A weary wave from Beck as MacReady pulled alongside the kerb. The Coroner's Office behind her, steel frames and blue cladding and serious faces behind seventies-era tinted windows.

Standing beside Beck: Klaudia Solak.

MacReady lowered the CID car window, flashed a quick smile at the journo. He wanted to take a longer look, forced himself not to. To Beck: 'Thought you were with Harrison?'

'Was. He's buggered off to do some actions. Not answering his radio now.'

'It's lunchtime. He'll be otherwise engaged.'

'How did it go with,' Beck glanced at Solak, 'the missing person's people?'

Solak chuckled. 'I can speak in tongues too, you know.'

'Well, he's still missing,' shrugged MacReady. 'How about your floater?'

'Well, he's still dead.' Beck opened the passenger door, climbed in. She waved at the offices. 'And the coroner wants everything yesterday, as per.'

Solak crouched at MacReady's window. Nudged his elbow with her own. 'So is it true the dock body had been decapitated? Arms and legs chopped off?'

'Klaudia,' Beck sighed.

'It's not my case,' said MacReady. He stared ahead. Thought *Megan. MeganMeganMeganMeganMegan.* 'Sorry.'

Solak's fingers brushed MacReady's forearm; the hairs stood to attention, his skin prickled. He looked down at the offending patch of goose pimples, looked up at her: she'd noticed it, was smiling at him. 'People are talking about honour killings. Witchcraft, even. There was a similar case in London a couple of years ago, remember? The torso in the Thames? Come on, Will. You were at the PM. I have my sources.'

MacReady frowned at her. 'Sources?'

'People talk. Maybe we could talk too? Can I ring you?'

'*Klaudia.*' Beck urged MacReady to drive away.

Solak ignored her. 'Do you have a business card?'

MeganMeganMegan.

'Enough,' said Beck. 'You can't do this, all right? He's going to give you less than I have, so nice try. And he's not as green as you think.'

Solak smiled. 'I don't doubt that for a minute. Here, take one of mine.'

MacReady swallowed as he palmed Solak's card. Gunned the engine. Watched Solak stand, give him a small wave. Thought about dropping her a line sometime. *What could it hurt – it might prove useful and it's purely for business. Isn't it?*

'Don't even think about it,' Beck said. She leaned forward as MacReady raised the window. Shouted, 'Bye, Klaudia.'

'Ring me,' Solak shouted, thumb and pinkie finger either side of her mouth.

MacReady eased into the Kingsway traffic, Beck flipping through notes and fidgeting beside him. 'You can talk now,' she said, frowning at her paperwork.

'Not much to tell,' MacReady said. He shifted up a gear, Cardiff Castle's brownstone walls drifting past his window. Left into High Street, out of the queues, then south along Saint Mary Street. Shoppers. Delivery vehicles and buses. People scarfing panini on pavement tables, hunched against the chill sea air blown up from the bay. 'Purely because they wouldn't tell.'

'Wouldn't tell?'

'Or couldn't. Something wasn't right there. Nathan Brissett is the new man of the house –'

'Oh, he's a right darling. Fond of punching uniform after a few pints. Fond of punching anyone, really.'

'Yeah? Well, I got the feeling he's knocking Tate's mother about. His sister too, maybe.'

'So?'

MacReady looked at her. 'Not very compassionate, Sarge.'

'I mean, numbnuts, it doesn't make sense. You think Brissett is beating them up to stop them telling the po-po where Jermaine is hiding? Why would he do that?'

He drummed fingers on the steering wheel. 'I really don't know. Perhaps they don't get on. Perhaps he doesn't want Jermaine back in the house.'

'Like I said, it makes no sense. Fletcher will have us hammering on their door every day now. Would be less hassle for all concerned if they just told us where we can find Jermaine.'

MacReady accelerated around a bus, rolled the car down the slope towards Callaghan Square, Loudoun House rising above the maisonettes and bungalows of Butetown in the distance, a grey slab against leaden sky. 'The DI's already looking to put a team on the house. If they can find a friendly nearby, that is.'

'In The Mellon?' Beck laughed, shaking her head. 'Brissett will have killed them both before any of the neighbours allow surveillance to camp out in their box bedroom.'

'I'm not too sure about that. Seems like Tate's mother can handle herself. The old man had his war wounds, too.'

Beck laid the case file on her lap. 'I just don't get it. So they're knocking each other about. Still doesn't explain why they won't divulge Tate's whereabouts.'

'They seemed scared. That's all I know.'

'Scared of what, though?'

MacReady shrugged, spun the steering wheel; the CID car drifted into Bute Street. He was thinking about the maisonette at Hodges Square, not half a mile from where they were. Garratt's ruined features floated in his vision as his mobile vibrated.

MacReady flicked his eyes down, saw the unknown number on the screen. 'Get that for me?'

'What did your last slave die of?'

'Not doing what I asked?' he grinned.

Beck rolled her eyes, scooped up the phone from the storage tray next to the gearstick.

'DC MacReady's mobile. No, he's driving at the moment and is incapable of doing two things at once . . . Yeah. Yeah.'

MacReady looked at her. Face scrunched, listening over the rumble of the diesel engine. Nodding, blinking rapidly. Tips of her fingers white where she pressed the phone to her ear. Other hand slipping a pen from her folder. Scribbling something down on the corner of an MG form.

'Great. Great. That's . . . that's OK. Thank you for looking into it.'

Beck ended the call. Placed the mobile on top of her file. Leaned her head back.

'Anything interesting?' MacReady asked.

'Were you waiting for anything from the Department of Work and Pensions?'

He nodded. 'They're the only ones who haven't come back to me yet.'

She puffed air between her lips. 'Well they've come back to you now.'

'Anything?'

'Tate didn't have a bank or Post Office account, yes?'

'No bank, no building society, nothing.'

Beck showed him the scribble. 'Ever been here?'

He squinted. *3 Stockland Court.* 'Nope.'

'Well you're going there now.'

'I've just been to Saint Mellons with the DI.'

Beck smiled at him. 'They sent Tate's Simple Payment card to the address last year.'

A flutter in MacReady's chest. 'The benefits card? Please tell me he's still collecting his income support money.'

'Every two weeks. Without fail.'

MacReady put his foot down.

Thought: *shit, we've got him.*

12

The address was just two streets away from Tate's family's home. A townhouse carved into multi-occ flats and bedsits, eight dingy boxes within a slightly larger box situated at the bottom end of Stockland Drive.

'They fucking know he's crashing here.'

Harrison, one hand in jacket pocket. Fag in the other, leaning against a job car and eyeing the firearms officers strapping and buckling and checking kit just inside the outer cordon. The main road into the estate blocked. Response and neighbourhood deployed at junctions, every PCSO Care Bear they could find and separate from their comfort blanket walking buddies posted on points. Nothing in or out, pedestrians or vehicles. The maze of The Mellon locked down, and quickly too.

Garratt would have been impressed, thought MacReady.

'They might not know anything,' Beck said to Harrison. 'It's not exactly what you'd call a close-knit bunch.'

'Three minutes' walk between their house and this one?' Harrison said, exhaling smoke. 'Far too convenient. I was right to bail Dane Sillitoe,' a pointed look at MacReady, 'and I'll be right about this, too. Whole family need to come in.'

'My sister lives ten minutes away on foot,' said Beck, 'and I haven't spoken to her in months.'

Harrison sniffed. Threw the cig. 'You're making me jealous of your sister, Sarge.'

MacReady watched AFOs huddle around their Tac Advisor, recognised two of the entry team as the officers he'd spoken to at King's bedside at the UHW. He nodded at one of them; it wasn't returned. Game faces on, he supposed. Good. He wanted them ready. He wanted them to hurry it up. Jungle drums would be beating. All this commotion: if Tate was inside the target address it wouldn't be long before he learned that half the city's police were encircling his street.

He glanced at Beck. 'Is it going to take them much longer?'

'Fletcher's putting a call in to that mobile number you got from Sillitoe,' she shrugged. 'If that fails, we go in.'

'The mobile's a dud. We should pick up Sillitoe again.' He returned Harrison's pointed look.

'All in good time, Will,' she said. 'Why don't you stop the old I'm-still-in-uniform rubbish and take the tit off your head? You're making me look positively serene.'

Movement amongst the firearms teams. Fletcher emerging from the huddle, lifting police tape, striding towards MacReady and Beck, search warrant still in his hand. Ops Room calling for radio silence, which meant only one thing.

'Nothing on the moby,' Fletcher said. 'As I'm sure you've gathered.'

MacReady switched to the dedicated firearms channel on his PR. Listened to muffled instructions and replies. To AFOs confirming they'd plotted up on black, on white, surrounding the target house. Watched other groups of helmeted storm troopers advance further into the cordon. MP5s, Glocks drawn. Ballistic shields raised.

Harrison shook his head. 'Let's hope the goons don't shoot him, eh?'

'Quiet,' snapped Fletcher.

MacReady held his PR close to his ear, heard the hiss of dead air. Checked around, saw Beck and Fletcher do likewise. Saw Harrison climb into a CID car and yawn.

'*Echo Tango Two One, approaching target premises now.*'

Robotic, distorted. MacReady's chest thumped.

'*Roger Two One, any movement inside address?*'

'*Negative as yet. No movement. Request permission to call out occupant?*'

'*Proceed.*'

The shout echoed along house fronts, back to the outer cordon. *Armed police . . .* Beck looked up at MacReady. Hitched her eyebrows, her expression anxious.

'*Echo Tango Two One, no response from occupant. Proceeding to front door.*'

'Please let him be inside,' muttered Fletcher.

'*Echo Tango Two One we are about to force entry. No transmissions on this channel until I say otherwise.*'

A stillness at the cordon. PRs placed to ears, fingers pressing earpieces. All eyes on the street curling away in front of them. Cold wind fluttering tape and suit jackets and fluorescent tabards.

No sound for what seemed like an age.

Then a sharp clap from further down the street, like a wet towel slapping meaty flesh.

The voice, higher, louder: '*Echo Tango Two One, entry gained.*'

MacReady closed his eyes.

Waited.

Waited.

Found himself crossing his fingers inside his trouser pocket.

Heard: '*Echo Tango Two One we have one person making off.*'

'*Roger, Two One, any description?*'

'*Male, mixed race, wearing red tee. Is on foot going over the neighbouring fences.*'

MacReady turned to a wide-eyed Beck.

Sprinted towards the house.

From behind him, Fletcher yelling: 'Will, *no* . . . Charlie . . .'

MacReady's shoes slapped on pavement, tie flapping over his shoulder and behind his ear. PR to his other ear, listening to the transmissions.

'*Male now three gardens away . . . We're losing ground because of our kit . .*'

'*Roger, Two One. Direction of travel?*'

'*South along the backs of houses. Towards the top end of Stockland Drive.*'

'*Divisional units to standby, repeat, standby and do not approach.*'

No way to know if the man was armed. MacReady knew it was all kinds of wrong but kept running anyway, took a sharp right into an alley between two bungalows, hip banging the cycle barriers at its entrance.

'You bloody idiot.'

Beck, breathless, running alongside him, PR clutched in hand.

'He's heading towards us,' MacReady grunted.

'Let firearms deal.' Her free hand gripping MacReady's sleeve, pulling at him to stop. 'If he's the one who shot Garratt he won't bat an eyelid about shooting anyone and anything to escape.'

He pulled his arm clear. 'We can't let him get away.'

'*Echo Tango Two One, we have a total loss, repeat, total loss.*'

'*Roger, Two One. To stations, male no longer in sight. Last seen heading south at rear of houses, described as male, mixed-race, wearing –*'

'Red tee,' MacReady breathed.

He grabbed Beck. Crouched and took her with him, pressed himself flat against the high garden wall. Placed a finger to his mouth and turned down his PR. Urged her to do likewise. Held up a finger and pointed along the alleyway.

A pair of jeans and trainers, dangling off the wall halfway down the alley. Bushes rustling, shrubbery leaves sprinkling the ground. The man emerged, back to them, red T-shirt spiked with twigs and creased with dirt. He brushed himself off, headed away from them, towards the trees that lined the back of Stockland Drive. Beyond them lay the endless drainage reens and marshes of the Wentloog Levels; if he made it past the treeline he could go to ground in any of the fields and farmhouses dotting the area.

'Shit,' Beck whispered.

'See anything in his hands? Weapon?' MacReady asked.

She shrugged and shook her head.

Ran.

It threw MacReady for a second. Enough for Beck to get well ahead. Scuttling low, towards the male who'd just jumped down from the wall. He followed, bent at the waist, weaving, trying to keep his footfalls light.

The man was about to reach the treeline when Beck launched herself at him. Hit him hard from behind; MacReady heard the *oof* as he was winded, the hoarse *What the fuck* as he went down with Beck in a blur of arms and legs.

He sprinted again, jaw clenched, teeth bared, shouting their location into his PR, readying his Kwik-cuffs with his other hand, praying the man didn't have a pistol or knife or even a Phillips screwy to plunge into Beck's eye socket, his Sergeant wrestling with all she had, his fists flying at her midriff, her arms locked around his head and neck.

MacReady yanked at the man's arms, clamped one cuff on, twisted and pulled at it. He rolled onto his back with the man propped against him, tried to get him nice and compliant, heard him curse and writhe and kick out and promise to find out where MacReady lived and burn his fuckin' house down.

And then he went limp.

MacReady held his captive for a moment, listening to the high-pitched keening coming from his mouth.

Looked up to see Beck launch another kick at the man's balls. MacReady felt nauseous just watching it happen.

'Got you,' Beck said, and placed hands on knees as she gasped for breath.

MacReady eased from under the man's torso, finished cuffing him behind his back.

Spun him around, smiling.

Felt the air go out of his lungs.

It wasn't Jermaine Tate.

MacReady ducked in through the ruined front door and into chaos.

'Wonder boy strikes again,' Harrison breathed into his ear.

MacReady jerked his head towards him.

Beck: 'Fuck off, Warren, all right? Ten minutes ago you were sure the family knew he was here.' A glance around the gloomy bedsit. 'And can somebody please turn that shit off?'

Drum 'n' bass and nicotine-stained walls and blacked-up firearms officers, wide-eyed behind goggles, weapons lowered, a swarm of helmets and tactical gloves waiting for somebody to tell them what to do next, the carpet worn and sticky beneath MacReady's feet, beer bottles and baccy and blunts, the muted TV showing hardcore porn, a three-guys-one-girl job, the broken sofa littered with balled, crusted toilet paper and across the room there was more of the shit, dozens of brutal sex DVDs and wank mags picturing women's twisted features and in the middle of it all a smirking Harrison.

A big old sigh at MacReady. A *tut tut*.

Fletcher, shouting: 'Is there anybody else? Anybody at all?'

The firearms stripey yanked a plug from a wall and the music died.

He looked at MacReady. 'House is clear. Just the one you've got.'

13

They brought Tate's family in.

Locked up for *assisting an offender*. It was bollocks, Mac-Ready thought, because he was convinced they'd done nothing of the sort, and seeing as though they were yet to speak to Jermaine Tate it wasn't confirmed he was responsible for committing any offences anyway. But what MacReady thought was irrelevant. Fletcher had taken the call from the Major Crime Detective Super while they were still inside the Stockland Court flat, his face drawn and eyes unblinking as he'd listened, before placing a hand on MacReady's shoulder and telling him *not to worry, we'll get him soon enough*. MacReady had seen it in the DI's pained appearance, though: the brass had had enough of the wild goose chases and it was time to put the arm on Marie Tate and company.

It was time, too, for the DI to pass down the bollocking he'd received from the Major Crime suits.

Fletcher was still tense and, MacReady sensed, not a little angry. Fingers rubbing at temples in front of an office window filled with blackening sky, the DI stared out onto the streets below; at what, exactly, MacReady couldn't see, as Fletcher had his back turned to him, and MacReady was folded into one of the low chairs lined before the DI's desk.

He noted Fletcher hadn't drawn his office blinds after calling MacReady in and waving him towards the chairs he was swiftly learning to detest. Outside, in the MIR: eyes on him. Harrison swivelling his own – considerably higher – chair back and forth, burger in hand and to mouth, an amused expression wrapped around the flaccid meat and bun as he watched and waited.

'I see me in you,' Fletcher said without turning around.

MacReady flinched at the DI's voice. The room had been silent for several minutes, the white noise in his ears lulling him a little as he mulled over the day's events. It was an odd comment and he didn't know how to respond so kept quiet, studying Fletcher's broad shoulders. Rain speckled glass; beyond the DI the city skyline was fogged with low cloud.

Fletcher shifted on his feet, turning slightly so MacReady could see his face. Weak light from the window cast deep shadows, accentuating the dark crescents beneath his eyes.

'Lost my old man too, in a way,' Fletcher said.

MacReady fingered his collar, pulling it away from his neck. Warmer in the room all of a sudden. At the mention of fathers. 'I didn't know he was over the wall too –'

'He was Old Bill,' Fletcher sighed, and stepped over to his chair. He dropped into it, hooked a heel onto the edge of his desk. 'Job pissed too, you know? Lived and breathed it. Thirty and out without a scratch. Didn't mean there wasn't any collateral damage, though.'

MacReady nodded. 'Your family.'

'Yup,' Fletcher said. His chair creaked as he leaned it backwards and looked heavenwards. 'Never saw him. Work or asleep, mostly. After years of his overtime bandit nonsense and never coming home, things fell apart.'

MacReady swallowed. 'No offence, sir, but . . . my old man's over the wall for murder. It's not really the same.'

'It's exactly the bloody same.' Fletcher dropped his foot to the floor. Leaned forward, elbows on knees, face scrunched with frustration. He jabbed a finger at MacReady. 'It's about losing somebody who's supposed to be there for you. To guide you. To show you what you're supposed to be doing just to get by. It's a big, bad, fucked-up world and all that, right? So you need someone to show you the ropes, and they're not there for you, for whatever reason. And for whatever reason it drives *you* mad, drives you to do things sane people wouldn't. Like run off in the middle of a firearms operation.'

'I'm sorry –'

'*Towards* a possibly armed suspect.'

'I've apologised,' MacReady said, and glanced through the window. Harrison, burger demolished, chuckling away as he watched.

'You fucking needed to,' Fletcher said, his voice louder now. Jaw working, trying to keep a lid on it. That finger jabbing away. 'Major Crime wanted me to do your legs. Professional Standards, the works. But I fought your corner. Because I get it, Will, all right? Like I said, I see me in you. That drive, that hunger which makes you work like a cunt to fill whatever void needs filling. But let me tell you, all that happens is you end up repeating history and replicating your sorry old man and losing all you've loved and fought for . . .'

MacReady sat back, reeling. Thought of Megan. Thought of explaining about doing his best. About always trying just that little too hard to compensate . . .

Fletcher lowered his finger. 'So what I'm saying, for your sake and mine, is wind your fucking neck in, all right? Whatever's driving you to do these things – and I appreciate you're trying to help, to impress, to do whatever it takes to work through those absent daddy issues you have – just stop it.'

Fletcher rose from his seat. Stepped back to the window and crossed his arms. Spoke quietly at the glass.

'Because you don't want to end up like me, Will. Truly you don't.'

Beck slid a mug in front of MacReady. He glanced up from a computer screen he'd been pretending to read, studied her face. Warmth there, her lips forming a gentle smile. Behind them the MIR murmured with conversation, with the faint rattle of keyboards.

'Don't beat yourself up about it,' she said eventually, and sipped at her mug. 'You did a ton of legwork. It didn't pan out but that's the way it goes sometimes.'

MacReady rubbed the heels of his palms into his eyes. 'I'm considering becoming a professional tea boy. Easier on my blood pressure. Less chance of pissing everyone off, too.'

'Not everyone.' Beck placed a hand on his shoulder. Left it there for a moment as she took a seat next to him; a small gesture for which he was incredibly grateful. 'And there's one body out of it, at least. I can put you down as an assist on the crime report if you like. Just benefit fraud, but it all counts. Mind if I . . .?'

She gestured at the computer; MacReady had it switched to the force intranet, its community messages and insipid good news items scrolling horizontally: drugs raid in the Valleys, commendations for a couple of PCSOs down west after they'd talked an attempted suicide from a motorway bridge, finger-wagging diktats concerning inclusiveness and diversity and generally being nice to everyone everywhere forever just in case they complain.

'Go ahead,' he said. 'I've had my fill of smiley HQ nonsense.'

Beck logged herself in to the Niche system, brought up the case file, selected the nominal page. 'This is him,' she said.

MacReady stared at the mugshot of the man Beck had hoofed in the testicles just two hours ago. Early forties, the baggy face and veined, fleshy nose of a drinker. She'd interviewed him while MacReady was sitting in Fletcher's office. 'Karl Haines? Not come across him before.'

'He's a scrote, but not up to much,' Beck said. She slurped at her tea. 'Been around on the fringes for years. A few thefts, some deceptions, but he's no master criminal. I got the impression he finds this life thing a little . . . trying. Bit of a sad sack really. Fond of the hard spirits.'

'Looks it. He going to complain about you booting him in the plums?'

She waved it away. 'Haines is old school. Knows it's part of the game. Was laughing and joking as we bailed him.'

'Does he know where Tate is?'

Beck shook her head. 'Says not. They weren't exactly best buds. Says he was just crashing with Tate in the bedsit for a bit, then Tate went off to Portugal and that's the last Haines saw of him. That was over a year ago.'

'You believe him?'

'I do,' she said, and placed her mug next to MacReady's on the desk. 'He coughed to it all. No solicitor, either. Just wanted it done so he could go back to his mucky films. Says he waited for a while for Tate to come back, then time went on and his own benefit cash wasn't going the distance at the supermarket booze aisle so he chanced Tate's Simple Payment card in the local store. Happy days, the PIN he'd found worked and he got Tate's benefits too. Kept doing it each fortnight until we came knocking today.'

'I can't believe the DWP didn't know about it.'

'Shock horror, there's an organisation as inept as ours. But in fairness, how could they have known? Haines had Tate's card and number to withdraw at any PayPoint. And it's not as if Tate has updated anybody about his circumstances.'

'What about the bedsit? The landlord?'

'Warren's spoken to him and it's a negative. Bills and rent were paid direct to the landlord by the benefits people on Tate's behalf. They were on time every time, so there was no reason for the landlord to go there. He had no idea Tate was no longer at the address. He didn't seem to care anyway, according to Warren. Long as he got his money.'

MacReady nodded to himself. The first throbs of a headache in his temples. 'Eighteen months though . . . that's a fair chunk of change.'

'Seventy-six at just over fifty quid a pop. Plus his own dole money.'

MacReady whistled. 'Buys a man a lot of whisky and porn.'

'You look jealous.'

'I am. Insanely. I just don't fancy the jail time that comes with it.'

'Jail time?' Beck spluttered a laugh as she flipped through her new case file. 'I see a conditional discharge and costs. Again.'

'Got to love those magistrates,' MacReady said, but could see she was lost in her paperwork. The mug of tea sat in front of her, already forgotten.

He fired up the terminal in the corner of the MIR – his corner, he'd come to think of it as, an apt spot for him in the room. On the fringes where he wouldn't cause any more aggravation. He watched a gloomy Fletcher stride out of his office and leave the MIR before turning back to the screen. His emails, the usual junk from departments he'd never heard of and duplicating the crap that had scrolled across the intranet screen: HR nonsense, reminders to complete Development Profiles, final warnings to complete NCALT training packages he had no need for, notifications of deaths in service, a *positive news* item about the brass at HQ raising a flag to celebrate the forthcoming Black History Month.

Nothing, nothing, nothing. Marie Tate and Nathan Brissett and Tate's kid sister Soraya, all down in the bin and being interviewed by Major Crime while he sat here clicking through pointless directives and vacuous diversity bleatings from people who hadn't experienced real policing in two decades.

He stood. Checked Beck. Head down, filling in exhibit labels for the Haines fraud. Glanced around the MIR. Bored indexers and typists, dead phones and the rattle of air con. The Office Manager – an old sweat Detective Sergeant who was yet to acknowledge MacReady's existence – streaming an episode of *Dexter* on a tablet computer, belly wobbling as he hooted at the plot.

MacReady ducked into the DI's office.

Took the property store keys.

Headed for the stairs.

There had to be something.

Something amongst the evidence bags or personal belongings that they'd missed. Something they'd not realised was relevant when the last checks were made.

Leon King's belongings. The detritus secured by CSI after Garratt. Spread across the property store floor once again. Car radios, cannabis blims, trainers, watches. MacReady sifted through it all, turning plastic sacks over in his hands, staring at the array of contents, willing something to make itself clear.

King's mobile phone.

A battered BlackBerry, sealed inside a small evidence bag.

MacReady squeezed at it through the plastic. Tried to turn it on. The battery, dead. All other roads had come to an end as far as Jermaine Tate was concerned. And Tate had been at the maisonette with King.

There just had to be something.

'Fuck it,' he said, and shoved the bag into his pocket.

At the front desk MacReady collared a passing uniform about getting hold of a charger, was pointed in the direction of the parade room. He pulled one from a wall socket, found a quiet office nearby. Out of sight, as well as out of mind.

He swallowed as he ripped open the evidence bag. Checked over his shoulder at the office door. Plugged in and pressed.

King's mobile booted up. Not passcode protected, a sign of the boy's arrogance. Probably a disposable anyway, but MacReady still shook his head.

Multiple missed calls and unread texts. MacReady checked the messages: over a hundred of the things. Terse, generic text speak. No names or locations. *Need 2 get togetha bro bell me ASAP*; *Where you at L?*; *Hey man, we need to hook up soon will call*; *Seen news, this true about you bro?* And on they went. All unsigned or just signed off with initials or nicknames: *JS. BigD. VirgDaMan. CP.*

Several from *S*.

Sillitoe? MacReady thought.

He scrolled back to the start of September. Lots from *S*. More than from any other contact, it seemed. More expansive, too. And a different tone to them.

Hi, can you ring me when you're free please? Hey, Leon haven't seen you in a week can we get together? King had replied to them, but the replies had been deleted.

On the night before the Garratt shooting, a final text from *S*: *Meet me at HS after you're done, it's urgent Leon . . .*

MacReady stared at the message. King's work was thieving and sneaking around other people's houses while they slept. He went to the maisonette after *work*. *HS*. HS had to be Hodges Square. Had to be. MacReady pictured Dane Sillitoe. Wondered if Sillitoe had lied about cleaning up, about going legit. If he was still running with King. Or just running King full stop.

Are you S? he thought. *Why did you want to meet King at the maisonette? What was so urgent?*

MacReady chewed at his bottom lip. Eyes on the BlackBerry. On the mobile number attached to that final text message.

He selected it, pressed dial. Listened to it ring, and ring. Voicemail. The recorded message in his ear, the voice warm and inviting, ending with a playful laugh. He closed his eyes: the voice didn't fit with the face he now pictured.

MacReady killed the call, yanked up the landline in the office. Dialled the custody suite.

Was told by the CDO: 'We bailed her ten minutes ago.'

He took Beck with him.

'You'll have to replace the evidence bag,' she said. 'And quickly.'

MacReady, hunched over the steering wheel. He nodded, scanning pavements, side streets. Headache roaring. 'Soon as we're done with this. She's on foot, refused a panda cab home, so can't have got very far. Bus stop somewhere, I'll bet.'

'And where are you going with *this*, exactly? Tate's sister was seeing King, so what? It doesn't mean she knows where Jermaine is hiding out.'

'I told you something wasn't right at that house. There might be a connection.'

Beck looked heavenwards. Fingers flicking. '*Might*. And you've tampered with evidence in a murder case on a *might*, straight after Fletcher bawled you out in front of the whole MIR.'

'I just want to check, Sarge, all right?' He looked at her. 'Just check, and keep it low-key, and see if it actually comes to anything before I take it to the DI this time.'

'And what if it comes to nothing?'

'Then I replace the bag, put everything away and go back to sitting in the naughty corner with nobody the wiser.'

'Except me,' Beck sighed.

'I just need you for this one thing. She could be more likely to open up with, you know . . .'

'A female speaking to her?'

MacReady shrugged. 'Yes. Sorry. But I promise I'll keep you out of it if the wheel comes off. Cross my heart.'

Beck was silent for a moment. 'Good,' she said eventually, and leaned forward. Squinted through the windscreen. 'Because there she is.'

Soraya Tate stood in the bus stop, alone. Bright red gilet against green metal and shatterproof glass. She turned towards the sound of the diesel engine: the familiar rumble of plod.

MacReady drew the CID car to a stop, clicked on the Police Park Anywhere hazards.

'You owe me for this, Will,' Beck said.

'And I appreciate it,' he said, and climbed out.

Resignation, frustration on Tate's face. 'You lot've just let me go.'

'Just a couple of things we need to firm up on,' MacReady said.

Tate threw a look at MacReady. 'You stalking me? At my house, now here?'

Beck, over the roof of the car. 'Sorry, Soraya. It won't take long.'

Tate closed her eyes. *A pretty girl*, MacReady thought again. Nineteen, twenty. Tall and slim, hair straightened and lengthened with extensions, skin a dark caramel, huge hooped earrings dangling. The bruises Fletcher had noticed: ugly blotches beneath her jaw, on her collarbone.

'That's what you always say,' she whispered.

MacReady glanced around, ushered Tate further into the bus stop. Mindful of CCTV that the Major Crime staff could be looking at right now. 'Tell me about Leon,' he said.

Tate opened her eyes. 'Leon who?'

Beck had made her way around the car and into the bus stop. 'It's fine. It's not as if we don't already know.'

Tate looked from her to MacReady. 'I've told the other ones everything.'

'Did you tell them about your relationship with Leon King?' MacReady asked.

'What relationship?'

'We've seen the texts, Soraya,' Beck said, her voice soft. Softer than MacReady had ever heard it. 'You were seeing him, weren't you? How did you meet him? Through your brother?'

Tate folded her arms high in front of her. 'This has nothing to do with you people.'

'But it might have something to do with Leon getting shot,' MacReady replied. 'How does that make you feel? Your boyfriend getting shot?' A low blow; he cringed inwardly.

Tate swallowed. Looked at something in the distance.

MacReady lowered his head at her, tried to meet her eyes. 'I saw the texts, Soraya. "*Meet me at HS*"? You sent it the night before he was shot. *HS* is Hodges Square, isn't it? The maisonette? Why did you ask to meet him there? What was so urgent?'

'You don't understand,' Tate said. An almost imperceptible shake of her head, her face tightening for a moment.

Beck stepped towards her. 'We can help you, Soraya. If there's something you know, something about Leon or your brother, we can help work it all out. You just have to help us first.'

'Just leave it,' Tate said. Her eyes glassy, blinking. 'There's nothing you can do for us now.'

MacReady reached out to her: his business card between two fingers. She shifted away, pressing against the back wall of the bus stop. 'What is it? I know there's something wrong. I know you're scared. You and your mother, it was obvious this morning. What is it you can't tell us about?'

'Just fucking leave it, will you?' Tate yelled. She crumpled. Head lowered, sobs like small hiccups making her shoulders hitch. 'You gave your card to Mum and she'll never ring you either.'

He turned to Beck, rolled his eyes. Shoved the card in his pocket. Stooped, tried to see Tate's face beneath the curtain of her fringe. 'Even if you don't want to talk about Jermaine, you can tell us about home, OK? About what's going on there? With your stepdad?'

'You . . . you don't know what you're talking about.'

'Then help us, Soraya.' Hands on his knees now, bent at the waist as he spoke. 'We can drop you home. Talk some more. You can tell us everyth—'

Tate screamed. Placed her hands to her face. Walked out of the bus stop.

'We can lock him up for you,' MacReady called after her. 'Take him away and he'll never do it to you or your mother again.'

Tate stopped. Spun around to face him. Cheeks blackened with mascara.

'My stepdad's a good man,' she said. 'A *good man*. And he's never laid a finger on either of us.'

'Soraya, we know everything –'

'You know everything about nothing,' Tate said. She paused, as if about to speak again, then shook her head and walked away.

MacReady stepped after her, felt Beck's hand on his arm.

'Let her go, Will,' she said. 'Let it go, for now.'

'I don't get it,' he said. Tate's red gilet, disappearing into the stream of pedestrians heading for the main shopping drag of Queen Street. 'If Brissett's not beating on them, then who is?'

Beck squeezed his arm through his sleeve. 'We'll work it out.'

'I don't get it,' he said again.

Beck stepped in front of him. Checked her watch. Looked up into his eyes.

'Replace the evidence bag then go home, Will,' she said. 'That's an order.'

14

A day off where he couldn't switch off.

The morning spent scribbling notes and pacing. Mentally working through what they knew, what he suspected, what none of them on the investigation could work out: the location of Jermaine Tate. Tate was the key that would unlock everything, MacReady was convinced of it.

Megan had tolerated it until lunchtime. Had listened quietly as he'd muttered and cursed, nodding as he wittered on while they sat together on the settee, rolling TV news reports unwatched by both of them this time, the sound muted. Had prepared their food while he stalked about the kitchen, running things by her, asking her opinion; during lunch he'd answered his own questions with more questions then sat, staring out of the kitchen window at a patio that needed some serious weeding. Megan had cleared away plates, loaded the dishwasher, placed hands on hips and turned to him.

'We need to get out of here,' she'd said, and he'd nodded, knowing it was as much for her as him. Despite the smile there was an edge to her voice. He'd been hard work since they woke and he sensed there was something more she wanted to say.

The park just a mile from their house. Pitted rugby pitches, the dust of summer-worn football fields, new play area for the local kids. The last of the warm weather filling it: a dog walker hurling a tennis ball for her frothing mutt to collect and return and repeat ad nauseam. Young mothers cooing over infants in expensive buggies. Grandparents pushing squealing toddlers in swings.

Guilt tugged at MacReady's insides.

They were yet to discuss anything to do with the adoption. The papers he'd found in the recycling bin. Her decision not to press on with it. It just seemed like there hadn't been time over the last couple of days. But there should have been time. He should have made time.

He linked arms with Megan. 'I'm sorry.'

She didn't reply; just leaned her head on his shoulder as they walked. Hips bumping, crossing the cricket pitch, the treeline and the shallow curve of the river in the distance. The forestry and mountains beyond. He had no idea where they were heading and that was fine. As long as he was moving. Keeping going. Going somewhere.

'I'm not just talking about work, either,' he said. 'Our plans . . . I wasn't here to talk it through. I don't want you to think I left you to make the decision on your own.'

Still leaning into him. She took his hand. 'It's OK, Will.'

MacReady stopped. Turned to face her. 'It's not OK, though. I was the one to suggest going for the adoption. I know you were nowhere near keen but let me keep nudging you in that direction. I'm grateful you tried for us. For me. But I should have been here. Instead I've been wrapped up in things that are totally out of my control –'

'You can't be in control of every little thing,' she said. Her eyes dropped to the ground and she squeezed at his hand. 'Sometimes other people have to make the big decisions.'

MacReady cocked his head. 'Are you all right, Meg?'

A pause. A twitch in the corner of Megan's mouth, as if she wasn't sure if she should smile or frown. Her eyes shining, adrenalised, as if she was . . . excited?

Then: 'I am. I am now, yes.'

MacReady looked away. Listened to the happy screams and faint chatter. The whisper of traffic from the main road. The yelp of the dog for its tennis ball. 'Why *now*? What's changed?'

The dog, going berserk. He watched it, a chocolate Lab, skittering to and fro on its front paws. Its owner holding its collar, one hand raised and ready to throw the ball. The Labrador straining, pulling, wanting to be let go.

Going batshit crazy.

MacReady felt a numbness in his chest. His mouth, dry.

Vaguely aware of Megan shaking her head. Of her taking his hand in hers and pressing at it, of her looking up at him and talking, other hand reaching into her jacket pocket and feeling around for something, telling him something, her mouth moving, no sound coming out, the Labrador all he could see now, struggling to free itself from its owner, barking and growling and foaming at the mouth.

MacReady thought of the dog handler at the Garratt shooting.

Of Beck: *And it's not as if Tate has updated anybody about his circumstances.*

He felt the world tilt a little.

'I have to go back to work,' he blurted.

'Will?'

He pulled his hand free. 'I'm sorry. Go home, Megan. I won't be long.'

A lie. He knew it.

Megan stared after him, mouth open, as he walked away, his hand fumbling for the mobile phone in his pocket.

By the time he reached the park gates MacReady was running.

Part 2

What Depths We Plumb

Bairro Martim Moniz,
Lisbon, Portugal

The children slept in the darkness behind him.

Just a short run from the airport into the heart of Lisbon. Aleksandar pulled on a cigarillo. The flight had been long and trying, despite the attentions of the crew and stewards. They had wanted for nothing yet the children had been uncontrollable in their excitement. His teeth ached; five hours spent grinding them, wondering if he'd had enough of this life. That meeting this one child, this child who reminded him of his baby brother, would prove a turning point.

He lowered his window and exhaled, let smoke drift up and out into the night. Felt warm air on his face. Felt the burn in his lungs, his throat.

'Não fume,' said the minibus driver. Gesturing at Aleksandar's lap. 'As crianças. As crianças.'

Aleksandar knew what he was saying but chose to ignore him. A little secondary smoke would make no difference now. He rolled his neck, heard the click of his bones. Stared out of the windscreen, temples throbbing as he puffed on the Villiger. They were heading south, the seven hills looming around them, black hulks against blacker sky. The city lit up, glowing, magical. He'd never taken in the sights.

Never walked to a miradouro *and drunk it in. Always so quick: airport to clinic for the delivery, then back to the airport where he'd wait and pace and sometimes steal sleep on one of the awful metal benches before flying back to the humidity and filth of Lagos.*

Everything so quick. So efficient.

So detached.

But not tonight. Tonight he would walk hilly streets he had only ever seen from the air, or through a minibus window. Maybe take a tram up to the famed Bairro Alto. Find a quiet bar, sit and listen to the chatter, to the Fado music he'd read about. Spend some time in this place that he visited so frequently yet had experienced so little of.

It was only now that Aleksandar realised: anything to delay going back. To delay leaving the little boy alone.

He tossed the cigarillo as the minibus slowed.

'*Estamos aqui,*' *the driver muttered.*

We are here.

The huge oblong of Praca Martim Moniz in front of them. The fountain's water jets turned off. Local kids gathered in clutches across the square, suffused in the golden glow of floodlights as they swapped cigarettes and jabbered.

Five more minutes to the clinic.

Just five more minutes.

Aleksandar lit another Villiger, sucked hard on it. Paid no attention to the reproachful look from the driver. Glanced down at his lap.

Bepeh.

Sleeping, head on Aleksandar's thigh. Soft breaths escaping from his pursed lips.

He placed a hand on the boy's head. Dug his fingernails into the tight curls.

Closed his eyes.

Just five more minutes until he had to deal with the doctor.

'*You are still here.*'

Irritation in the doctor's voice; he did not look at Aleksandar as he spoke, his English fluent and clipped, his polished nails seemingly of more interest. The children filed past, faces puffy with sleep, no chatter now, the day a long one for them. Soft footfalls on tiles as they disappeared down a corridor. Clinic staff ushering them away, out of sight, their smiles betrayed by dead, uncaring eyes.

Aleksandar held Bepeh's hand. Held it tight. Strip lights itching his eyelids. The chemical stink in his nose. His stomach pulled into a fist. He looked out of the open doorway, into the night. The mini-bus sitting there, engine idling. He thought about leaving with the boy. Taking him away from all this. Dealing with the consequences when he had to.

'*Your work is done. Go, please.*'

Aleksandar turned to the doctor. A small man, rake-thin, his features sharp and unkind. His arrogant, impatient air. The way he spoke to people as if they were shit on his heel, never meeting their eyes. As if it was beneath him. Aleksandar disliked the man but tonight felt it something closer to hatred.

Luís Tristão Gonçalves.

O Cona Pequena.

The Little Cunt.

Aleksandar thought about snapping Gonçalves' neck. Breaking it, just as he'd done to that chancer's fingers at the airport. It would be easy, over in a heartbeat. But the repercussions would be enormous.

It was one thing to disappear with the boy, another thing entirely to remove somebody so essential.

They would come for him.

'Is everything ready?' Aleksandar asked. A pointless question; of course it would be. He didn't want to leave, though. Didn't want to abandon Bepeh to Gonçalves. Needed to work through his options before there wasn't an option.

Gonçalves bristled. Still not looking at Aleksandar. 'It is not your concern.'

'But the other deliveries –'

'By errand boys such as you,' Gonçalves said, and looked up. 'Errand boys who know better than to ask questions that will confuse them. Confusion causes problems, yes? And we don't want any problems . . .'

His eyes dropped to Bepeh. Narrowed.

'Give him to my staff,' Gonçalves said.

'I do not think he is strong enough –'

'Hand him over now, cabrão.'

Aleksandar hesitated. Looked to the doorway again. To the minibus. Squeezed Bepeh's hand, shifted his weight. Ready to run.

Gonçalves heaved a sigh. Yelled something in Portuguese, his voice echoing off the tiles, travelling down the corridor. Figures appeared. Advanced from the bowels of the building. Clinic staff, coming for the boy. Six or seven of them. Too many, and prepared. Coshes, a scalpel glinting. The boy too valuable to lose after all this effort. More valuable than Aleksandar would ever be, because there was always another waiting to replace people like him.

The doctor closed the clinic door and resumed studying his nails.

Bepeh leaned into Aleksandar; he felt the boy's heart thump against his waist. Looked down, saw wide, dark eyes staring up at him. Glassy and fearful. Looked around, saw clinic staff surrounding him, hands already reaching.

If he took the boy his life would be over. Even if they escaped these white-coated thugs it would be a matter of weeks before somebody found them. He'd seen it before, had stood and watched and even held people down while fingers were removed, eyeballs were punctured with screwdrivers, diesel thrown over battered bodies, had once lit the match and walked away laughing with his companions, their former colleague's agonised shrieks still in his ears as they drove away.

It was the price you paid for failure. For carelessness. For the most minor of indiscretions.

Aleksandar swallowed. Knelt down before the boy. Held onto his hand. Brushed at his hair, looked him in the eyes. If he couldn't take him, at least give him something to carry with him. Something to reassure him.

He reached into his shirt, unclasped the necklace. Tihomir's necklace.

'For you, Bepeh,' Aleksandar said, and placed it over the boy's head. It hung on his skinny frame, thick gold ropes against the red of his fake football shirt.

The boy blinked, his face creasing as he wept.

'You must go,' said Aleksandar, and released his hand.

The staff pulled Bepeh free. Aleksandar clenched his fists. Stared at the floor. Tried not to listen to the boy's wailing as he was led away.

Gonçalves' voice, flat and uninterested: 'How very sad.'

Aleksandar stood. Stepped towards him, fists swinging at his sides, his breath ragged, watery eyes bulging and on Gonçalves' unconcerned features. 'O cona pequena,' he growled.

'The animal speaks some Portuguese,' Gonçalves smiled. 'Well done.'

He opened the clinic door.

Nodded towards the Lisbon night.

Gone midnight but the city still warm and alive.

Aleksandar walked, the rage not subsiding. Shouldered through groups of youths at the praca, willing them to retaliate, wanting them – just one of them – to say something he would recognise as an insult. Something he could react to.

Nothing. They eyed him sullenly as he stalked onwards, crossing roads, ignoring car horns, a brutish stranger with face lifted to dark sky, meaty hands wiping at wet cheeks, chest hitching.

The minibus, gone. His flight waiting on the runway where it could wait until morning. Aleksandar headed north through Rua Palma, the street he'd been driven along so many times, the street he'd never set foot upon until now. Passers-by stared at him, nudged their partners, pointed, their faces warped through his tears, their voices drowned by his sobs.

At Intendente he stopped. Glanced around. A neon sign flashed down a side street. Tables and chairs on the pavement, the low thrum of guitar.

A shot of tequila inside the bar. He gestured for another. And another. The alcohol burn in his chest. Demanded the bottle, threw notes at the young guy working the drinks, listened to him mutter in broken English. Grabbed the bottle by the neck, sucked at the glass lip, chugging what was left of the clear liquid. Glanced around at the bemused faces of the other patrons, cursed them all over the music lilting from an ancient stereo system behind the bar. Pointed at bottles in the chiller cabinet, barked give me three, *dropped more Euros on the counter.*

Aleksandar took the Super Bocks outside, flopped into a chair.

Felt like a coward.

Felt lonelier than he'd ever felt in his life.

He drank the lager, puffed on a Villiger. Tired now. His head fuzzy. People walking past. Ghosts. Drifting through the haze of his vision. Ghosts like Tihomir. So many years ago but still so raw.

And now Bepeh. After he'd promised himself never to get close to anybody ever again. The void he felt was immediate.

Aleksandar finished the Super Bock, leaned forward. Placed his head in his hands. His eyelids heavy. For a moment he felt he might drift off, cigar still burning between his fingers.

'Você está bem?'

The voice was girlish, amused. Aleksandar heaved his head up. Squinted. Focused.

She was about fifteen. A tumble of dark hair over bony shoulders. Faded jeans, mismatched denim jacket. A jangle of multicoloured plastic bracelets, the pop of chewing gum between crooked teeth. Aleksandar smelled strawberries on the balmy air.

The girl babbled at him, hands busy, eyes shining. Jittery. Wired. He knew the signs well enough.

A bang on the window behind him. Aleksandar craned his neck, saw the young bartender waving the girl away, his face twisted and angry.

She didn't move. Continued to gabble at Aleksandar.

'Inglês,' *he said.* 'Falar Inglês.'

She shrugged. Screwed up her face.

No English, then.

The door opened. The bartender stepped out, shooing her, the pair of them arguing in Portuguese. Aleksandar rubbed at his forehead, at the tightness of his skin.

'Ask her,' *he said, tugging at the young guy's sleeve,* 'how much.'

The bartender stopped arguing with the girl. Stared down at Aleksandar, lip curling.

Aleksandar jammed Euros into the man's hand.

'Ask her,' *he said again.*

The bartender looked at the money. Sniffed. Turned to the girl, his fingers slipping the notes into his pocket. 'Quanto custa?'

A cock of the head. As if deliberating. That black hair kinked and curling at the nape of her neck as she studied Aleksandar. 'Setenta.'

'She says seventy Eur—'

Aleksandar stood. 'OK.'

The bartender rolled his eyes, disappeared back into the bar.

He was finding it difficult to put one foot in front of the other. Placed a hand on the table to steady himself. Stepped across to her. She looked up at him.

More wide, dark eyes.

Aleksandar reached for her hand. Her fingers so tiny, curling through his.

No bigger than Bepeh's.

15

Sun pulled itself across the garden as he waited.

Figures in the surrounding lanes, hovering. Grim faces above folded arms framed in overlooking flat windows. Black eyelets of mobile phone cameras aimed in his direction. Couple of twenty-something wide boy shottas, all 'ball caps and spring-stepping this way and that at the far end of the alleyway which ran alongside the maisonette, shooting the shit loud enough for him to hear, the *gotta be po-po* and *he on his ownsome, lessdoim* rattling along brickwork towards him. So they knew who he was. What he was. The jeans-and-sweatshirt off duty cop attire he wore, no doubt. What they didn't know was why he was here.

It was a question MacReady was starting to ask himself.

'Please hurry the fuck up,' he muttered, and fingered the mobile in his pocket. Three nines already buttoned in and ready to dial if things went awry. Twenty-five minutes alone here already, enough time for doubt to nibble at him. Enough time for the guilt he felt at leaving Megan to turn his guts sour. More than enough time for word to fly about a lone Five Oh just itching for a beating.

I'm gonna reef on you, pig, reef on you hard.

Les get down there, bra, serious. Nobody will say fuck all.
Here, piggy piggy.

Louder now. Closer. Cajoling each other, winding themselves up, MacReady knew how it went, knew they were just a few more back slaps and knuckle bumps away from advancing on him. He pulled the mobile from his pocket. If he dialled, brought in the cavalry and was proved wrong, this was over. He would look a fool. Meddling in something he shouldn't, when he'd been specifically warned against it by Fletcher, and on a rest day, of all things. And then the questions would come. The finger-pointing during the old interview without coffee. The hushed sideways shift to file prep or prisoner handling or all the way back to uniform and long night shifts where people would fall silent when he entered the parade room.

Better to do it himself. Quietly, after all that had gone on. Just to check. Just to put his mind at rest so he could go back to the MIR and resume dogsbody duties with nothing nagging at him. No harm done, nobody knowing. But at least he'd know for certain.

Silhouettes inside the alleyway now. Bouncing on heels and sucking their teeth, a high five, a pull on a baseball cap, *what you doing here in my ends, bruv, what you snooping round for on your lonesome you got some front . . .*

'Come on, Emma, come on,' he said. Shifted back a ways, on to the patio, the French doors with their second set of chipboard shutters behind him. Hand squeezing the mobile. No cuffs, no ASP or CS Spray. Making the calculations: even if he put a call in now it would take several minutes for assistance to arrive, if not longer. Plenty of time for him to get rolled, for the men coming at him to pummel him senseless and walk away laughing.

Thumb hovering over the call button. Eyes on the mouth of the alleyway. Footsteps on concrete, the men's voices high and excitable, goading each other, just a few feet away now, just about to emerge into the garden where MacReady was slinking further backwards, pressing himself against the chipboard, *come on, Emma, where are you, come on . . .*

Heavy footfalls. The men, running.

And not towards him. Away, up the alleyway, out onto Hodges Square, their whoops and catcalls drowned by the grumble of a diesel engine.

MacReady bent over, hands on knees, as the dog van pulled alongside the garden wall. 'At last,' he breathed. Cleared the nines on his phone. Slipped it into his pocket.

A smile from the dog handler as she climbed out of her wagon. Emma Ellis. Shades on, black overalls matted with hair, streaked on the sleeves with what looked like saliva. They joined the job together, back in the day: same intake, same first station, a mutual appreciation that once led to a drunken kiss on a dance floor which they both squirmed about during their next shift. He'd called her on his way back in to work.

'Sorry I'm a bit late, Will,' she said. 'Been at headquarters to collect some sperm.'

MacReady's eyes widened. 'Oh. Right. Beats picking up spare epaulettes, I s'pose.'

Ellis lifted her shades onto the frizz of her blonde hair, cocked her head. 'It's for training the dog. Sexual offences?'

'Not here to judge,' he raised his hands. 'I'm just glad you turned up. Was starting to get a little troubled hanging around here on my tod.'

She checked around, squinting in the sunlight. 'Well you've already gathered an audience. What am I here for, Willy boy?'

Blunt as ever. MacReady took a deep breath. 'A favour. Off the books, so to speak.'

She looked him up and down. 'I was wondering where your cheap suit had gone. You on a rest day?'

'Yup.'

'Off the books, on a rest day.' Ellis nodded slowly. 'Just the kind of talk to make me nervous.'

He arched an eyebrow. 'Says she who's just handled a strange man's semen. Look, can you let your dog have a sniff about? I'm not really sure how it works, but I'd be really grateful if you could let it –'

'Him.'

'Let him check the area.'

Ellis placed hand on hips. 'This scene was released weeks ago, Will. There's nothing left for us to do.'

'There might be something we missed.'

'We didn't miss anything.'

'You were here after Garratt was killed. When he was still on the patio. And your dog. It was going nuts.'

'Lots of people around, it gets him excited.'

MacReady glanced about. The sun, dropping towards the rooftops already. They needed to hurry. 'Did you update Ops Room with your location?'

'No. I never tell them where I am if I can help it. There's nobody left on response nowadays so they'd be sending me to all sorts if I did.'

'Good,' he said.

She held his gaze for a second. 'Major Crime don't know we're here, do they?'

MacReady shook his head. 'Nobody knows.'

Ellis paused, as if deliberating. Chewing at the inside of her mouth. A sigh. 'Then I was never here, all right?' She dropped the shades back over her eyes. 'Once I've done whatever it is you want, I'm gone.'

'Understood.'

If this turned out negative Ellis had nothing to worry about. If he was right – well, he'd deal with the fallout when the time came. He watched her pull kit out of the van: lead, harness, bright orange ball, metal spikes. The dog whimpered in the darkness at the rear.

'What are the search parameters?' she asked over one shoulder.

MacReady made a vague gesture at the maisonette, the garden. 'Round here, really.'

'That's incredibly specific, Will, very helpful.' Ellis turned, handed him the spikes. 'Go stick these into the ground in a few places. Just to get things up and running.'

MacReady stalked into the long grass, feet unsteady on furrows and mounds of sodden earth, of rusted paint tins and rubble. He had no clue what he was doing. Jammed the spikes in the soil as he went. Behind him he heard the van's cage door open and shut, Ellis cajoling her dog, *come on, boy, come on, let's take a look for the crazy man . . .*

'This OK?' he called. 'I've set up the markers.'

She pinched the bridge of her nose beneath the sunglasses. Other hand gripping the lead, the German Shepherd sitting at her heel. 'They're not markers, Will. They're probes. You're sup-posed to take them out now.'

'Ah.' He retraced his steps, pulled out the spikes. Handed them to her as the dog eyed him suspiciously.

Ellis knelt, rubbed one of its ears. Muttered something MacReady couldn't hear. The dog skipped forward, darting towards the maisonette wall, towards the alleyway. Ellis fed the lead through her hands; Macready could see knots along its length.

'To measure distance,' she said, before he could ask.

The German Shepherd skittered along concrete, pausing at the mouth of the alleyway. Turned, headed back towards the boarded French doors. Nose down, tail up, zigzagging, its snorts audible. Ellis fed the lead, watching from behind her shades. MacReady stepped over to the side of the van to give them room.

'He's not showing a particular interest in anything at the moment,' Ellis said after a while. 'If you can get the boards off he can do inside. Again.'

MacReady watched her gather the lead, the dog pacing over to him for a quick sniff at the bottom of his jeans. Ellis placed her hands around her mouth, did that telephone *tch tch tch* thing and the dog ran to her side.

'Can you let him off the lead for a mooch about?' MacReady asked.

'Free searching, you mean.' She unhooked the harness, dropped it at her feet. Held the dog by its collar. Showed it the orange ball; it tensed immediately, forelegs bunched muscles as it barked at her hand. Ellis struggled to keep hold of him. It reminded MacReady of the woman and her Labrador in the park.

'Find it,' Ellis said, and let go of the collar. She threw her hand out, not letting go of the ball.

The German Shepherd bolted into the long grass.

'Ball pissed,' she smiled. 'Will do anything to get his mouth around the thing.'

They watched in silence as it sprinted back and forth, a blur of black and tan, its thick tail skywards. It stopped to nose the fence on one side of the garden, to investigate broken house bricks and solidified concrete bags, to scratch itself behind the ear before moving on. An impressive sight, MacReady thought.

'You do know I finish at four today?' Ellis asked.

'Won't be long,' MacReady said. He turned to her. Hands in her overall pockets, sun on her face, a satisfied smile as she watched her companion go about its business.

As relaxed as he was anxious.

This is fucking stupid, he thought. And he'd left Megan at home for it.

'I think we can call it a day, Em,' he said to her after a few more minutes of canine snuffling and sniffing had passed. 'Sorry to drag you down –'

'You've got a PI,' she said.

MacReady screwed up his face. 'I've got a what?'

She was walking into the grass. MacReady watched her go, saw the German Shepherd frozen halfway down the garden, eyes fixed on a point MacReady knew he'd jabbed with a spike not ten minutes ago.

'Positive indication,' Ellis said. She raised her hand; the orange ball still gripped in her fingers. 'Here, boy. *Tch tch tch.*'

MacReady was vaguely aware of the dog sprinting towards Ellis, of it jumping to catch the ball she'd flipped into the air, of it hunkering down to chew on the thing. He pushed through the weeds and ryegrass and stopped at the point where the dog had indicated.

'Here,' Ellis said from behind him, and handed him a marker flag. It was the size of a tent peg; MacReady pushed it into the earth.

'I'm not sure about this,' he said to himself.

'Wait one,' Ellis said, and jogged to the van. The sound of items being shifted around on the metal floor of the wagon, Ellis bent at the waist, rummaging. After a moment she straightened: in her hand was a well-used shovel.

MacReady hacked at the grass with it. Cleared chippings and dust from topsoil. Dug into the earth, shoulders working the shovel a few inches deep. Used a foot to press it deeper, yanking the handle to remove mud and soil and thin seams of clay, the sun on his back, his neck a ring of sweat, Ellis with her shades up again, watching him dig a foot square hole, shoving the dirt to one side, the shovel working deeper, MacReady hunched over it, grunting, not speaking, not saying anything.

Until he stopped. Stood upright. Stared at the hole. Dropped the shovel into the grass.

Placed a hand to his nose.

The German Shepherd watched him with dull eyes, jaw working the ball.

Ellis shrugged. 'What?'

'You'd better make yourself scarce,' MacReady said, his voice hoarse. Shaking fingers reached for his mobile. 'Because the whole world is going to be down here as soon as I make this call.'

Dusk and dirt and the choke of generator diesel.

In the cone of light beneath the arc lamps the Crime Scene Manager stood silently, making her notes, watching her staff slip in and out of the tent, nodding as they spoke to her. The Major Crime Detective Super a few feet away, hands in pockets, still bitching about the interruption to his evening catching up with Sky+ recorded *Midsomer Murders*. Uniform ringing the garden, tying tape to lamp posts, shining Dragons and Maglites into locals' faces as they pushed out the cordon perimeter, *back away, move back, stop your fuckin' shoving or I'll lift you, you cunt* and then the scuffles, the teenagers dragged to the back of a van, the cries of *police brutality*.

MacReady walked among long shadows on the patio, soil inking his fingernails, the folds of his hands, shoulders knotted and numb from digging, tension in his neck, waiting, waiting. Fletcher and Beck, heads close together, talking in hushed tones, glancing at him occasionally, the evening air chilly now, their breaths backlit by torchlight.

'Suppose I should be thanking you,' Harrison said. He stood, leaning against the maisonette's back wall, one foot raised against yellow brickwork. A nod of his head towards the over-grown garden, to the CSIs trampling grass, to the tent erected over the small hole dug by MacReady. 'Nice bit of ovies for this.'

MacReady didn't reply. He didn't care about overtime or money. On his phone: three text messages from Megan. A voicemail from her. *Are you coming home? We really need to talk.* He'd answered none of them.

He closed his eyes. Pictured material. Faded red. Rolled. Disintegrating. Thought of the missing square of carpet in the maisonette's lounge.

A hand on his arm.

Fletcher. Leaning in to him, so close MacReady could smell the sourness on his breath, the faint tang of single malt. 'You should've called me, Will.'

Beck stood behind the DI, chewing at the top of a pen, watching.

'I wasn't sure, after, y'know . . .' he began, but it dissolved into a shrug.

'There'll be questions from above,' Fletcher said. 'Questions I don't have the answers to. Whatever the outcome here, it's going to make me look foolish.'

A click of the fingers from Harrison. 'Supernintendo.'

The Detective Superintendent strode towards them, face drawn and serious, eyebrows a pissed-off V above tired eyes. A paper-suited Gordon Barnard, the smoothy pathologist, walked beside him, stripping his hands of latex gloves.

'It's as you thought,' Barnard offered as they reached the patio. He glanced at the Superintendent, waited a beat. When the Super said nothing he continued. 'You've got a body in the ground. Shallow burial. Wrapped in carpet.'

Fletcher grimaced. 'Early thoughts?'

Barnard rubbed at bristled cheeks. 'I've poked and prodded now your colleagues have uncovered a little more. I believe it's male. It's pretty well preserved, which I would put down to the environmental conditions and soil makeup. But it's been there a while.'

'About a year?' MacReady asked.

Fletcher shot him a look.

Barnard eyed them. 'Way too early to say.'

The Detective Superintendent sighed. Looked skywards.

Said to Fletcher: 'Tell me how the fuck we missed this, Danny.'

16

MacReady had grabbed a few hours, Megan already asleep when he arrived home from the maisonette scene and slipped into the warm bed. He'd finally drifted away, his dreams punctuated by a screaming Soraya Tate wrapped in a blood red gilet, a shadowy figure behind her, silver gun barrel glinting.

When he woke, groggy and vaguely annoyed, he wished he could just pull the quilt back over his head. He reached across, patting at the mattress as he went: Megan gone already. He sighed and rolled the other way. Six twenty a.m. on the bedside clock. Beside it, affixed to his phone, was a pink Post-It note. Her handwriting:

We must talk. Tonight. Please.

X

He had no idea what time he would be home. Quick shower, change of clothes, bite to eat, no messages from work – unbelievable, given last night's turn of events – and MacReady was in the hallway and heading for the front door before quarter to seven.

Then he stopped.

Megan's note. The desperation in the scrawled spikes of her handwriting. He remembered the day before, in the park, her talking at him, reaching into her jacket pocket for something.

The jacket that hung on the coat stand tucked in the corner of the hallway.

MacReady turned one pocket out. Found nothing. Rifled through the other.

Pulled out a folded piece of paper.

Opened it.

Read the letter.

Felt his legs weaken. Felt bile in his throat.

Shoved the letter back in the jacket pocket.

Thought: *how*?

Beck made the call to Soraya Tate.

MacReady picked up hot drinks from a petrol station on Newport Road. Chocolate for Beck, more coffee for him. Waited for the early-morning rain to ease off, gave up waiting and sprinted back to the CID car. Beck talked into her mobile alongside him; he sat quietly in the passenger seat, not listening, forehead against fogged window, car roof thrumming above him. Wet and tired enough to feel it in his bones. A caffeine headache now, ice behind his eyes, mainlining three sugars and black even before they left the station at 7.30 a.m. He looked at the cardboard cup in his hands: anything to keep him going. Anything to ease the roar of static in his ears.

The letter. After reading it he could barely concentrate on what he was doing. Had staggered from his house to the car. Almost lost control of it on the drive into work, drifting into the opposite lane, missing an oncoming motorcyclist by inches. Found himself sitting in his motor in the car park of the nick, engine running and a uniform tapping on the window to check he was all right.

He'd nodded. A smiling zombie. 'All fine here. Cheers, mate.'

All fine here. But it wasn't fine. It didn't make sense. Unless . . .

MacReady shifted upright. Willed himself to focus on something other than his wife. Flipped open his file of paperwork and studied the printout on top.

An email to the MIR from Barnard late the previous night: the full PM yet to be done, but from prelims the body recovered from the maisonette garden was a black or mixed-race male, late teens, early twenties. Six foot, slim build, decomposed but not putrefied. Surgical pins visible in the ball and socket of the gleno-humeral joint of the right shoulder. They'd picked the email up this morning, MacReady too exhausted – too distracted – to do anything other than nod as he read it.

The final paragraph from Barnard, though. An afterthought, almost.

By the way, it may be worth your while if Detective Sergeant Beck calls in once the full post mortem is complete. It's still to be done, but there are some very interesting things to discuss already.

MacReady turned to Beck as she ended the call. 'And?'

'She'll meet us.'

He handed her the chocolate. 'I'm impressed.'

Beck prised the lid, took a tentative sip. Closed her eyes for a moment; MacReady couldn't be sure if her reaction was one of delight or disgust at the machine-produced gloop. 'I told her we'd take her to see Leon King,' she said.

MacReady fixed her with a frown. 'Did you run it by the DI?'

No response from Beck. She dumped the cup in a holder. Started the engine and pulled off the petrol station forecourt.

'How're you going to get that one past Major Crime?' Mac-Ready asked. 'She's not immediate family.'

'Our little secret,' Beck winked, and shifted up a gear. 'Thought you might like that, given what you've been up to the last couple of days. And it means we don't have to wait for Easyman's medical records to turn up for ID purposes. Besides, it's the only way she'd agree. She's spooked enough as it is.'

The Tate house. The damage. The bruising to Marie and Nathan Brissett. Soraya, yelling at them in the bus stop. *My stepdad's a good man. And he's never laid a finger on either of us.* 'Did you tell her anything about the new body?' asked MacReady. 'That we've found her brother?'

'That we *think* we've found her brother,' Beck said. 'No, I didn't.'

'You know it's him,' said MacReady. 'I can see it in your eyes, Sarge.'

Beck drove them onto Eastern Avenue, merged into traffic. 'We'll find out for sure in a little while, won't we?'

'Please don't tell me we're meeting at the house.'

'Panic not, Will. No Nathan Brissett tantrums to deal with. She's on her way to work. Wasn't keen, but agreed to talk as long as it's away from the family and she gets to hold hands with her boyf. She's RVing with us at the hospital now.'

They drove in silence, windscreen wipers flopping, the dual carriageway choked with civvy workers heading for the city centre, tired and puffy faces hanging over steering wheels, gathered behind misted bus windows, queuing to reach places they didn't want to be.

'Odd, though,' MacReady said after a while. He wiped the inside of his window with the sleeve of his jacket, saw the sign for the University Hospital of Wales turnoff.

Beck sounded the horn at a Transit van as it cut into their lane. 'What, you, miseryguts? You've been away with the fairies since you came into work.'

'Barnard's email,' MacReady replied, ignoring the remark. 'Don't you think? "*Some very interesting things to discuss*"?'

'I have no clue,' Beck said. She turned to him. Grinned. 'But we could always pop in and see him, if you like.'

'Think I'll pass.'

'Yeah, *out*, you lightweight,' Beck said. She slowed, the UHW concourse entrance in front of them. 'Anyway, there's our girl.'

MacReady squinted through rivulets of rainwater on glass. Saw the red gilet. Soraya Tate, heading towards them. No umbrella, no hood, hair matted to her scalp. Drenched and stony-faced.

'She really needs to get herself a new coat,' said MacReady.

Beck glanced at him. Shook her head. 'Like that's the worst of her worries.'

A blast of cold air, the patter of rain into gutter water, as Soraya Tate climbed into the back of the CID car. Beck reached across the seat; in her hands, MacReady saw the cup of hot chocolate.

Soraya Tate looked at it, then to Beck. Eyes unblinking. 'Thank you,' she said eventually, and took the drink. With her other hand she wiped rainwater off her cheeks and forehead.

'No, thank you,' said Beck. 'We appreciate you doing this.'

Tate dropped her head. Stared at the cup. 'I just want you to find Jermaine.'

Beck looked at MacReady. He widened his eyes for a second.

'Was your brother ever in an accident, Soraya?' Beck asked.

Tate brushed a straggle of hair behind one ear. Looked up at Beck. 'Accident?'

'Injuries, something that required medical treatment . . .'

She looked at them blankly for a moment. Then: 'He was always getting lumped up. Had a temper on him, y'know. Wouldn't take any disrespecting from anyone so kept getting into fights an' all.'

'Did he ever end up in hospital?' MacReady asked.

Tate shrugged. 'I don't know. Jermaine was . . . We never knew what he was up to half the time. Sometimes we wouldn't see him for a week, then he'd rock up and sleep for two days straight, not even eating, nothing. Then he'd row with my stepdad and disappear again.'

'I take it they didn't get on,' Beck said.

'Was the drugs,' Tate said. 'Jermaine was pretty fucked up most of the time. You lot know my stepdad was a lot of things, but he wasn't into all that.'

'Did Nathan ever hit him?' Beck asked.

'Already told you, he never laid a finger on any of us.'

MacReady shuffled around to face her. 'The bruises, Soraya. I can still see them on your neck. I saw them on your mother and Nathan when I came to the house.'

Tate's face hardened. She glanced out of the window. Said, 'You don't know what you're talking about.'

'Then help us out here,' MacReady said. 'There are things we can do.'

'I'm trying to help you,' Tate said quietly. 'And there's nothing you can do.'

Beck placed a hand on MacReady's knee, shushed him silently. He sighed, turned back to face the windscreen.

'Did Jermaine ever have an operation, Soraya?' Beck asked. 'Surgery after one of these fights?'

'Why do you keep asking that?' Tate said.

'Just firming up on a few loose ends,' Beck replied. 'Might not mean anything.'

Tate drank some of the chocolate, licked at her top lip. 'This stuff is rank.' She handed it back to Beck, who dropped it into a holder. 'Worst one was back when he was about fourteen, fifteen, I think. Came off a mini motorbike on the old railway line not far from our house.'

'What happened?'

'Bust a few bones. He was here,' she gestured at the UHW, 'for a whole weekend, I remember. Maybe longer. They had to stick all these pins in his arm and shoulder.'

Beck nodded at her. Gave a gentle smile. 'OK,' she said. 'OK, that's fine. Do you want to go see Leon now?'

MacReady was dialling the MIR as Beck and Tate climbed out of the car.

So they'd found him.

During the phone call Fletcher had pretty much agreed the body located at the maisonette was that of Jermaine Tate, and told MacReady the Major Crime Super was of the same opinion. *We're waiting for the PM, but it looks like that's a formality now. Just get yourself back here soonest. It's me and thee doubling up for the first set of interviews with you know who.*

MacReady felt energised from the rush of adrenaline, sensed Beck was on the verge of punching the air. Except now wasn't the time.

Soraya Tate sat sobbing uncontrollably at Leon King's bedside. Fingers clawed and clutching at King's bandaged hand. Forehead resting on a sunken, yellowing chest that rose and fell as machinery pumped air into lungs. Whispering something to King, something MacReady couldn't make out over the wheeze and hum of medical equipment.

'Bless them, it's so touching,' said one of the firearms officers. Another duo deployed to stand guard, drink coffee, read lads' mags and flex pecs at passing nurses.

The other ARV officer nodded in agreement. 'Bet this month's overtime that Bob Garratt's wife and kid have been totally forgotten.' A pointed look at MacReady. 'Why we bend over backwards for these shithouses is beyond me.'

MacReady thought of his brother. 'They're just people when all's said and done.'

The officer snorted as he glanced across at King's bed. 'What're you, a *Guardian* reader? My heart fuckin' bleeds.'

Beck's hand on MacReady's sleeve. He swallowed the anger. No fuss, no scene: Soraya Tate wasn't supposed to be there. He rolled his eyes at Beck. Stepped away from the ARV officers, closer to King's bed. Listened.

I'm sorry I'm sorry I'm sorry . . . Tate, rocking as she repeated the same two words.

'What's she saying?' Beck, at his side.

'That she's sorry.'

Beck listened. 'For what, though?'

MacReady didn't reply. Watched Soraya Tate until he couldn't watch anymore. *All this, and we've still got to tell her about Jermaine.* He walked over to Tate, lowered a hand to her shoulder. The shake of bone and cool skin beneath his palm. 'We really have to go, Soraya.'

She swivelled her head towards him. Wet eyes, streaked mascara, a silver globule hanging from one nostril. She wiped at it with the back of her hand. 'Is he going to die?'

'I hope not,' said MacReady after a moment. 'I really hope not.'

'For different reasons to me though, right?' she asked, and stood. Her tone clipped, now. She yanked up her gilet, pulled it on, zipped it to her neck, to the bruises colouring her jawline. One final look at King. 'I'm so sorry,' she breathed.

'You've got nothing to be sorry about,' Beck said, speaking softly, a hand moving to Tate's back. 'None of this is your doing.'

Tate shrugged the hand away. Turned to Beck. 'He only went to the maisonette because of me,' she said. Her face crumpled. Fresh tears as she dropped her head into her hands. 'I sent him there.'

'We saw the text,' MacReady said. 'It doesn't mean you're at fault.'

'You haven't got a clue, have you?' Tate cried. She raised her face to the heavens, shook her head. 'Oh God, you don't know anything, and not even people like them,' she pointed at the ARV officers, 'can help you.'

Tate walked towards the exit. MacReady and Beck fell in alongside her, exchanged glances as Tate jabbed at a button to call the lift.

'We need to talk about Jermaine, Soraya,' MacReady said.

Tate hugged herself, arms tight around her midriff. 'I've already said too much.'

A faint ping and the doors slid open. Tate backed into the lift, shaking her head, shaking her head and laughing humourlessly as she pressed for the ground floor.

She stared at MacReady. 'I just want you to find him. 'Cos maybe then you'll start to understand what you're dealing with.'

The doors closed and she was gone.

17

Busy in the custody suite for a Tuesday morning.

Cells full, civvy detention officers microwaving detainees' breakfast meals, processing prisoners, a conveyor belt of cheap haircuts and Asda George tracksuits and body sweat. A constant *ratatat* on metal doors and calls for fag breaks and cups of tea, *two fuckin' sugars an' all*. No-bail warrant arrests waiting to be shipped to court where they'd be released on bail yet again and breach their conditions within the day. Drunks and toms, juvies in overnight for Take and Drive, their parents disinclined to attend for the eighth time that month and Social Services yet to arrive at their office despite it nudging 9 a.m. Every other cell taken by football fans, home and away. Pre- and post-match rumbles in city centre pubs had run the previous night shift uniforms ragged. Resources across the capital had been stretched to their limits again, and the SMT coffee and buns brigade who'd slept peacefully while the wheel came off were yet to pick over the wreckage during the blame game of the morning Tasking Meeting.

MacReady raised a hand to hide a yawn. Glanced at the DI standing next to him. Rumpled, unshaven, paperwork jammed under the arm of his charcoal suit, less ready to go than ready to fold. Fletcher was to take the lead in the interview, MacReady having been allowed to sit in by the DI after much consultation with the Detective Super. He wasn't sure if it was a grudging thank you for finding what they now knew were Jermaine Tate's remains, or as a means to keep him the fuck out of the way in the pokey so he didn't embarrass anybody else on the team.

Dane Sillitoe stood at the booking-in desk, face blank and pale as he unclipped an expensive-looking watch, handed it to the CDO for bagging with the rest of his property. While Mac-Ready and Beck were driving to meet Soraya Tate at the hospital, the traffic black rats had picked up Sillitoe on the M4 heading east towards Bristol; before he clocked off last night Fletcher had circulated him force wide and on PNC as wanted.

Sillitoe's overconfident air was noticeably absent, but then being arrested on suspicion of murder could certainly take the wind out of anybody's sails.

The custody sergeant tapped at her keyboard. 'Legal representation?'

'Just the duty sol,' Sillitoe said, voice quiet.

MacReady stepped forward. Thought of Malcolm Gill, the toothpick-thin brief who'd sat with Sillitoe a couple of days before. 'You have a family solicitor. Should we give him a call?'

'Duty sol,' Sillitoe said again.

'This is a serious matter,' MacReady said. He tried to look him in the eyes; Sillitoe turned away, head lowered. 'Murder, Dane. You're in the bin for murder and you want the on-call brief?'

A cough from Fletcher. 'His choice.'

'Duty solicitor it is,' the custody sergeant said. She gestured to a CDO. 'Russ, take Mister Sillitoe to cell seven, would you?'

Sillitoe got both.

The phone call from the front desk came half an hour later; Fletcher clearly thought a petty squabble was beneath him, so MacReady put down his just-brewed mug of tea and made his way to the foyer.

Malcom Gill was shaking his head at a woman, his ruddy face darkening. 'We've only just been made aware, Fiona. I don't know what he's playing at.'

'It's irrelevant,' she said. 'He asked for a duty solicitor and that's why I'm here.'

'We'll handle it. We'll cover any expenses you've incurred.'

'Not the point, Malcolm.'

'You seriously think Dane's father is going to allow your firm to represent him?'

'Not his call. And we're more than capable, you know that perfectly well.'

MacReady leaned on the counter, waited for them to finish. Neither had noticed he was there. Impatient faces behind them: MOPs queuing to sign bail, to produce driving documents, to report dole money 'lost', their lies lager-scented as they demanded a crime number for replacement booze funds.

'I've tried to explain to Dane how serious it is,' MacReady said, loud enough to make both solicitors jump. The custody clock ticking already; no time for this.

Gill turned to him. 'Serious? Fiona advises me you've arrested him for murder. *Murder*? Whose murder?'

'I can't disclose anything to either of you at the moment,' MacReady said. 'Not until, y'know, you guys have finished arguing about which of you gets to look after him.'

The solicitors stared at him. Turned to face each other.

'A quiet word,' Gill said to the woman.

They retreated to one corner of the foyer. MacReady watched as Gill leaned into the duty solicitor, talking at her, eyes narrowed. She argued with him, shaking her head, Gill leaning in closer and muttering quickly, more forcefully. He dug out a mobile phone, made a call, handed the phone to her. She nodded as she listened to the voice on the other end of the line. People grumbled in the queue; MacReady ignored them, his bewilderment at Megan's letter having morphed into a simmering anger that he was struggling to keep under control.

'I've taken advice,' the woman said when they returned to the counter. She swallowed as she spoke, eyes shielded and studying the floor. Her neck was mottled with red, flushed and angry-looking. 'Malcolm can do the necessary.'

MacReady studied her for a moment. Nodded. 'Right.'

Gill's mouth flashed a fake smile. 'I'd like to speak with my client, please.'

Something was amiss.

MacReady sensed it. He left Malcolm Gill drumming his fingers on his expensive briefcase in the foyer, made his way back to the custody suite, asked the sergeant to log a visit to Sillitoe's cell.

He slid open the suicide hatch.

'The duty solicitor has gone, Dane.'

Sillitoe sat on the edge of the wooden bench, elbows on knees. He jerked his head up at MacReady's voice. 'What d'you mean, gone?'

'Malcolm Gill is here. He's going to sit in with you again.'

'I don't want him.'

'I think your family may have had something to say about that.'

Sillitoe placed hands over his face, pushed them back through his hair and spread his arms wide, exasperated. 'Shit, man. Shit.' He stood, paced over to the hatch. Ducked his head to look at MacReady. 'I asked for the duty sol, and you can't even get that right. I do not want Gill, do you lot fuckin' understand?'

'He's at the front desk now.'

'How did he find out I was here?'

MacReady shrugged. 'Beats me.'

'Please don't tell me you've briefed him.'

'We've said nothing. He knows nothing other than what you've been arrested for.'

Sillitoe's eyes closed. 'That's more than enough.'

'What's going on here, Dane? I know something's off.'

'Get rid of him,' Sillitoe muttered. 'Get rid of him, please, before you do any more damage.'

MacReady watched him shuffle over to the bench, lie down and face the wall. After a moment he slid the hatch closed and walked back to the custody suite desk.

'Problems?'

Fletcher, leaning on the doorframe, coffee in hand. From the kitchenette behind him, MacReady heard amused female voices on a television set, the discussion seemingly centred on health problems for women in their fifties.

'None at all,' MacReady replied, but couldn't be sure if it was the truth or not. 'We might need the Sarge to ring the duty sol again, get her back here.'

'You're joking, right? Tick tock and all that.'

At the front desk he walked out into the foyer.

'Is he ready?' Gill asked.

'He doesn't want you,' MacReady said.

Gill chewed at the inside of his mouth, eyes tapered behind glasses as he mulled this over. Then: 'It matters not what young Dane wants, it's what he's given in order to look after his and everybody else's best interests. This is out of my hands.'

A smattering of people on chairs, waiting for appointments, to give statements, to pick up stolen property. They listened in as Gill's voice rose in volume.

MacReady was losing what little patience he had left. 'It is out of your hands. Dane's no juvenile –'

'I'm acutely aware of that, *thank you.*'

'Then you'll be acutely aware that he can choose his own legal rep, that he doesn't have to disclose anything to anybody outside these walls, and as he doesn't want to speak to you I would say that your work here is done. So unless there's something you'd like to tell me about why he doesn't want you . . . *thank you.*'

MacReady proffered a hand. Gill ignored it. Hovered in front of MacReady, blinking, clearly making mental calculations. There was the briefest of twitches in his left cheek, the shadow of something MacReady couldn't quite identify passing across his face.

He watched as Gill swept out of the station and into James Street, pulling his mobile out of a pocket and dialling. One glance back at the building, fingers cupped over his forehead, and he was out of sight.

One of the MOPs stretched and yawned in his chair, the bottom of his tracky bots gathering around his shins, his dirty trainers untied and squeaking on the carpet as he shuffled. 'This goin' take long, mate? Been waiting here for an hour already, like.'

MacReady took no notice. Swiped his pass card, buzzed himself back into the station.

Pictured Gill's face. The flash across his features.

It was fear he'd seen there.

Sillitoe went no comment.

Four tapes over three jittery interview sessions, the two words repeated endlessly until, as the wall clock nudged one in the afternoon, his voice was a robotic, uninterested drawl in response to anything they put to him.

'D'you need a break to stretch your legs, Mister Sillitoe?' Fletcher asked at one point.

'No. Comment,' Sillitoe had replied, such was the amount of listening going on.

'Going to be a long one,' Fletcher said now.

No Comment interviews were irritating at the best of times; with the day he'd had already MacReady felt like screaming inside.

'Yup,' he nodded, nibbling at the inside of his cheek.

* * *

On the kitchenette television: twenty-four-hour news again, the squat maisonettes of Hodges Square framed by grey sky, techies and Major Crime and a couple of pips passing across the screen, the voiceover female. Female and familiar. It cut to a live feed from the scene; the reporter appeared, finger pressed to her ear, wind snapping at her fringe as she spoke to camera.

It's unclear at present what the police have found here, Nick, because they are telling us very little. It's difficult to say what they know, if anything at all.

Klaudia Solak. An incredulous, provocative tone to her voice. The ambition stark in her eyes, her face.

You have to remember that this is where a serving officer was shot dead. Shot dead, and the police are no further forward, it seems, despite a huge deployment of staff and resources. And it must be said, Nick, that people within the Butetown community are starting to question the abilities of the detectives involved in the investigation . . .

'Fuck's sake,' MacReady said, and reached for the remote. He muted the television, slumped back into the battered chair. Watched as Solak nodded a brilliant, encouraging smile at one of the stuffed-shirt rankers whose mouth moved silently as he told her things he probably shouldn't.

'Media,' sighed Fletcher.

'We've got neighbourhood teams up the wazoo in Butetown trying to smooth things over,' MacReady said. 'She's just looking to whip things up, for an angle. She makes that Kay Burley muppet look like a shrinking violet.'

Fletcher looked over at him. 'You're a bit excitable, Will, aren't you?'

'Doesn't it wind you up, though?'

'Media,' he said again, as if it explained everything. 'So you going to tell me how you found out about Jermaine Tate's old surgery details a full four hours before his medical records are due to arrive?'

MacReady fidgeted in his seat. 'The Sarge ... we did some digging together.'

'Like your digging, don't you?'

'Just keeping busy.' He checked the time on his phone: a reflex, to shift the conversation elsewhere. 'When do we go back in?'

Fletcher sat slouched, heavy-lidded and with legs crossed at the knee. Folder splayed on one thigh, calm as you like. As if he was about to nod off. 'Want to wait for the Eighteens to come back. Something else to work with, hopefully.'

The Section Eighteen searches. Post-arrest, Fletcher had dispatched teams to Sillitoe's swanky flat down the Bay, to the vehicle recovery centre, where they'd impounded the limousine Sillitoe was driving when tugged by traffic. Dusting, bagging, tagging. Logging anything and everything. And nothing from any of them as yet. Just Scott Sillitoe, ringing Ops Room and Cardiff Bay front desk every ten minutes demanding his vehicle was released: *I'm losing fucking business here* ...

MacReady got up, found there was no room to pace inside the kitchenette. Made his way out of the custody suite, to the parade room, knowing it would be empty. Mid-afternoon and Ops Room would be stacking calls, plugging gaps, dragging uniform from one unfinished incident to the next.

He dug out Solak's business card. Stared at the contact number. Still angry about what she'd said on air. Still angry with her. A chance to put the record straight.

And angry with Megan, too. Furious now.

MacReady pulled out his mobile phone. Brought up Megan's contact details. His thumb, hovering over the call symbol. Hovering. Knowing he didn't trust himself not to let on that he knew. He wanted to catch her cold tonight. Confront her.

Klaudia Solak's voice in his head.

People talk. Maybe we could talk too?

'You told us Jermaine Tate was in Portugal, Dane.'

Sillitoe, shrunken in the chair, tieless, reeking of fag smoke and desperation, wet eyes blank and bloodshot and fixed on the wall clock, on a second hand sweeping silently, endlessly. Hands brushing through mussed hair, teeth clicking at the nubs of fingernails.

'No comment. I keep telling you, no comment.'

'I think we should move on, gents.'

Fiona Noble, the duty solicitor. Elfin fifty-something, sharp black business duds, stray blonde hairs curled on the lapels. Still buoyed by her recall, a dinner party story filed away, the time she got one over on the infamous Malcolm Gill.

MacReady preferred her being there; Gill was obnoxious and unpleasant to be around. Noble, not so much. At least for a scrote's brief. She knew it was a game and played it so: efficiency tinged with world-weary humour. MacReady liked her immediately. He also sensed she held criminals in as low regard as he did, although he doubted she'd ever be upfront about it. Whatever pays the bills, he supposed, although he could never imagine stooping to such levels to put food on the table.

Fletcher, palms spread: 'With respect, your client is failing to answer any of the –'

'Of course he's answering,' Noble cut across. She looked up from her notes. Smiled, added a hitch of the eyebrows. Playful, almost. 'Just not in the way that you'd like.'

MacReady shifted forward in his seat. 'Dane, you know we've found what we believe to be Jermaine Tate's body at the maison-ette. The maisonette you've been to before. Have you got any-thing to say about that?'

'No comment.'

'Your friend is dead, Dane. Your other friend has been shot and is lying in a coma in hospital. We have a woman and child who lost a husband, a father, the same time Leon King was almost murdered. If you had nothing to do with any of it, now is the time to tell us. Now is the time to tell what you know.'

Sillitoe folded his arms. Shook his head.

'Do you know who shot Leon King and Detective Sergeant Robert Garratt?'

No response.

'What about the drugs we found in the limousine?' Fletcher asked. 'Appears to be cocaine.'

Noble sighed. 'My client has already indicated to me that it was for personal use. The amount found is minuscule. He's prepared to accept any penalty for that. And we discussed this following disclosure.'

MacReady threw his pen onto the desk. 'This is ridiculous. *Ridiculous*. You're giving us nothing, Dane. Absolutely noth—'

'Careful, officer,' Noble said, staring hard at him. 'I would hate to halt the interview for oppressive behaviour.'

'You're only in here because he,' MacReady gestured at Sillitoe, 'was too petrified to let his normal brief represent him. Why is that, Dane?'

'DC MacReady, I should warn you –'

'What are you so scared of? What are all of you so terrified about? Everybody we talk to has fear in their eyes, even Malcolm Gill.'

'DC MacReady –'

He snapped his head to Noble. 'For God's sake, what?'

'I'm removing my client from the interview,' Noble said.

Fletcher rocked back in his chair. 'Hoo boy.'

MacReady watched Noble gather her things, motion for Sillitoe to follow her out of the interview room. He noted the time for the recorder, switched it off as they left.

Fletcher said nothing for a moment. Sat quietly, nodding to himself. The wall clock showed quarter past three. Then: 'Been a long couple of days.'

'Sorry, boss,' MacReady said. He slipped paperwork and photos into his file. Knew what was coming.

'Yeah,' said Fletcher. He rubbed at his eyes. 'See you tomorrow, Will.'

'We can still throw another interview into him. Once he's calmed down.'

'And are you going to calm down? What on earth has got into you today?'

'Once everyone's calmed down, I mean. Something might come out –'

'He's not going to give us any more than he already has. We've got him for the gear in the limo. His flat is clean. What more do you want?'

'He's given us nothing.'

Fletcher stood. Opened the interview room door. Stepped back to allow MacReady to leave. 'I'm releasing him,' he said, almost a whisper. 'He can have a charge sheet for the drugs, another for obstructing police. Conditional bail. That'll do for now.'

'That'll do?' MacReady asked. He shook his head. Checked around the doorframe, saw Noble and Sillitoe waiting at the custody desk. He lowered his voice. 'With respect, boss, he's going to walk out of here laughing.'

'I know,' said Fletcher. 'That's why I'm putting a surveillance team on him as soon as his arse goes out the front doors. Let's see where he takes us, all right?'

18

Megan looked up as MacReady entered the lounge.

'Hey,' she smiled, but it faded as quickly as it had appeared. 'You're home early.'

MacReady draped his jacket over the back of the settee. 'Nothing left for us to do today. Nothing for me, anyway.' He studied her. 'At least not at work.'

She was sitting stiffly, hands on knees, fingernails working fabric. She was nervous, he realised. Breathing rapidly, audible flutters in her throat. She glanced at him then dropped her eyes to the floor. Her nails, almost as bad as Beck. Scratching and working at the thighs of her trousers.

'We should talk,' she said, voice so quiet he almost missed it.

A faint shiver in MacReady's stomach. The days and evenings away, stretching for weeks, worse than when he was on response, and that had been bad enough for their relationship. He steeled himself for the bullshit all spouses dreaded: Megan telling him she'd been unhappy for too long, that she was lonely and he hadn't even noticed how abandoned she felt, that his absence this last month had tipped her over the edge, and his inability to provide her with what she really wanted was the final straw. That she was beyond desperate, and it had driven her to do a terrible thing.

That he was the ultimate cop cliché with a failed marriage because of The Job.

That there was someone else.

The letter he'd found in her jacket pocket this morning.

Confirming Megan's booking appointment with a midwife.

She was pregnant.

'Then talk,' he said. Trying to keep his voice steady despite the anger already spiralling around inside him. *Let her talk. Let her dig her own hole. She doesn't know you know.* Just like being in work, prepping for interview. Give them enough rope, as his old tutor constable used to drum into him. MacReady noticed Megan was rocking gently, small movements back and forth as one incisor nibbled away at her bottom lip.

'Have you ever . . .' she started, then took a sudden deep breath, chest hitching. 'Have you ever done something that you thought was the right thing at the time . . . but afterwards . . .?'

'Plenty of times.' MacReady lowered himself into the chair opposite. Kept his eyes on a face that shifted and turned away repeatedly, unable to look directly at him. Clasped his hands between his knees. Pictured himself running after a man who he thought was an armed Jermaine Tate. Digging up a maison-ette garden without the knowledge of his senior officers. Getting himself – and his colleagues – into trouble.

Not the same, though. Nowhere near the same as this . . .

MacReady couldn't contain it any longer.

'Who is it?' he blurted, mouth dry.

Megan looked at him now. 'I don't understand.'

'No, Meg. You do understand. It's a simple question. Who is it?'

Her fingers, continuing to scratch away. 'Will, I –'

'I found the GP's letter,' he said. Curled his lip. Leaned towards her, neck straining. 'I fucking *know*, Meg. And it isn't mine. It can't be mine, can it? Because,' he flicked his fingers towards his crotch, 'I can't have kids. And you're having a kid, aren't you?'

She crumbled. 'Yes,' she cried.

And there it was. And it cleaved his heart to hear it. MacReady blinked at her. For a moment thought he might burst into tears. 'So the most obvious fucking question, which you seem incapable of understanding –'

'You're scaring me now –'

'– is *who is it*? Who is the father?'

'Please, Will, please stop shouting, I can't think –'

'You fuck somebody else and they knock you up and you expect me to be *calm*?'

'Will, please, I've been trying to tell you, you don't underst—'

A sudden hiss in his ears. Red whorls in his vision. MacReady scrambled upright on unsteady legs. Felt winded, almost, the pain of the realisation doubling him over. Numb with fury, with the knowledge that if he stayed a minute longer he might not be able to control himself, that things would deteriorate into something far worse than anything Stuart and Kirsty had done to one another. He staggered towards the door. Flailed at the handle, slammed it down and opened the door to the hallway.

'*Will . . .*'

Megan's voice, hoarse and thick with tears.

MacReady hesitated at the front door. Just for a second. Closed his eyes, could see nothing but his smiling wife coupling with a faceless stranger.

'No,' he said, and stepped out into drizzle.

MacReady slammed the front door behind him.

Rain lashing sideways, buffeting the car as MacReady killed the engine.

His thighs shook as he climbed out and into the downpour, slammed the car door shut, stalked across the garden with its pathetic lawn and abandoned, broken children's toys. His fists hammered the front door, the sound loud and shocking as it echoed around the quiet cul-de-sac.

Curtains would be twitching. MacReady didn't care. He had nowhere else to go. Time for his brother to return one of many favours. To do the decent thing and let him crash here. Just for tonight. For a few nights. Until he could think straight. Until he could wrap his head around what had happened.

Yet the door remained closed. He thumped at it again, kept thumping, a dull and rhythmic beat accompanied by the patter of rainwater spilling from a downpipe.

'Open the fucking door, Stuart,' MacReady shouted, and kicked at the bottom panel; the UPVC shuddered in its frame. Inside, Kirsty's raised voice. It was clearly an argument with someone else, someone talking quietly enough not to be heard.

A metallic click from inside the door. A louder *thunk*, the bolt sliding across.

Kirsty swung the door open, dirty tea towel in hand. 'Will? What's going on?'

'I'm sorry,' MacReady said, and pushed past her and into the house.

His brother in the lounge. A tracksuit splayed on the settee, eyes on a football simulation on the TV, console controller in hand. Something good cooking in the kitchen out back: Mac-Ready smelled garlic, red wine, red meat. Stuart gave him a perfunctory once over before his eyes swung back to his computer game; his kid brother turning up unannounced – and the reason why – clearly not troubling him.

'What's up, baby bro?'

'We're just about to have something to eat,' Kirsty said, heading into the kitchen. 'Stu had some winnings at the bookies so we're treating ourselves. You staying?'

MacReady called after her. 'Something to eat would be good. If that's OK. As long as I'm –'

Stuart's mobile, sitting on the coffee table between them, gave a text alert. MacReady glanced down at it. Frowned when he saw the name on the screen: Megan.

The football game went silent; Stuart had paused it, fingers frozen around the controller, his eyes on the mobile, on the name displayed there.

'What's this . . .?' MacReady asked, confused. Looking at his brother, back to the battered phone on the table. 'Why is Megan . . .?'

Stuart made a grab for the mobile. MacReady beat him to it.

'Fuck you doing, bruv? Give me my moby.'

Stuart's hand now grasping; MacReady snatched the phone out of reach, opened the message.

Will knows. Don't say anything until I speak to him.

The sudden adrenaline shiver in his thigh muscles. Barely able to breathe as he stared at his brother. Quickly making the calculations. Counting the days, the weeks. How far along Megan was. The last time Stuart stayed over: the night after Garratt was shot dead. Megan at the end of her tether. MacReady had gone to work the next day leaving them together in the house.

How far would you go, Will?

MacReady slumped to his haunches, placed one hand on the carpet to steady himself. With the other he pushed at his closed eyes, pushed at that image he could see again, of Megan rolling around with another man, except this time it wasn't a faceless stranger – it was his older brother. He was desperate for it to go away.

'Tell me why,' was all he could manage.

'Tell you why . . . what?' Stuart asked. He sounded genuinely puzzled, but his eyes shifted about, looking at everything bar MacReady. 'I'm trying to play FIFA here, bro. What you on about?'

MacReady sprung upright. 'You think I wouldn't have found out?' he roared.

'Whoa, wind your neck in now, Will,' his brother said, hands raised. He glanced towards the kitchen. 'Found out about what? And keep your voice down, yeah? You're going to get me into more trouble with the missus.'

'So Kirsty doesn't know.'

It wasn't a question.

His brother pushed himself up from the settee. Threw the controller across the room. Squinted down at MacReady. 'I don't understand what your fuckin' problem is, Will, but you'd better start dealing with it a little better than you are, yeah? Coming into my home, shooting your mouth off –'

'Does she? She doesn't, does she? It'll ruin her, Stuart. You have kids. You've ruined everything. Women aren't your personal baby factories. Three with Kirsty? Two more with different women that you've walked away from?'

Stuart giggled. 'What the actual fu—?'

MacReady threw the punch, saw his fist flying forward before he even realised what he was doing. His knuckles connected with his brother's chin, a dull and sickly crack, knocking him back to the settee where he sat, stunned at what had just happened.

'Are you for real?' his brother said. One hand wiped at his lower lip. He eyed MacReady for a second, teeth bared, blood smeared across the whites.

He didn't give MacReady a chance to answer. Launched himself from the settee. Took MacReady above his hips, shoulder-first into the ribs, both of them rolling towards the opposite wall. Just like the bad old days. The knuckling-up in the High Riggs flat after their father had administered his bi-weekly thrashing, Stuart bleeding and beaten and seeking release, finding it in a younger, smaller William MacReady.

His brother on top of him now, too strong still, knees jammed alongside MacReady's flanks, wiry arms holding MacReady's to the floor. He strained against Stuart, fought with everything he could muster, but it wasn't enough. The anger and frustration screamed through him and he thought he might burst into tears.

'You. Think. I. Fucked. Your. *Missus*?' His brother banged MacReady's arms against the carpet with each word, stared hard into MacReady's eyes.

'You're a scumbag, Stuart,' MacReady rasped.

His brother gave a humourless laugh. 'And you're a mentalist, bro.'

MacReady arched his back, tried to throw his brother off. Knew it was pointless. Looked into Stuart's eyes. Felt a strange calmness. Felt his body go limp.

Said: 'And you're just like Dad.'

His brother's lips squashed together, his jaw grinding, his eyes wide and furious. Raised tendons on his neck. His head drawing back, further away from MacReady's face.

MacReady knew what was coming. Closed his eyes. Heard the kitchen door open. Heard Kirsty's scream.

Felt his brother's forehead connect with his cheek.

Then nothing.

19

Barnard's office.

Gloomy, windowless, cramped, as far from the hi-tech chromatorium nonsense of *Silent Witness* as you could possibly get. Tucked off a corridor in the hospital mortuary, an airless and cluttered box of file boxes, certificates, family photographs and ten-year-old computer equipment. Walls a drab green, ceiling tiles polystyrene, cracked and stained with nicotine from a time when smoking in poky workplaces was compulsory. The tang of antiseptic and coffee, the grace notes of soured human flesh.

Grim, but MacReady would have happily swapped the place for the interior of his old motor. Spending the night inside it hadn't been high on his To Do list yesterday, but there'd been no other place for him to go. He could have crashed somewhere at the nick, or called Beck and couched it in her lounge, but then tongues would have wagged and the comments would've come and MacReady didn't trust himself to be able to deal with any of it in a calm or measured way at the moment. So when he'd come round from the headbutt to find his brother absent and Kirsty pressing a packet of frozen peas to his face he'd thanked her and driven away. Driven to the foreshore east of the city, parked up on an industrial estate, flopped the driver's seat back as far as it would go. Had lain back, arm over his eyes, thinking. Hours working through it all, crying and thumping at the steering wheel while ignoring the throb in his cheek and the buzzing from his mobile phone. Then there was a tap on his window and Mac-Ready had opened his eyes to find a security guard telling him in no uncertain terms to clear off. He was surprised to see the grey light of morning behind the man's looming face; at some point he'd succumbed to exhaustion and collapsed into sleep.

Texts and missed calls from Megan. He'd deleted them without reading. Just seeing her name on his phone had made his pulse quicken. He'd called home, not getting a reply, which he was happy about. Drove there, a quick sweep down the road to make sure Megan's car was missing: she'd left for work. The house empty, no note from his wife, no idea where she was, most of him not caring at that moment. A quick shower, a change of clothes, a snatched glance in a mirror at the ever-growing lump under his left eye. Some more clothes and deodorants and shower gels thrust into a kitbag, because he didn't know when – if – he'd be coming back.

Beck had caught him sneaking into the MIR that morning. She'd eyed MacReady's swollen cheek and tilted her head to one shoulder, eyebrow cocked.

'I don't even want to know,' she'd said. 'Grab a coffee. We're leaving for the mortuary in ten.'

MacReady was surprised to find Barnard's office so slovenly; the professor was a particular man, borderline fussy even, always turned out immaculately, never seen without suit and tie. During the PM on the dock torso Beck had asked the professor why he bothered, given the dead didn't care how he looked.

But their families do, Barnard had replied.

The office was the antithesis of the man who occupied it, but everyone needed a place to breathe, MacReady thought. From the doorway, he glimpsed *World of Warcraft* on the laptop sitting on the desk. Barnard had been stealing longing glances at the screen while Beck and Fletcher shrugged off jackets and settled in chairs.

'That thing will eat up your days,' Beck nodded at the laptop.

Barnard scratched long fingers at his chin, the nails pristine and clipped. 'It's certainly adding to my credit card bill. Do you play?'

'My partner seems to spend more time in the realm than the real world.'

The professor shifted his bifocals onto the top of his head, gave a rueful glance around the office. 'I can't say I blame him.'

'Her.'

'Oh.' Barnard sat back in his chair. A sideways look at Fletcher. Nodded to himself as he eyed Beck. 'Right.'

Beck's hand up to her mouth, pulling at the corners of a smile. 'You seem . . . surprised.'

'More disappointed, Detective Sergeant,' said Barnard. 'Such an awful waste . . .'

Beck chuckled. 'I'll take that as a compliment. I think.'

'Terribly unreconstructed, no?' shrugged Barnard. 'Much to the chagrin of my wife. Hence,' he gestured at the frozen image, 'I'm frequently banished to other worlds.'

'So what do you have for us?' MacReady asked from the doorway.

'Let me log out of this,' Barnard sighed, and rattled at the laptop keyboard. He turned to face them, laced those spindly fingers across a trim belly. A metallic squeak from the base of the chair as he rocked it back a ways. 'An eager beaver,' he replied. 'Your supervisors must be very pleased to have you on the team.'

'Debatable,' said Fletcher, throwing a look over his shoulder at MacReady.

Barnard squinted as he studied MacReady's face. 'That's an impressive shiner you've got blossoming there. Did somebody do that to you in work?'

'We've thought about doing it,' Fletcher muttered.

MacReady reached up, touched the swelling. Pain shot through his eye, his temple. Shook his head. 'Rugby match.'

'Didn't know you played,' said Beck.

'A true man's game,' Barnard nodded. To Beck: 'No offence, of course.'

She waved it away. 'I can still appreciate the thighs on display.'

'Indeed,' Barnard replied, looking mildly nonplussed. Files suddenly being shifted about on the desk, the professor shuffling paperwork. Business time. He glided on the chair to a desktop computer, clicked at a mouse and made a strange ducking movement with his head; the bifocals dropped neatly onto his nose. 'We've cross-checked dentals and med records. It's this missing man of yours. Jermaine Tate. Trussed up in a roll of carpeting bound with electrical flex.'

MacReady watched Beck's hands tighten into fists on her thighs. Pictured the cracked concrete floor in the maisonette, the square of missing carpet. None of them thought anything of it at the time of the shooting, of the burglary.

'You've been pretty lucky with the garden,' continued Barnard. 'There was barely two inches of topsoil before several feet of clay. Whoever buried the young man couldn't have known it would preserve him quite well.'

'Or cared,' said Beck.

'Well that, and the makeshift shroud helped to keep a lot of him intact.' Barnard looked at MacReady. 'At the scene you asked how long he'd been in the ground?'

MacReady nodded. 'A year would be good.'

'I'd go along with that,' Barnard said. 'And that's about as far along as I care to go at the moment. But I've made a few telephone calls, particularly to a forensic entomologist friend of mine. Do you know what a Phorid fly is, Detective Inspector?'

'Coffin flies,' Fletcher replied. 'Seeing those things in a window at a *concern for occupant* call always used to make me shudder.'

'Yes, those stinkers do tend to cling to the nostrils for a few days,' Barnard winked at him. 'So: quantities of dried pupal cases were found inside the carpet. Not a huge amount, but my esteemed colleague tells me there are enough to suggest that there had been at least two life-cycles of Phorids inside the shroud. They'd eaten away some soft tissue.'

Beck turned to MacReady. 'Sure you don't need to sit down?'

MacReady flashed her the finger, his knuckles aching as he did it. *Stuart*. Punching him yesterday. He wondered where his brother was now. What he was doing. If he'd told Kirsty and they were now trading blows in the kitchen while their kids screamed at their feet.

'Small colony of woodlice, too.' Barnard was studying a screen which was reflected in his glasses. 'I'm advised they're always attracted by the fungus on de-fleshed bones, but as the Phorids hadn't done much damage there was little to draw them in. Not a well-established colony either, and certainly not several generations. I've sent samples and a report to my acquaintance for a definitive answer, but she is of the early opinion that your body has been in the ground for around twelve to fourteen months.'

'That ties in with the last time Tate was seen,' said MacReady.

Fletcher scooted forward in his seat. 'Can you tell us about injuries?'

'Multiple,' Barnard replied. *Click, scroll*. Those thick eyebrows working as he rolled notes up the screen in front of him. 'In layman's terms: serious head trauma, multiple fractures to the skull, jaw, orbital sockets, forearms, fingers . . . I could go on.'

'So he had a right shoeing then,' Fletcher offered.

'Quite,' said Barnard. 'I would say the injuries to his skull alone were more than enough to kill a grown man.'

'No gunshot wounds at all?' asked Beck.

'None,' replied Barnard. 'This was a sustained and brutal assault. To cause that amount of damage takes time. The number of injuries are on the same level as those someone would suffer in a serious car accident. But they're not consistent with such an accident, if you see what I mean. They appear more . . . targeted. Deliberate.'

Fletcher: 'Someone was beating him for a while.'

'I'd go as far as to say it was akin to torture,' Barnard replied.

Beck exhaled. 'Jesus.'

'Could it have been more than one person?' MacReady asked.

Barnard shrugged. 'Quite possible. Some of the trauma is minor – wrist injuries, for one – which means he could have been restrained while others hit him. Difficult to tell, though, because even though the Phorids had little time to gobble soft tissues they'd eaten enough away to make pinpointing any ligature marks, for example, almost impossible.'

'At least we know why Tate's blood was found in the maisonette now,' MacReady offered.

Fletcher dropped his head, rubbed at his buzz cut. 'Wasted time and money from our ever-shrinking budget looking for him though. Thinking he was out there somewhere, still thieving oxygen.'

'It sounds about right,' Beck said absent-mindedly. Her thumb riffled through case papers. 'Kill him inside the place, wait until dark, shallow grave in the garden not ten feet from the back doors. There're walls on three sides to keep out prying eyes.'

'But why kill him?' MacReady asked.

'More importantly,' Fletcher said, and looked up, 'who killed him?'

'King?' MacReady replied. 'Could've been why somebody tried to take him out. Revenge for killing Tate kind of thing?'

'Why would Leon King kill Tate, though?' asked Beck. 'Because of a stolen video camera that linked them? I don't buy it.'

Fletcher puffed air out of his cheeks. 'And even if that was the case – and I don't for a minute think it is – who would go after King? One of Tate's family? Dane Sillitoe, because he was on the recording too?'

'Nathan Brissett has got a mean temper on him, we all know that,' MacReady replied. 'Perhaps he did it, and that's why they're refusing to speak to us.'

'We're grasping here,' Fletcher muttered. 'And this is driving me beyond nuts. It just doesn't make sense, Will. Nathan Brissett is all kinds of bad if you're thinking of pub brawls and general twattery, but murder? He's not the type. And we already know he and Jermaine loathed one another, so do you honestly believe he'd shoot some shithouse as revenge? This would mean Brissett – and quite probably the rest of the family – already knew Jermaine was dead, and not one of them has told us anything of the sort.' He sighed. 'I'll task someone to cross-check his swabs with the hits we found in the maisonette and on King's clothes, but it'll come back negative. It wasn't Brissett. End of.'

MacReady exhaled. Leaned against the doorframe. More unanswered questions. Two steps forward, one back, and still the rapes and aggravated burglaries of the normal CID world continued to stack up back at the ranch, the incident reports unopened and ignored alongside the threatening emails from BCU commanders about work not being done.

Silence for a moment. The room seemingly gloomier.

Beck flinched in her seat when Barnard cleared his throat.

'So.' He was smiling. A pleased-with-myself thin grin. 'Would you like to hear the interesting aspect to your garden friend?'

Beck straightened. 'Your email.'

'My email, yes,' Barnard nodded. He turned to Fletcher. 'You wanted to know about injuries?'

Fletcher spread his arms wide, palms out. 'All ears.'

'The multiple fractures we've discussed were all pre-mortem,' Barnard said. He sunk back into his chair. Hooked an ankle onto one knee. 'It's the post-mortem injury that piqued my interest. Brought back fond memories of a windswept afternoon a few weeks ago.'

He was staring at Beck.

'Please don't tell me –' she said, and stopped herself. Placed a hand to her mouth. Chewed at one fingernail, her skin ashen.

'I couldn't quite believe it when I saw it,' said Barnard. 'But it's the same, I'm afraid. The young man in the garden was disembowelled. Cut open in exactly the same manner as the torso you people dredged up from the dock.'

20

At three in the afternoon Fletcher appeared in his office doorway and motioned for Beck to come over. MacReady watched as they spoke quietly, heads close, eyes shifty. Became aware of Harrison powering down his workstation, rising from his desk, hand already reaching for his jacket as he threw furtive glances around the room. The MIR went about its business behind him: civvies updating and cross-referencing, SMT rubbing chins while looking devoid of answers, Major Crime just looking well-pressed and serious, a second whiteboard already filling up with pictures and question marks and dashes of marker pen, a large corkboard now joining the line-up of office presentation tools seemingly taunting them from one corner. The air seemed stale and unmoving, the staff going through the motions with bleary eyes and fluorescent tans.

Beck walked across to MacReady as Fletcher locked his office. 'Act casual so none of the bosses notice you.'

MacReady looked up at her. 'If I danced on my desk in a studded thong they wouldn't blink.'

'Humour,' Beck nodded. 'Excellent attempt, miseryguts.'

He said nothing. Leaned back in his chair. Thought about explaining to her. It was sitting inside him, like a cancerous lump in his guts, and he wanted it out. Wanted to spill it to take some of the pressure off. What good it would do he didn't know. And it would be the old police officer's secret – everybody would know and pretend otherwise, and he would know they were doing so. That was the way the game worked. He couldn't bear the whispering, the glances each time he walked into the room. He batted the idea away.

'Anyhoo,' Beck said quietly, 'the DI's knocking it on the head for today. Time for a group huddle so we can think straight.'

'Here?' MacReady asked.

'The other office,' said Beck.

'Other office?'

'Pub,' Beck said. 'Grab your things.'

Tucked away on a side street, The Pen and Wig sat in a row of grand old Victorian three-storeys a stone's throw from the Civic Centre; it was the bolthole of choice for discerning Cardiff Uni students and legal types whose musty chambers littered the main drag alongside the city's museum. MacReady knew of the place, had turned out for an assistance shout back in the day when a judge, of all people, in his cups and presumably after a trying day adjusting his wig, took it upon himself to dispense instant justice via a pint glass to the face of another punter. He'd never drunk in there, but as he stepped through the front door MacReady thought it perfectly pleasant: oak panelling, high-backs and chunky sofas in nooks of bookshelves, pumps aplenty lining the lengthy bar.

Sky Sports on the widescreen in one corner, but muted, leaving a murmur of conversation from the twenty or so patrons sitting with drinks and bar meals.

'All right here,' he said, looking around. 'Nice atmosphere.'

'You'll enjoy it,' Harrison said, checking the lengthy selection of ales. 'They hire kids' board games. You can have a go at Downfall while the grown-ups talk business.'

MacReady glanced at Beck. 'Downfall?'

She shrugged. 'Mine's a dry white, by the way. Large.'

'I'll have two Brains SA,' Harrison said. 'Boss?'

'Two,' nodded Fletcher. 'Saves time.'

Harrison turned to MacReady. Held up four fingers. 'Skull Attack. Two for me, two for the boss. Get them in, new boy. We'll be in the beer garden. And try not to get into any more punch-ups while you're sorting it out, there's a good lad.'

MacReady rocked on his heels and watched as they sauntered off to the rear of the pub. A twenty in his wallet, his funds for the week. The barman, a cheerful chap in black tee, already pulling at the pumps.

'I take it you heard,' MacReady said.

The barman nodded. MacReady looked at the twenty. Made the calculations.

'And I'll just have a small Coke,' he said.

He struggled to let go of the money when the barman reached for it.

Chilly outside now, the sky dull and ribboned with blackness. Beck had chosen a table next to one of the patio heaters; above it, a parasol creaked and fluttered in the breeze. Harrison, off to one side with a cigarette gripped between wet lips. Fletcher muttered a thank you as MacReady placed drinks in front of him, then hoisted a glass to his lips and sucked at the beer with relish.

'So,' he said, top lip an amber froth. He glanced from Harrison to Beck to MacReady. Arched an eyebrow. 'Care to share your thoughts?'

'Might get meself a burger,' Harrison said as he sat, studying the menu.

Beck looked sideways at Harrison, shook her head. To Fletcher: 'Anything from Dane Sillitoe?'

'*Nada*,' Fletcher replied. 'Got the secret squirrel squad on rotation, following him about, but he's been very boring so far.'

'Or very careful,' offered Beck.

'Maybe. And if that's the case I hope he makes a mistake pretty soon, because the surveillance is eating up our budget and giving the Major Crime rankers palpitations.'

'Every cloud,' said Harrison. He'd flipped the menu, was running a finger down the list of desserts. 'Wish they had some peanuts on these tables,' he grumbled.

'I met with the Super this afternoon,' Fletcher said to Beck. 'Understandably, he's folding your torso case into the main inquiry. I've forwarded him everything you've given me.'

Beck nodded to herself. 'That everything isn't much.' She sipped at her wine. 'But it's one less for me to deal with on my own, I suppose.'

'You're still going to deal with it, Charlie,' Fletcher said. 'Folding it in is just the usual arse-covering exercise by the higher-ups. Things have taken a turn for the very shitty and HQ are making lots of noise. Two more bodies. And both with the same wounds? It was hard enough when we just had Garratt, but thanks to Miss

Marple here,' he tipped his head at MacReady, 'and our little meeting with Barnard we're fucking swamped with dead people and somehow, somewhere along the line they're all linked. And none of us has a clue how or why.'

He necked the rest of his pint, looked off into the distance. 'I have a horrible feeling about all of this. This is our patch, and pretty soon Major Crime will get bored and the money will run out and there'll be another high-profile job at the other end of the force so we'll be left to deal with all this crap ourselves.'

'And we won't deal with it,' Harrison said. 'Like always.'

Fletcher reached for his second pint. 'I'll never make the next rank after this.'

'Thought you never wanted the extra pip anyway?' asked Harrison.

'Course I fucking don't,' Fletcher grunted. 'Especially the lobotomy that comes with it. But that's not the point.'

'I think we should go back to Tate's family,' Beck said. 'Bring them all in again if need be.'

'For what?' Fletcher asked. 'Genuine question.'

MacReady cradled his glass, lemon slice bobbing amongst bubbles. He'd drunk none of it. Didn't think his roiling stomach could take it. 'There's more going on than they're telling us. We all know it.'

'Again, bring them in for what, though, Will?' Fletcher asked. 'They thought Jermaine was in hiding, and if they knew where they were less than inclined to tell us, for no other reason – that I can see – than they're anti. But it's all irrelevant now, isn't it? The kid is dead, but if you want to pop up there and arrest them for the offence of being a bit unhelpful then fill your boots.'

MacReady felt Beck's eyes on him. 'You OK, Will? You look a bit . . . off.'

'True dat.' Harrison slapped the menu down on the table. 'You're not your usual over-keen, fucking irritating self.'

Megan. Stuart. MacReady closed his eyes, pictured the unimaginable. His skin prickled. He couldn't be sure if it was the cold air in the beer garden or not.

'I . . .' he said, and opened his eyes. Fletcher, Beck and Harrison frowning at him. His face suddenly warm, eyes welling.

'Will?' Beck asked. Her hand on his forearm, hunched down a ways, looking up at him from under her blonde fringe. Concern on her face.

MacReady thought of the chunk of change in his wallet. Of his pitiful bank account. Of the credit card tucked behind the picture of his wife. *For emergencies only*, she'd drilled into him. *For those rainy days.*

He looked skywards. Said, 'I think I need a drink.'

Fletcher studied him for a moment. Nodded.

'Attaboy,' he said.

Somewhere along the way he'd lost them, shortly after they'd lost themselves.

A head-spinning haze of lager bottles and whisky chasers, of strobe lights and 4x4 beat squawking divas, of another trip to a cash point for more funds via the credit card and where he'd struggled, blinking and stretching his face, to punch in his PIN, of Beck arguing with Harrison, snarling and grabbing at each other's jacket collars in the middle of yet another bar, drinks spilling, *you fat wanker, you bull dyke what a waste of a good pair of tits* before staggering out together, arms around shoulders, of Fletcher, bored of queuing for curry and chips, strutting out into Caroline Street with cock swinging in the evening air and spittle flecking his chin as he pissed into a gutter, yelling *I demand a fucking taxi*, and MacReady didn't know how long they'd been caning it but not one moment had been spent discussing the case and the evening was all the more enjoyable for it and now it was dark and chilly and he was alone.

Clambering out of a taxi in Cardiff Bay, in front of Le Croupiers Casino, thrusting a ten into the driver's hand, turning and walking towards the oh-so-modern edifice of glass and steel tubing. Carefully putting one foot in front of the other, fumbling for his wallet, wondering what he was doing here, what he was hoping to achieve, brain fogged, thinking about his wife and his brother, *did they didn't they*, about Leon King, *there must be something, King used to come here, there must be something we missed*, thoughts colliding with such force he swore he could hear them clattering about in there.

'Y'alright, bro?'

Door security. Some no-necked 'roid goon in a quilted black bomber jacket, toy walkie-talkie clipped on his belt. Watching him with mild amusement.

MacReady licked sticky lips, squeezed one eye shut. Steadied himself. Flashed his warrant card. 'CID. Making some enquiries. Serious, serious enquiries.'

'You shitting me?' the goon laughed. He checked about. Leaned in, mock-conspiratorial. 'You don't have to pretend it's all official to get in for free, y'know. There's no entrance fee.'

MacReady studied the man's face. Something familiar about him. 'I know you?' he asked. 'Dealt with you before?'

The man placed a hand over his heart. 'Never been in trouble. Honest.'

'Yeah, I'm sure.'

MacReady pushed past him, glass doors parting, up the stairs, the security guy chuckling after him, *Sure you don't want a membership form*? then the gurgle of slot machines, the hubbub of conversation, the drone of sportscasters from widescreens, the smell of lager from the bar, of desperation from the tables.

Full. Mostly men, jeans and short sleeves and rope necklaces, hunched over slots and Blackjack and Punto Banco while penguin-suited staff calmly drained them of money that, like MacReady, they could ill afford to lose.

MacReady felt quite at home. Exhilarated, almost. A small part of him, free now. No responsibilities whatsoever. No guilt. Nobody. Nothing.

He pulled out the card from his wallet. Fumbled with his mobile. Dialled. Spoke briefly. Felt his tongue mangle the words, too thick and heavy in his mouth. Ended the call. Knew he'd sounded pissed, didn't care. Thought about what he'd just done and swallowed. A step into the unknown.

At the bar he ordered another drink, held a note out between two fingers, snatched it away when the barman reached for it. 'I'd like to speak to the manager.'

It came out *manja*, and he winced.

The barman looked at him, face sullen. MacReady put him at about seventeen, eighteen. Thin goatee which didn't quite reach all the way around his mouth. 'I'm afraid she's not available, sir.'

'I'm sure she's available for the police,' he said, and let the kid take the five-pound note. Pulled out his warrant card. Patrons either side of MacReady began turning towards him. Muttered comments. The curling of lips, nudging of elbows and gestures in his direction.

'She really isn't available,' the barman said, one hand reaching under the lip of the counter.

MacReady sighed, took a slug of lager from the overpriced bottle. 'You're telling me this place is open with no management supervision whatsoever? Who's in charge, then?'

The barman handed him his change. 'Well, just me for now.'

'No offence mate, but you look like you should be in school, not running a city casino.'

'Tch,' the barman said, mask slipping. 'You can fucking talk, what are you, like some baby CID or something?'

MacReady bristled. Leaned an elbow onto the counter. The barman took a step backwards. 'Listen to m—'

'Everything good here, Tobes?'

The voice, from behind MacReady. Knew who it was before he turned. The door security staff. Tobes – Toby, MacReady assumed – must have buzzed him, pressed a panic button. His hand, disappearing under the counter.

'This guy saying he's law, Daryl,' Toby said. 'Didn't think they were allowed to get munted on duty, though.'

'Nor me,' Daryl replied. He looked at MacReady, a well-practised smile forming beneath narrowed eyes. 'What can we help you with, sir?'

MacReady half turned towards him. 'Manager?' He concentrated this time, making sure the word was clear.

'Not here,' the doorman said. 'You'll have to come back. When you're . . . thinking more clearly. OK?'

'I'm not going anywhere,' MacReady said, and fought against a hiccup. 'I want to view CCTV recordings. And we can either do it nicely, or I will bring a ton of shit down on this place, starting with,' he gestured at Tobes the barman, 'the licensing department for leaving a juvenile in charge.'

All eyes on them now. A broad, dead smile from Daryl the doorman. His fingers clamped around MacReady's upper arm, pulling him upright. 'Let's go somewhere a little more private, yeah?'

MacReady thought about shrugging him off. Knew he wouldn't be able to manage it, even if he'd been sober.

'Lead the way,' he said as he was yanked through the crowd of onlookers.

Daryl pushed through a door marked *Staff Only*, slammed it shut and turned to face MacReady. They were standing in a corridor: breezeblock, concrete floor, air con and electrical cabling, the distant hum of a generator.

'I'm going to talk to you nicely,' said Daryl, square on to him. 'Because that's how we work together, yeah? Cordial, right? You help us out when there's a rumble at the doors, we help crack a few skulls if the punters start getting the better of you. Time-honoured tradition, and all that.'

MacReady nodded slowly. 'Except we hate each other really.'

Daryl laughed. 'S'just business.' His face became serious. 'But you coming in here like this is bad for my business. And you've got some front having a go about the manager not being here when you're on duty and pissed as a skittle with a face that came second best to a wall. It could be bad for *your* business, you get me?'

'What d'you care?'

'My brother's po-po, mate,' Daryl sighed. 'And my old man was job for thirty years. So I know what the score is, and what you lot have to go through. But neither of them would ever have done something like,' he waved a hand up and down at MacReady, incredulous, 'like this.'

'I'm working on something serious,' MacReady said. He felt very tired all of a sudden. 'I really need to check your CCTV. Going back to August. There's a man who used to come here, I need to find out if he was ever with anyb—'

'My brother's already had the DVD recordings collected. All the way back to June.'

MacReady blinked. Squinted at the man in front of him. Cocked his head. So that was why he looked familiar.

'Danny Fletcher?'

'Yup.'

MacReady placed a hand on the wall to steady himself. 'Shit.'

Daryl chuckled. 'Belled me earlier to say he was going out tonight. I take it none of his mob warned you about trying to keep up with him.'

MacReady shook his head. Wiped at the drool forming on his bottom lip.

'Man oh man,' Daryl laughed. 'Well if he's in anywhere near the state you're in, he's going to be in big trouble with his new lady.'

'Please don't tell him about this,' MacReady asked.

'I'll cut you a deal,' Daryl smiled, placing a hand on MacReady's shoulder. 'You spend a few more quid at the bar, maybe tip old Tobes for the sterling service he's carrying out, and we'll keep this as our little secret, yeah?'

'I really don't think I can drink any more,' MacReady groaned.

'Of course you can,' Daryl said, and opened the door. He gestured for MacReady to walk through it. 'You're CID. It's in the job description.'

MacReady walked back into the main hall, ignoring the amused stares and wrinkled noses. He turned to Daryl.

'A bouncer, though?' he said, looking about the place. 'Here?'

The man shrugged. 'You're thinking: *underachiever,* right? Maybe *he's the failure in the family.*'

'I just . . . You never thought about joining the job, like Danny?'

'Thought about it, sure,' Daryl said. 'Then I stopped thinking about it when my older brother turned into a pisshead with a broken marriage and kids he never sees, just like my old man.'

MacReady blinked away an image of Megan. 'It happens.'

'You don't have to let it.'

MacReady nodded slowly.

'And besides,' Daryl grinned. 'I get to beat people up for a living. Just like you lot, right? Except there's no paperwork and all the bar snacks are free.'

'I want your job,' MacReady slurred.

Daryl gave a loud laugh. Slapped MacReady on the arm: a friendly gesture but it hurt rather a lot.

MacReady gritted his teeth and fought against the urge to rub his stinging flesh. He watched the bouncer walk away, then pause at the top of the stairs. A look over his shoulder.

'Don't forget Tobes,' he winked at MacReady, and tapped his nose.

The casino's sports bar: groups of slack-jawed punters staring up at multi-screen Sky blarting stats and match updates, their drinks and conversation forgotten, the atmosphere increasingly muted as they mentally totted up their losses. MacReady's eyes lingered on their sagging bodies for a moment, sensing the glowing gloom, like a bad bruise darkening and spreading.

He found an empty table, slid into a tub chair, fighting to see straight, more tired now than he'd ever been. Checked his phone. No new messages from Megan. From his bastard brother. He contemplated ringing them, but it was a fleeting thought, and swiftly suffused by an almost incandescent burst of rage that he knew would get him into serious trouble if he rode with it. He batted the idea away. His lager bottle – he'd tipped *Tobes* when he bought it, costing him a fiver – dangling near the floor, untouched but for a forefinger wedged into its neck. A triple scotch that he neither wanted nor needed sitting on the low table in front of him. Nearly 10 p.m. and dark outside, but he couldn't see out of the floor-to-ceiling windows; athletes of various disciplines adorned the glass, the lithe, pumped sports-people towering over clumps of squat, beer-bellied clientele.

He'd been thinking about Leon King. Why he came to Le Croupiers. Picturing his acne-scarred face tightening over a

Craps game, willing the dice to fall in his favour. From what they knew, King was like most of the people in here: struggling, anxious to get the right hand of cards, for electronic dials to clunk into the jackpot place on the slots, blowing what little cash they had because maybe, just maybe . . . A windfall on the tables would beat screwing OAP houses or pummelling students for their mobile phones. Less risky, anyhow, even if the odds of grabbing a wedge of coin were lower here than out on the streets.

Maybe King owed money to somebody. Maybe he hadn't paid up, and whoever it was that shot Garratt had been there to put the arm on King? MacReady was au fait with the concept of debts you could barely repay, and how it could drive you to despair. But owed money to whom, and for what?

MacReady took a reluctant slug of lager, head rocking back as he tipped the bottle to his mouth. Shivered as the bitter liquid ran over his tongue; he'd reached his limit hours earlier. He shook his head and muttered to himself, 'Why did they come to get you, Leon?'

From somewhere above him: 'My, aren't you looking handsome?'

MacReady swung his head upwards. It took his eyes a moment to catch up.

Klaudia Solak.

He squinted: she was dressed down. Jeans, bright red woollen sweater, hair swept into a ponytail. Still enough to make the breath catch in his throat. Still enough to make him feel guilty despite all that had gone on.

'Holy shit,' he said. 'You came.'

'You rang,' she replied. 'Again.'

She narrowed her eyes at him as he motioned for her to sit down.

'I've had a few,' he said, and rubbed at his face; it felt doughy and cold beneath his fingertips, the first stiff bristles forming at his chin.

'No, really?' she said, and dropped into the chair. 'What on earth are you doing here, Will? And why did you ask me to come?'

He leaned forward, elbows on knees, dropped the lager to the table. 'I'm not really sure anymore.'

A faint smile from Solak. 'About why you're here? Or asking me to come?'

'Both.' He exhaled. Scratched at his jaw. 'D'you want a drink?'

'I'm driving,' she said. 'And I'm sitting here waiting for you to rant at me again for doing my job.'

'You annoyed me yesterday. All that bollocks on the news, making us out to be clueless. That's why I rang.'

'When you rang I was in the middle of a press briefing with your Assistant Chief Constable. You bloody annoyed me, Will. It was unprofessional. And you lot do seem a bit clueless, to be frank.'

MacReady lifted the whisky, sipped at it, savoured the sour warmth. Held the glass in front of his face, thought *fuck it* and gulped the rest of it down. 'There've been . . . Things have moved on. We're getting there, just so's you understand for next time.'

'Charlie says otherwise.'

'Ah,' MacReady waved a hand in the air. 'What she know, eh?'

'More than you, it would appear.' Solak tilted her head. 'So do you want to talk about it?'

MacReady felt the whisky burning his insides. Everything a little fuzzy now, blurred at the edges. Even Solak seemed to be a little hazy. He was dog tired. Drunk. 'Whatever I tell you will be all over the news tomorrow. Won't it? That's what you do.'

'We could work something out. Help each other. Who knows what could come of it if we got specific information out there?'

'They'd turf me out of the department. The job, even. You know what it's like now, after Leveson.'

'We could keep you anonymous.'

MacReady laughed, the sound loud and bitter in his ears. 'They'd find out. And it would ruin me. Not that there's much left to ruin.'

Solak leaned in closer. 'I'd look after you, Will. You seem like a nice guy –'

'I'm a fuckin' mug, is what I am.'

She sat back. Studied him.

'I could tell you something,' he said. Head feeling loose on his neck now. His brother's face, Megan's face, there each time he blinked. 'Tell you a story for your news report. The mug DC and how he missed all the clues. That'd go down a storm, wouldn't it?'

'Maybe we could talk through the clues,' Solak said.

'He's got a hold over me now,' MacReady slurred. 'He's a shit, never achieved anything in his life, and he's got a hold over me for the rest of *my* life. Turns out he's the real man after all. Talk about fuckin' irony.'

A small shake of the head from Solak. 'I thought we . . . I don't really follow you, here. I think maybe you should go home, Will.'

'I think you should mind your business about that,' he said.

'This is so unprofession—'

'I want to go home with you,' he blurted.

Solak paused. Stared at MacReady. One painted fingernail brushed at her bottom lip as she sat, thinking.

'This is unprofessional,' she said again.

'I want to go home with you,' MacReady repeated. 'Now.'

Solak looked to the floor. Up at the ceiling. At him, something going on behind those dark eyes of hers. MacReady sighed, waiting for her to stand and bawl him out and leave, mentally prepared himself to go see Tobes and order more drinks and even buy one for Doorman Daryl and he'd catch some late football highlights with the rest of the casino losers before grabbing a taxi back to his car in the basement of the nick to grab some sleep.

'OK,' Solak said finally.

It made MacReady flinch.

He nodded.

'OK.'

Bairro Martim Moniz,
Lisbon, Portugal

Gonçalves woke early.

The woman, curled into pillows beside him, clucked softly as she slept. Weak light bled into the bedroom around Venetian blinds, casting everything in grey shadow: furniture, champagne flutes, discarded clothes on the floor. The city, still dead outside his apartment above the clinic.

Gonçalves sat amongst ripples of quilt, trying to make sense of things. Trying to make sense of why he felt so . . . off kilter. It was unlike him to rise at such a ridiculous time. Routine was all, his life carefully managed, controlled, efficient, and yet he'd jolted upright a full hour before the pulse of his alarm. The first time he'd done so in an age.

He studied the sleeping form next to him. Thought of the day that lay ahead. Thought of his family. His son, in particular. A wide-eyed ten-year-old, so innocent, so harmless, a boy who looked to his father for everything.

Gonçalves brushed at the curve of the young woman's hip, her skin warm and burnished beneath his fingertips. Recalled the previous night and what they had done to each other. What she had done to him in her drunken, feral state. Thought how strange and sometimes frightening it was the way people could touch others.

She rolled over, mumbled his name out of the corner of her mouth, eyes still closed.

'Sleep,' he whispered, and as he eased out of the bed knew without doubt it was the last time he would see this woman.

Gonçalves gathered clothes, closed the bedroom door on her, padded to the kitchen. Scribbled a note on kitchen towel, handwriting spiked and careless, the message curt. Enough for her to know. What she knew of him already was enough to stop her causing problems, enough to stop her coming back here after today.

He pulled his mobile from the tangle of his trousers, called home. Closed his eyes when his wife answered, her voice thick with sleep. Spoke quietly as he poured juice with his free hand.

'Beatriz, it's me.'

'Luis?' A pause, the phone moving away from her mouth: checking the time on the screen. 'Are you still in work?'

'I'm sorry, we had to press on through the night. One of the patients was quite sick.'

'My goodness, those poor children. Is everything fine now? Are you coming home?'

Gonçalves swigged at the juice. 'I have to stay here. Just for a little while. There may be further work to do this morning.'

'Oh, Luis,' she breathed into his ear. 'You must be exhausted.'

'Is Teo awake?'

She chuckled. 'It's too early. He's still asleep. Worn out from kicking that ball about with his friends, no doubt. He's so good at it now, Luis, you should see him –'

'Please give him my love, Beatriz,' he said, and lowered his head. 'Please tell him that I love him and will see him soon.'

Her breathing on the line. Then: 'Is everything all right, Luis?'

Gonçalves nodded. Inside he felt as if something had shifted. 'Please tell him,' he said, and ended the call.

In the bathroom he spun the shower on, locked the door. Leaned over the sink and stared at himself in the mirror, the hiss of water behind him, the low hum of the extractor fan. The mirror began to fog, condensation creeping in from its edges, creeping in on his reflection, fading him, whiting him out, until at last he couldn't see himself anymore.

And for that he was grateful.

Gonçalves pictured the brute who'd come to the clinic. Stinking of cheap cigars, his eyes welling, not wanting to let that one child go.

That one child. Little Bepeh.

It was time to go downstairs.

It was time for the boy.

'Everything is prepared.'

Gonçalves' assistant, standing in the anteroom with hands laced over the paunch at his midriff. He'd been at the bottle overnight again, his breath drifting hot and bitter from cracked lips, the pouches of his wine face like small bags sitting at the corners of his mouth. The whites of his sunken eyes threaded with blood, thinning hair mussed and greasy from the sofa he'd probably passed out on, several Trincadeira tintos sitting empty at his feet as he'd twitched and dreamed of all that he had lost.

'Are you prepared, Felix?' Gonçalves asked, but it was a weak rebuke, and hypocritical to press him further. Coming down the stairs from the apartment it had finally struck him how the clinic had begun to take its toll, and he'd paused, hand on the handrail, doubled over and suddenly breathless as he pictured his family and the dangerous position he had placed them in. Reckless. Stupid. And for what?

More money than he could ever have imagined. More money than he could earn walking the wards at São José: austerity cuts still biting, stripping hospitals of staff, of equipment, of interest in the very people they were supposed to care for.

That was why he'd started. Convinced himself it was for his family. But at some point he'd lost his way: the money he'd been putting aside for Beatriz and Teo and Thalia increasingly diverted to drink, then drink coupled with the odd line, then that first whore, and from there a hazy segue into what seemed a life of work, of detached rutting, of absence from home, until finally last night where he found himself – lost – snorting coke off the breasts of a woman he barely knew. And now he was at risk of losing everything: just a few months, a few steps, it seemed, behind Felix, a man he'd considered pitiful until now.

It had taken the boy to make him understand.

Gonçalves glanced through the glass at the small form beneath sheets on the bed. Motionless, helpless.

He didn't feel ready for this at all.

'I could ask the same of you, Luis,' Felix said, his tongue clicking on the roof of his mouth. He extended a hand towards Gonçalves. 'I found this on him.'

Gonçalves glanced at the hand. Saw the necklace hanging from two fingers. Remembered the brute giving it to Bepeh the night he'd dropped him here.

Gonçalves swallowed. Gestured at the sinks. 'Put it there. I'll return it to him afterwards.'

Felix arched an eyebrow. 'If there is an afterwards.'

'The boy will be fine,' Gonçalves said. 'I know he will.'

21

Tongue pasted to the roof of his mouth and the smell of bacon in his nostrils.

MacReady pushed himself onto his elbows, blinking, for a panicked second or two not knowing where he was: stark white walls, couple of arty black and white prints hanging, parquet wood floor, thick quilt tangled cocoon-like around his naked torso.

Images from the previous night flashed before his eyes.

'Shit,' he muttered, and placed his head in his hands. *What have I done*?

A dull throb in his temples as he threw on clothes, splashed water over his face in the en suite, squeezed toothpaste into his mouth and rubbed at his gums with a finger that tasted of hops and sweat. Stumbled back into the bedroom, found her sitting on the edge of the bed.

'You look peachy,' Solak smiled up at him. She was dressed in work duds, had showered, hair silken and already drying, and he'd slept through it all. A mug of black coffee in one hand; she held it out to him.

MacReady took it gratefully. 'I'm really sorry.'

'For what?' she asked, grinning. She stood. 'Breakfast is ready in the kitchen.'

MacReady watched her go, eyebrows raised.

Solak's apartment was in the Bay; from the panoramic lounge window he could see across the water, the islands of Flat Holm, Steep Holm, the vague outline of the English coast, of Weston-Super-Mare bathed in morning sunlight. He munched on the sandwich, holding the plate to his chest to catch any stray crumbs. After last night's behaviour he suspected dripping bacon fat on the plush carpet would tip Solak over the edge.

'This must have cost a fortune,' he said, turning to look at her.

She was perched on a stool at the breakfast bar, grimacing at her laptop screen. She didn't look up as she spoke. 'Not too expensive. They can't sell these things because of the economy. I managed to snag a bargain.' She tapped at the keyboard.

'But still,' he said.

'No, Will. You couldn't afford it on your police wages.'

He finished the food. Walked across to her. 'Klaudia . . .'

She glanced up at him. 'Is this The Talk? Because I thought we were pretty chilled, here.'

'We should talk about it.'

Solak closed the laptop. Took a deep breath and sighed. 'Will, all you need to know is that I'm not in the habit of bringing home men I barely know to let them have their wicked way with me. Married men at that, who are too drunk to remember their own name, and drowning in self-pity. This was a one-off.'

MacReady blinked. Her bluntness stung him, but it was the truth. 'So . . . why let me come back here? I don't get it.'

Solak held his gaze for a moment. 'Believe it or not, I felt sorry for you. Every time I've seen you working you're like a rabbit in the headlights. A bit lost, perhaps. Charlie talks a lot, as you know. And she's talked about you. I must admit, I am interested, Will. Very interested. And I enjoyed last night, but that was last night and this is today.'

'Very business-like,' he remarked, almost sulkily.

'I have to be. You have a lot on your plate. More than I realised. Some of the stuff you talked about –'

'Please don't tell me we discussed the Garratt case.'

'We didn't.' She pretended to think, finger against her cheek as she looked up at the ceiling. 'Or did we?'

'Is this why you brought me home? For information?'

She looked annoyed. 'Of course not.' Then smiled: 'Or was it?'

'Please, Klaudia,' MacReady said. 'Don't play games. If I spilled my guts about work, you can't use it. They'd crucify me. And we're close to something. I know it.'

'For goodness' sake,' Solak said. 'You moaned about your wife and your life all the way from the casino to my front door, nothing else. Your misery rant almost killed any designs I had on shagging you, so consider yourself a very lucky boy. All right?'

'I'm sorry,' he said again.

'Wow. Who said romance isn't dead?' she said.

'That's not what I mean,' MacReady said. 'I'm really grateful for this.' He waved a hand around at the apartment. 'But things at home . . . they're pretty complicated at the moment. I don't want to add to it.'

'Yeah, your brother and your wife,' Solak nodded.

MacReady's eyes widened. 'I told you?'

'All the gory details. But you're not sure if it's true or . . . something.' She shrugged at him. 'Anyway, if it is, you were right to say he'll have a hold over you now. Tricky stuff.'

He slumped onto the stool next to her. 'Jesus.'

Solak reached across, took his hand in hers. MacReady went with it; it felt strange and good and a terrible, wonderfully simple thing to enjoy, all at once, her skin soft as she brushed a thumb across his knuckles. 'You'll work it out. I'm sure you will. And if you don't, if it doesn't, then maybe –'

MacReady kissed her. Darted his head across before he could think himself out of doing it. It was awkward, Solak moving to turn her cheek to his lips, changing her mind mid-turn, the kiss more of a quick bump of lips.

'Oooo-K,' she said, nodding to herself. She let go of his hand, slipped down from the stool. 'I've really got to go to work.'

'I'm sorry,' he said for what seemed the twentieth time, and for what he couldn't be sure anymore. Megan? Stooping to her level? This, with Solak? It was a mess.

'Don't be,' Solak said. Checked her phone, her car keys. Picked up a large shoulder bag. 'D'you need a lift? I know the station is a five-minute walk away, but I'm not sure you're capable yet.'

MacReady smiled. It was weak, uncertain. 'I'll be fine. Fresh air and all that.'

'See yourself out then, lover,' Solak winked, skipping towards the front door. 'And thanks for the info on the Garratt case . . .'

'Hang on, I thought I didn't –'

'You *didn't*,' she laughed, and opened the door. She hesitated, pretended to think again. 'Or did you?'

And then she was gone.

MacReady let out a long, low groan. Shook his aching head. Couldn't believe he'd shot his mouth off about Megan and Stuart. And to a journalist, of all people. Better that than anything about the Garratt case, though, he reasoned. Although he couldn't be sure whether he had or not, thanks to Solak.

His phone buzzed in his pocket. MacReady checked: a text from Beck.

You are late, numbnuts.

She was right, it was gone 8 a.m. He dropped off the stool, glanced around at the apartment again, looked out of the window and across the sea. Leaned against the glass, arms out, palms spread, head lowered as he let it all sink in. Despite what Megan had done to him he still felt unclean, somehow. Dishonourable. He'd cheated on his wife. Whatever the outcome, it would stay with him forever.

MacReady jerked his head upright. Something nagging at him now.

Thought about what Solak had just said to him. About his brother.

He'll have a hold over you now. Tricky stuff.

MacReady closed his eyes and pictured Soraya Tate.

He ducked into the uniform locker room, weaved along metal rows, checking he was alone. Found an open locker near the showers; a female PC's kit, but it would have to do. Rifled through the shelf, found a selection of in-an-emergency toiletries all cops kept at the nick, the wipes and sprays and smellies used after a gutter roll-around with a drunk or to clean the remnants of skin-slippage from fingernails after handling a month-old corpse.

Stripped to the waist at a basin. Washed and sprayed and wiped at his hair with something that promised *texture and a hi-shine*. Stared at his reflection in the mirror. Hangdog, dark circles under his eyes. Skin dry now, flaky. His left cheek plum-coloured and engorged, the bruise spiderwebbing to the side of his nose.

'What the hell are you doing, MacReady?' he asked himself.

In the MIR he walked straight into the DI's office.

'So you're not dead, then,' Fletcher said. Coffee steaming on the desk in front of him. Ibuprofen blister packs next to the mug. He looked as tired as MacReady.

Beck, seated on the edge of the desk, feet dangling and not quite reaching the floor. One shoe twitching up and down. She nodded at MacReady.

Neither mentioned the previous night, MacReady assuming it was an embarrassed case of *What Happens on the Lash Stays on the Lash* or, more worryingly, that it was the norm for the team and therefore in no need of further discussion.

'I've been thinking about Soraya Tate,' MacReady offered.

'*Sorry for being late, sir*,' Fletcher said. '*I know I'm a trainee detective and supposed to be impressing everyone, but what the hell, right?*'

'I apologise,' MacReady said. 'I got . . . waylaid.'

'You were wearing those clothes yesterday,' Beck smirked.

Fletcher raised an eyebrow. 'And you smell like one of those nonces in Special Branch. What's going on with you, Will? Your face, turning up late looking like shit? Do I want to know?'

'Not really,' said MacReady.

'Let me put it another way: is it going to get me in trouble?'

MacReady hesitated. 'No, boss.'

'Then I don't want to know. So, Soraya Tate. Thrill me.' He sipped at the coffee and leaned back in his seat, mug resting on one thigh.

MacReady turned to Beck. 'Remember the hospital?'

'What about it?' she asked.

'Soraya,' MacReady said. 'I've been thinking about what she kept saying.'

'That she was sorry to King?'

'That's part of it. But there were other things. Like the way she defended her stepfather. It seemed genuine to me. I don't think Nathan Brissett is roughing the family up.'

Beck looked at the ceiling, thinking. 'She did seem pretty adamant. OK. So we assume someone's been putting the arm on them.'

'Who, then?' asked Fletcher. 'And, I'm thinking more importantly, why?'

'Another thing,' said MacReady. 'Soraya kept saying *I just want you to find Jermaine, I just want you to find him*. At the time I assumed she honestly didn't know where he was hiding,' he looked at Fletcher, 'and was asking for help.'

'That's what it seemed like,' Beck said.

MacReady looked her in the eyes. 'But what if we misunderstood, Sarge? What if she already knows her brother is dead? What if they *all* know he is dead? What if, by *find him*, she meant find his body? So the family could give him a proper burial?'

'Closure for them,' Beck nodded. 'And hope that it would lead us to the person who did this.'

'Exactly,' MacReady said. He turned to Fletcher. 'She knows Jermaine is dead, and I'd wager the twenty-seven pence I have left in my wallet that she knows who killed him.'

Fletcher studied MacReady for a moment. Glanced down at his drink. Scooped it to his lips, took several slugs. 'God bless sugar,' he mumbled. He raised his eyes to Beck, shifted them to MacReady. 'And whoever did it has been beating his family to ensure they stay quiet?'

MacReady nodded. 'I reckon.'

The DI rubbed bleary eyes. Stared out of his window for a moment. Swivelled back to MacReady and Beck.

'Lock up the Tates again,' he said to her. 'I'll ring you with what for when you're on your way and my head has stopped hurting. And go grab a couple of the Major Crime people. Handful of uniform, too. Big, hairy-arsed ones, preferably. You'll need them.'

He tossed a folder across the desk at MacReady.

'That's for you,' he said. 'Seeing as the rest of us are going to be busy wrestling with Nathan Brissett and his dog.' He gestured through the door, to the MIR. 'Harrison's waiting for you.'

MacReady fought against a groan. 'Yeah. Cheers.'

Close and cloying inside the car.

Late-September sun hanging low in a cloudless sky, warming them through the windows. Harrison, all ashtray stink, seemingly happy to roll through traffic with a solitary half-clogged fan producing a pitiful wheeze; it was doing MacReady's recovery no favours, his throat still whisky-bomb raw, guts griping, clothes day-old rumpled and smelling of Chanel's *Coco Mademoiselle*.

The usual no-talk from Harrison as they headed north, towards the Lisvane area of the city, the CID car growling across the flyover at Gabalfa interchange, beneath them the slip roads and junctions choked, the A48 a crawl of tin-canned commuters inching their way to work. MacReady flicked his eyes across at his colleague: no outward sign of any residual effects from the twelve-pinter but he couldn't be sure if it was a case of the booze barely touching the old sweat's insides, or if Harrison was deliberately hiding how ill he felt just to make MacReady feel worse.

He flicked through the folder Fletcher had given him; there was little to the contents. Couple of printed sheets, no photograph.

'Gregory Nelms?'

A shrug from Harrison as they waited at a red.

'Not much on him,' said MacReady, scanning the PNC printout, the antecedents. 'Thirty-eight years of age, no previous. Works at the crematorium in Northwood cemetery.'

'Which must be nice,' said Harrison.

'No spouse or kids. Says here that he lives at home with his mother.'

'Gay, then,' grunted Harrison, accelerating through the junction.

MacReady sighed, head feeling heavy. 'Or perhaps he's, y'know, divorced? It happens a lot.' *Could happen to me*, he thought, and had a vision: not of Megan and his brother, but of him and Klaudia Solak, a tangle of limbs and sweat beneath thick quilt. Of Solak's thumb brushing across his knuckles. Of him, despite everything, dutifully explaining where he'd been – the awful thing he'd done – to an uninterested, pregnant Megan. No matter what his reasons, no matter what she'd been up to with Stuart, he still felt guilty, and not a little afraid to go home.

'Doesn't have to,' Harrison said. 'Helps if you don't play around, too.'

He tilted his head and looked towards MacReady, eyebrow arched.

MacReady knew nothing about Harrison's home life other than he had a – presumably long-suffering – wife, and anyway was in no mood to argue so ignored him. Tapped the folder with his forefinger. 'So why are we going to speak to him?'

Harrison took a right at a roundabout, the crematorium chimney poking over the treeline and swinging past the windows. They both gave it a quick glance before Harrison gestured at the folder in MacReady's hands. 'Because while you were fucking about with who knows what this morning, we got a shout from the surveillance team.'

'Dane Sillitoe? They're still following him?'

Harrison nodded. 'He visited this Gregory Nelms first thing.'

22

The house was large but looked tired, slumped and greying in about quarter of an acre of overgrowth and behind a low metal gate in desperate need of a paint job. The bright sun only served to highlight the drabness of its once-white walls; it screamed of moderate wealth long gone. Six or seven bedrooms, MacReady guessed, and its occupants unable to afford to redecorate a one of them, never mind the crumbling façade and smattering of outbuildings.

'Shame,' he said, looking across a driveway more weed than cobble. 'Would need a pretty penny to fix her up.'

'More than you can afford,' Harrison said, opening the gate; hinges *skreeee*ed. 'Unless you get a jackpot at the casino next time you visit.'

MacReady's mouth flopped open. 'You know?'

'Course we fucking know,' Harrison said, and snorted laughter. '"*I wants to see the CCTV, maaan.*"'

'Jesus,' MacReady said. The sun felt hotter on his back. 'Why didn't the DI say anything when I got in?'

Harrison tapped his nose. 'Insurance, mate. All filed away. You ever do his legs, he'll counter with that. What did you think, Daryl wouldn't tell his older bro about one of his troops performing?'

'He virtually promised –'

'He was on the phone before Fletcher left his house this morning, you muppet,' Harrison said. He walked away, sandals grinding on loose chippings and rocking cracked cobbles.

MacReady waited a moment, cursing Daryl Fletcher, cursing himself for tipping the young lad behind the casino bar. He tucked the folder under his arm, trudged after Harrison through rows of dead potted plants, past a fence flaking in the sun.

'I'll run this,' Harrison said, not looking at him. 'You just sit there looking sweet and smelling like a tom's freshly washed foo-foo.' He rapped the front door with chunky knuckles. It echoed into the house; a minute later, and just as Harrison was about to thump the swollen woodwork with the edge of a fist, MacReady spied a figure through the frosted glass.

'Hold up,' he said.

The woman was in her late seventies, early eighties. Hunched and wrapped in a dirty cream cardigan, face pinched and carved with wrinkles, grey hair to her shoulders, knotted and thinning. She peered up at them, half behind the door, watery eyes above a wrinkled nose. 'Yes?'

'Mrs Nelms?' asked Harrison.

'That is me,' she said. Her voice a dry croak, but the words clipped, refined.

Harrison's mouth twitched into a brief smile, his warrant card thrust into the woman's face. 'We're the police, Mrs Nelms.'

She pulled the door open, clutched knotty hands at her chest. 'Oh, my goodness. You've arrested him, haven't you?'

MacReady and Harrison swapped a quick look.

'Your son?' asked Harrison.

'What?' An expression of horror. 'Which one?'

Harrison rolled his eyes to the heavens and made no effort to hide the exasperated sigh. MacReady could see it in his expression: *daft old cow*.

'We're just here for a quick chat,' Harrison said, looking down at her. 'D'you mind if we come in?'

She hesitated in the doorway. Deliberating. Eyes seeming to shift from dull and lifeless to sparkling, then back again, as if lucidity was intermittent.

Then: 'Please wipe your feet, gentlemen. I don't want you traipsing dirt all the way through the house.'

By the time he'd reached the lounge MacReady was wondering why he'd bothered shuffling his shoes on the threadbare mat: dust and grime everywhere, the carpets worn and soiled, the decor and furnishings at least thirty years old. Dark wood and faded floral patterns, curtains half drawn with dust motes hanging in weak light, the faint aroma of cooking fat and gone-over vegetables.

'Can I get you a cup of tea?' she asked, and gestured to the lump of a leather settee pressed against one wall. A dado rail ran above it, lined with dozens of miniature figurines; MacReady squinted at them, saw myriad cats frozen in various poses, some of them comedic efforts, the cartoon-like animals wearing top hats or pulling theatrical expressions. It was like a ceramic Internet.

'Not for me, thanks,' they replied in unison as they sat down; a long sigh came from the settee as it expelled air from somewhere.

The woman lowered herself into an armchair opposite, pulling at the sleeves of her cardigan as she perched on the edge of the seat. Her eyes had dulled again, and she cocked her head, staring at a spot on the carpet next to MacReady's shoe.

'Mrs Nelms,' Harrison said, his voice flat. Already bored of this woman, MacReady could tell.

She inhaled through her nose, looked down it at them. 'How can I help you?'

'Is Gregory home?'

'No,' she said. 'Why are you asking for him? Is it about the break-in?'

Harrison fidgeted, trousers squeaking on a cushion. He placed a hand to his forehead and pressed at it, kneading the skin. 'We don't know about any break-in, Mrs Nelms. We're here to talk to your son about . . . other matters.'

Life behind her eyes again. 'I must say I'm very disappointed in you both.'

Harrison tilted his head. 'Beg pardon?'

'How long has it been, now?' she asked. Her hand was raised, and she began counting on withered fingers: 'Three, four, five weeks? Perhaps longer? And nothing from any of you people.'

'Madam,' Harrison said. 'I haven't got the faintest idea what you're talking –'

'Who did you think we'd arrested, Mrs Nelms?' MacReady asked. He could feel Harrison's eyes on him as he flicked through the half-dozen sheets of paper in the folder. 'You mentioned it at the front door.'

Her lip curled as she turned away, as if in disgust. 'That man,' she said. 'The one who broke in here. I thought you were here to tell me you'd caught him. I'm very disappointed, to be frank.'

MacReady shifted his gaze to Harrison, was met with a *you started it* shrug. Asked the woman: 'Are you sure you rang the police when it happened?'

Her lips thinned, angry at the question. She glared at MacReady. 'I can assure you I haven't completely lost my marbles, despite what you two clearly think. Of course I rang the police, even though I was mortified. I *let him in*. That man lied to me, telling me he was here to repair the gas meter, and I can't believe I fell for it. Old now, I suppose. But not too old to learn from my mistakes. That's why I made sure you showed your police badge before I let you come inside. People take advantage.'

'That they do,' Harrison said, hand just about hiding a yawn.

She stared at that spot on the carpet again. 'My son Gregory, we have our differences, but if he hadn't arrived home when he did I dread to think what would have happened to me.'

MacReady felt something tug at his insides. 'Are you saying Greg caught this man inside the house?'

She nodded. Pointed to the area of carpet she'd been staring at next to MacReady's feet. 'That man hit him with a . . . club, or a truncheon, right where you're sitting. Kept hitting him, even when he was on the floor and wasn't moving. Just to get my handbag. Terrifying, and . . .'

MacReady tuned her out.

Thought of the statement they'd obtained from DC Masters after the Garratt shooting. The brief details of Leon King's activities: screwing OAP complexes, targeting the elderly, the time when he'd been disturbed, inside a house and blagging the octogenarian occupant, by the woman's son, a son who'd been beaten senseless by King before he made off with the woman's bag.

He turned to Harrison. Saw it in his face: this was the house.

'Mrs Nelms,' Harrison said. 'Do you know a man named Leon King?'

Wrinkles of confusion on her face. 'Never heard the name. Why do you ask?'

'When is Greg likely to be home next?' MacReady asked.

She glanced out of the lounge, in the direction of the front door. 'Quite soon, I hope. He's collecting my newspapers. I would imagine he'll be back shortly.' She turned to face them again. 'Are you sure I can't get you anything?'

Harrison waved the question away. 'Has anybody else been to the house this morning, madam?'

'The postman, presumably. Our mail was already on the hall table when I came downstairs.'

He shook his head. 'Anybody else? Driving an executive car, perhaps, like a limousine?'

'A limousine?' she chuckled. 'I wouldn't know, officer. I tend to sleep late, nowadays. Greg is the early riser, all that anxiety of his. You're better off asking him.'

'How is Greg now?' MacReady asked.

She rose from the armchair, using a hand to push herself upright. 'Still rather frightened. Always the timid sort, though.

My other son, he's the headstrong one, what some people would call a real man, out there making his money – he's in Dubai now, doing ever so well, do you know – but my Greg is a home bird. He tries,' she glanced around the lounge sadly, 'but there's only so much he can do, I suppose. I've told him, if he wants to keep this place after I'm gone he'll have to pull his finger out.' She paused at the lounge door. 'Are you certain you'll not have tea? I'm about to make some, Greg will be back in a moment.'

MacReady closed the folder. 'Why is he still frightened?'

She sighed, pulled the cardigan tight around her sunken chest. 'I haven't the faintest. But the money he's wasted on extra locks and those ridiculous lights that switch on and off when something moves outside. A burglar alarm too.'

'It's understandable,' MacReady said. 'Especially after what happened.'

She frowned at him. 'Young man, this was months ago.'

'He installed all these things *before* the break-in?' asked MacReady.

'Oh, weeks and weeks before,' she said. 'Started talking about home security and protecting ourselves. I found a kitchen knife next to his bed once, too. Told him it was completely unacceptable. But he didn't listen, as usual. And not a bit of it helped when that man came here, did it?'

She shuffled from the lounge; a few moments later they heard running water and the clink of crockery.

MacReady looked at Harrison. 'Talk about a coincidence. Why wasn't this mentioned in the paperwork? We've got King in custody –'

'In a coma,' Harrison said.

'But in custody, and nobody's been to tell these people yet?' MacReady shook his head, frustrated. 'This makes us look stupid, Warren. Aren't we supposed to be regularly updating victims of crime now?'

'Fucked if I know what's going on,' Harrison said, examining a fingernail. 'Though it's not as if we haven't been a little bit pre-occupied with other matters.'

'It's unprofessional. We should tell them now.'

'Cool your jets, Will,' Harrison said. 'I'll speak to Fletcher. I've got enough to worry about here with the old bat making me a cuppa in that grubby kitchen. She'll sit and make sure I drink it, you watch.'

The sound of a key in the front door. A burst of sunlight in the hall, then the door slamming shut.

A male voice: 'I'm back.'

Then he was in the lounge doorway: tall, gaunt, lank black hair framing sunken eyes, bundle of newspapers under one arm. His mouth opened a little when he saw Harrison and MacReady sitting in his lounge; he knew who they were.

MacReady recognised him straight away: Gregory Nelms was the crematorium manager he'd spent ten minutes talking to at Garratt's funeral. Had found him twitchy, nervous even then.

Now he looked ashen.

Harrison gave a quick nod of his head at Nelms. Introduced them. Said, 'Why don't you take a seat, Greg?'

Nelms stepped into the lounge. As he dropped the papers on a coffee table MacReady noticed the man's hands were trembling.

'Is there . . .?' Nelms asked.

'A problem?' MacReady said. 'Not at all.' He gestured for Nelms to sit in one of the other armchairs, sensing that if he took the seat his mother had just vacated she would be none too impressed.

Nelms' mother rattled in behind him, tray in hands, laden with cups and packets of half-opened biscuits. 'Did you get the *Mail*? I hope you got the *Mail*.' She turned to Harrison and MacReady. 'He's usually late at the shop and they've sold out.' Back to her son. 'I hope you got the *Mail*.'

'Yes, Mum,' Nelms said, looking at the floor as he sat. 'I got the *Mail* for you.'

'Thank goodness.' A dramatic huff and roll of the eyes from Nelms' mother. She placed the tray on the coffee table, scooped up the wodge of newspapers and tottered across to her armchair. 'Help yourselves to the biscuits, officers.'

MacReady smiled and raised a hand: *no thanks*. He could sense Harrison fidgeting beside him: food versus hygiene. He suspected food would win out.

'How are the injuries?' asked Harrison, eyeing the plate.

Nelms looked meekly at them from under the flop of his fringe. Touched his temple and ran fingers across the skin. 'Better, now. Much better. Thank you.'

MacReady pulled a sympathetic face. 'Sounds terrible, what happened?'

'Yes, it was . . . a shock,' Nelms replied. He looked at MacReady's cheek. 'I see you're in the wars, too.'

MacReady gave a weak smile. 'Perks of the job.'

Harrison capitulated and reached for a bourbon. Bit into the biscuit. Came straight out with it, crunching around the words. 'So how do you know Dane Sillitoe?'

There was a moment's hesitation, Nelms blinking rapidly, fingers still rubbing at his scalp. 'Dane Sillitoe?'

'He called here this morning. Bright and early. Remember?'

MacReady pulled out his notebook, a pen, ready to jot anything down. Stared at Nelms. Saw the sweat. A thin film on his forehead, his upper lip. He kept quiet, let it play out. Knew Harrison was doing the same. Nelms' mother sat to one side, feigning interest in her daily rag.

'How . . . how do you know he came here?' Nelms asked.

'We just do,' said Harrison, and Nelms swallowed. The rapid blinking again, as if making mental calculations behind those tired eyes. 'You were saying, Greg?'

'Mister Sillitoe, he does a lot of business at the crematorium,' said Nelms. His voice was robotic, almost. A drone. 'Their cars are very popular with bereaved families for the funerals of their loved ones.'

Harrison swallowed the last of the biscuit. Wiped at the inside of his mouth with a finger which he then began to suck the tip of. 'What did you talk about?'

'Nothing . . . exceptional,' Nelms said. He shifted back in the chair, crossed his legs at the ankles; it looked awkward, as if he was trying too hard for relaxed. 'We have a couple of services coming up and needed to go over a few things.'

Harrison was nodding. 'Bit odd, though, coming to see you at stupid o'clock? Most people would go to the crem to speak to you, right? Or ring? Email?'

'He was on his way to a job,' Nelms said. 'He just called in.'

'Seems like you're quite close, then,' MacReady offered. 'Him coming to your house to see you.'

Nelms' mother curled one edge of the paper over. 'I've never heard of this person before. I'd know if Gregory had a new friend.'

'And you people have just called in,' Nelms said. 'No email or phone call beforehand. Doesn't mean we're close, does it?' He gave a thin smile.

'We're the police, Greg,' Harrison said, eyes narrowed in annoyance. 'Turning up unannounced is what we do. Don't you watch those telly programmes?'

'We don't have a television downstairs,' Nelms' mother said. 'There's enough to do in a day without one of those things eating up the time.' She gave a pointed look at her son. 'But he has his own in his room, for those films he likes and whatnot.'

'I can't help you any further with Mister Sillitoe,' Nelms said. 'He's as busy as the rest of us, and thought it prudent to finalise a couple of pressing matters while on his way to an appointment. One of the funerals is for a Hindu gentleman, which of course requires special, and speedy, arrangements. I think it would be better if you spoke to Dane himself.'

'We've already spoken to him,' said Harrison. 'And we'll be speaking to him again.'

Nelms sat forward. Glanced at his mother. Appeared to gather himself a little. 'I really wish you hadn't come here like this. You should have contacted me by telephone beforehand and we could have agreed to meet at my place of work –'

MacReady tapped the pen on his notebook. Remembered the aggravation when they visited Sillitoe's father's offices. How Harrison had seemed to enjoy it. 'We thought it best to conduct this at your home. No need to cause ... difficulties with your job. Raise eyebrows and so on.'

'That's ... very thoughtful of you,' Nelms replied. 'But my mother is elderly and already extremely anxious after what happened during the burglary. And two strange men turning up at the door this morning does not help matters.'

'They gave me a fright, Gregory,' his mother sighed.

Nelms looked from her to MacReady and Harrison. Shook his head, like he was as disappointed with them as his mother professed to be.

'Have you ever heard of a man named Leon King, Greg?' MacReady asked, and felt Harrison tense next to him, hand hovering over the biscuits.

'I can't say it rings a bell,' Nelms replied, and gave an odd smile as he shrugged.

MacReady studied him. Saw the wringing of hands between his knees. The constant licking of his bottom lip. He reminded MacReady of Beck: fidgety and drowning in nervous energy.

'Your break-in,' MacReady said. A low groan from Harrison. 'We believe we have the suspect in custody. I thought you should know.'

Nelms' mother dropped the paper to reed-thin thighs. Her mouth was an O beneath goggling eyes. 'You've caught him?'

'Is it,' Nelms swallowed, 'this Leon King you mentioned?'

MacReady heard Harrison breathe loudly through flared nostrils. He nodded. 'He's in hospital at the moment. Has been for some time. But he's the man who broke into your house.'

'Have you interrogated him yet?' asked Nelms.

MacReady allowed a smile. 'No, we haven't . . . *interrogated* him, as yet. He's in a coma. We're waiting for him to recover.'

Nelms, blinking again. 'Do you think he'll pull through?'

'I'm sure he will,' said MacReady, not sure at all. 'He's in excellent hands.'

'Oh, thank goodness,' Nelms' mother wailed. She threw her hands in the air. 'Thank goodness, Gregory!' She pushed herself up from the chair; her *Daily Mail* slid to the patchy carpet. Nelms smiled awkwardly as his mother bent down and embraced him, patting her on the back and shushing her.

'I'll never forget it, my boy,' she sobbed. 'Never, ever. Seeing him hitting you, hitting you over and over with that thing of his –'

'It's fine, Mum,' Nelms said. 'It's all over. Quiet now.'

Harrison's mobile rang.

MacReady sunk back in the settee, utterly exhausted now, Nelms' mother crying in the background, her relief palpable, *his voice, I can't stop hearing it*, she was wailing, hands clawing at Nelms' jumper, *even now, after all these weeks, even in my sleep. So rough and that terrible language, effing and jeffing and 'why didn't you do it properly Greg, why didn't you'*, oh my word . . .

'Yeah,' Harrison muttered into the phone. Nodded. 'Yeah, yeah. Of course.'

He killed the call. Stood. Said, 'Thank you for your help, both. We'll be on our way.'

MacReady looked up at him, palms up, questioning.

Nelms' mother turned her head to them, cheeks wet, a small bubble of saliva in the corner of her mouth. 'Thank you, officers.'

'No problem,' said Harrison, and flicked his eyes to Nelms. 'We'll be back to finish this, Greg.' He held Nelms' gaze for a moment. Glanced at MacReady, tilted his head towards the lounge door.

MacReady followed him out, Nelms' glassy eyes on him all the way, the mother's sobs ringing in his ears.

Harrison sighed as MacReady slammed the car door.

'What now?' he asked.

'We can't fucking go,' MacReady said. 'You heard. Nelms kitting the place out with all sorts even before the burglary? For protection? He was keeping a *blade* by the bed, Warren. Something's well off here.' He looked out of the window. Shook his head.

'We'll finish up later,' said Harrison. He started the engine. 'Stop whinging.'

MacReady turned to him. 'Every person we speak to is shitting themselves about something. All of them, scared. Don't you wonder why?'

'I don't wonder about anything. When things happen I deal with them. Simple.'

'We should be dealing with Nelms,' MacReady said. 'Now.'

Harrison shoved the car into gear, pulled away. 'We're going to the Tates' place to RV with Fletcher.'

'That was him?' MacReady asked. 'What are the Tates saying?'

'Not a lot,' Harrison grunted. 'But then I s'pose you don't get much conversation from an empty house.'

MacReady turned to him. 'They've done a runner.'

It wasn't a question.

'Yup,' said Harrison. 'Packed what they needed and fucked off, by all accounts. And just to cheer you up, the DI's on the warpath. Blames you and the Sarge for putting the arm on the sister. Thinks you spooked them into doing a bunk.'

MacReady placed a hand over his eyes. 'I don't think today could get any worse.'

'Oh really?' Harrison said, and gunned the engine. 'Well suck this one up, trainee: you shooting your mouth off about Leon King has jinxed us. The hospital has been on the blower, too. He died half an hour ago.'

No sign of the Tates' guard dog; its rusted chain hung from the front wall.

They were gone, all right. MacReady knew Marie Tate would never leave behind her beloved beast to fend for itself.

He pushed through the gate, nodded at the Major Crime detectives hovering next to the rusted Ford Granada. They didn't return it, just stared reproachfully. One of them streamed smoke from his nostrils, a roll-up ciggie pinched between fingers that rested on the abandoned car's roof.

'Those things'll kill you,' Harrison said from behind MacReady.

The detective puffed on the rollie. 'Hopefully, tubs. Then I won't have to deal with CID amateurs anymore.'

Fletcher was pacing the lounge, phone clamped to ear and *yes sir*ing; he glared at MacReady as he entered. Beck perched on the windowsill, chewing at a thumbnail. She offered a wan smile before closing her eyes and shaking her head.

He glanced around, saw tell-tale signs of a hurried exit: black bin liners half full with clothes, a tatty holdall dumped on the settee, toiletries and shoes and carrier bags of foodstuffs strewn across the carpet. Cupboards open, drawers out, the television on and muted; a slick-looking reporter mouthed silently at the room, the Hodges Square maisonette washed in sunlight behind him.

Harrison dropped his bulk into the settee and smirked. 'All right, Sarge?'

Beck tilted her head and gave a sarcastic smile. 'Not really, no.'

MacReady thought better of sitting down.

Fletcher ended the call, slipped his mobile into a pocket. Looked at the floor for a moment, then placed hands on hips and raised his head to MacReady.

'I told you not to go harassing her,' he said.

MacReady looked to Beck, back to Fletcher. 'Is she answering her mobile?'

'No, she's fucking not answering her fucking mobile, Will,' Fletcher said, and MacReady blinked. 'Nor is Marie, nor Nathan Brissett. Maybe I should try the fucking dog's number?'

MacReady had never seen him so incensed. 'I'm sorry, boss –'

He looked MacReady up and down. Shook his head, jaw working as if weighing up the pros and cons of chinning his junior officer. 'You look like shit. I just don't get it. What's the matter with you? I've been sticking my neck out for you these last few weeks, fighting your corner when the higher-ups have questioned you going Tonto on your lonesome. But your constant running about and meddling are starting to get right up my chuff. And I'm a pretty patient guy.'

'Things . . .' MacReady pictured Megan. 'They've been getting on top of me.'

Fletcher gave a humourless snort. 'Don't give me that. We're all feeling the pinch. Don't you think I go home and sweat on this? I'm the DI for the area, for God's sake, and if this goes pear-shaped it's down to me. So what, Will, as a foot soldier, do you have to fucking worry about?'

MacReady looked away, looked for any sign of moral support. Saw Beck, head lowered. Turned to Harrison, but his glazed eyes were on the television.

'I'm just trying to do the right thing,' he said at last. 'We're close to something, I can feel it. We just left Nelms' house and it's obvious he's up to someth—'

'Enough, Will,' Fletcher said. He sounded tired. Beat.

MacReady looked him in the eye. 'But the mother, she told us Nelms was rigging security stuff at the house even before they were burgled. That Nelms was scared, as if he knew something was going to happen.'

Fletcher shifted his gaze to Harrison. 'This right, Wazza?'

Harrison shrugged. 'He's a weirdo anyway. Just look at where he works.'

MacReady spun to face him. 'You know as well as I do that Nelms didn't feel right, Warren. He went pale when he saw us sitting there in his lounge.'

'Just jumpy from the burglary,' Harrison yawned.

'It was more than that and you know it. The way he was looking at us when we told him we'd locked somebody up for screwing their house. He wasn't pleased or elated, just fearful. Even with his mother, crying on his –'

MacReady froze. Felt his skin prickle. Looked up at the ceiling for a moment, seeing Nelms and his mother embracing on the armchair in that musty old house.

Said to Fletcher: 'It wasn't a burglary.'

Fletcher screwed up his face, irritated. 'What?'

MacReady looked at Harrison. 'You heard her, Warren. Breaking her heart about King conning his way into the house then giving Nelms a shoeing.'

'Yeah, it was emotional,' said Harrison.

'I can't believe I missed it,' MacReady said. 'She *told us* what King was shouting. *Why didn't you do it properly Greg, why didn't you*, right?'

From the windowsill, Beck asked: 'If it was a straightforward distraction burglary, y'know, scrote picks random house, how come King knew his name?'

MacReady looked at her. Nodded a thank you. Turned back to Fletcher.

'King knew Gregory Nelms,' MacReady said.

'And King is dead,' said Fletcher.

'And Nelms knows Dane Sillitoe,' MacReady replied. 'It wasn't a burglary. Nelms spun us a line. They *all* know each other. Nelms, King, the Tates. And King was there for another reason. There's more to this.'

Fletcher placed his hands to his face and squeezed. Held them there for a few seconds. Dropped them to his sides and sighed.

'Go get Nelms,' he said quietly.

MacReady turned to Harrison.

'Uh-uh,' said Fletcher, and shook his head. He nodded at Beck. 'It's a simple pick-up job. Even you two couldn't balls that up. So bye-bye now.'

Beck sighed and pushed herself up from the windowsill.

MacReady followed her out of the lounge.

Heard Harrison mutter, 'Thank fuck for that.'

Above Saint-Pol-de-Léon,
French Airspace

The flight attendant lingered, hand on the glass of scotch and ice, one fingernail tapping. Her freckled face hovering near his, pale green eyes mischievous, expectant, as she bit at her bottom lip. Her perfume floral, hanging in the air with the question she had just asked.

'Thank you.' Gonçalves shifted in his seat. Thought of the times he'd spent with his head between the woman's thighs, lapping at her in the cramped toilet, pausing only to snarl at Felix when he hammered on the door for a piss.

He did not look at her now. 'But no.'

She blinked, unsure, because he had always been brusque with her, often toyed with her, and after a moment she realised he was not playing this time, that he meant it, and her face reddened as she straightened, clearing her throat.

'Is there anything else?' she asked. Angry, wounded.

Gonçalves shook his head. Reached for the tumbler of scotch. She was gone from his side before the ice rattled against his teeth.

Felix chuckled in the seat next to him. 'I think that might be the last drink she gets you, my friend.'

'I'll survive,' said Gonçalves, and fidgeted in his cramped seat. The aircraft's engines whined as it banked left, light moving across the insides of the cabin. As it levelled off Gonçalves' eyes shifted from Felix's bloated features to the window: brilliant blue that stretched into the distance. Soon they would descend into warmth and sun that would stay with them for the rest of the day; the pilot had already described the abnormally fine weather that awaited them. He pictured Beatriz at home, playing with Teo and Thalia, making the cookies and pastéis de nata they loved, the same sun illuminating a kitchen cluttered with mixing bowls and flour and chocolate chips the children would steal when their mother's back was turned.

Not long. Just twelve hours. And then he would be home.

Felix swigged at his red wine, finished it. Raised the glass at the flight attendant hovering near the cockpit door. She ignored him. 'My last too, I think, thanks to you,' he sighed, and glanced around as if expecting to find a mini bar somewhere.

Gonçalves pushed his scotch towards Felix. 'Take mine if you can't wait –'

'Warning light,' said Felix.

He was pushing himself out of the seat as Gonçalves checked behind them.

Four stretchers. Blankets covering the small frames curled on each one. Drips and monitoring equipment. A solitary amber light blinking above the nearest sleeping child.

Above Bepeh.

Felix was snapping open a kitbag as Gonçalves reached the boy. Knelt at his side. Checked for a pulse in his skinny wrist. Found it, *weak but rapid, his chest rising and falling quickly as he fought for breath. His lips tinged with blue.*

He clicked his fingers at Felix. 'He's splinting. Ventilator. Now.'

Felix flicked switches on equipment. Said, 'If he doesn't last, this is over.'

'He'll last.' Gonçalves glanced at the flight attendant. 'How long?'

She looked at him coolly. 'Twenty minutes.'

'Tell them it's urgent,' he said, and nodded at the cockpit door. He slipped the mask over Bepeh's head. Reached into his trouser pocket. Pulled out the necklace. Placed it in the palm of the boy's hand. Cupped the hand in his.

Whispered, 'Nearly there, child.'

23

Nelms had left for work.

'I want to thank you,' his mother had said to MacReady, her milky eyes red-rimmed from the crying. 'Greg's so relieved, he's calmer than I've seen him in weeks.' She'd taken his hands in hers, paper-dry and cold on his fingers, and he'd been desperate to pull free, to scream to the crematorium with Beck, but had waited a moment, the elderly lady silent and sucking at her cheeks as she gazed up at him with gratitude. As if he was her hero.

And he'd waited, he realised, because he needed it more than her.

They'd left, Nelms' mother waving them away, and he'd wondered how different her reaction would be when they told her Greg was in the bin because – and MacReady was certain of it – he was up to his neck in something.

Something.

Beck swung the car off the roundabout at Northwood and through the cemetery gates; the crematorium building hove into view at the end of the driveway. 'We're his shitty end of the stick duo now, you know that?'

MacReady nodded. Neat lawns and flower beds rolled past his window; beyond them the countless gravestones and interment plots of the garden of remembrance. Through a gap in a hedgerow he glimpsed a young couple hunched over a small mound, shifting flowers and teddy bears beneath Indian summer sun. Large letters carved into marble headstone: *Lauren*. The dates below made her out to be four years old.

He closed his eyes.

'Any crap that comes through the MIR, it'll appear on my action list,' Beck said. 'All the crank calls from psychics who've spoken to King's spirit, the rubbish the civvies normally sift through, Fletcher will give them to me to sort out.'

She nudged him with an elbow. MacReady looked at her.

'And guess what?' she asked, and slowed as they reached the crematorium. 'I'm going to give them all to you. Then I'm going to kill you. Then make you do more paperwork. Then kill you again.'

They climbed out of the car at the rear of the crem; MacReady heard the buzz of a lawnmower, saw groundsmen hacking at conifers. A breeze carried the faint yet constant hiss of traffic from the M4 motorway that snaked through the countryside at the rear of the site.

At reception they proffered warrant cards, the young woman behind the desk as unfazed as Nelms' mother had been startled. She gave a practised smile and held up a finger as she continued typing with the other hand, eyes narrowed and concentrating on the computer screen.

'How can I help you?' she said eventually. Chirpy and light, at odds with the sombre surroundings. Early twenties, hair an inky Louise Brooks bob; MacReady noticed the ends kept catching in one corner of her mouth when she spoke.

He stayed quiet. Considered it good form given he seemed to get Beck in trouble every time he said or did anything.

'Gregory Nelms?' Beck asked.

The woman arched an eyebrow. 'Ooo, interesting. What's he done?'

'Just routine enquiries,' Beck replied with a smile.

'Disappointed,' the woman said.

'Because you really, really want him to be arrested?'

The woman shrugged. 'We don't get much in the way of excitement around here. As you can imagine.'

'The dead don't give good conversation.'

'Indeed they don't. Not that I'd ever want to see one of our deliveries, never mind have a natter with them.' She gave a small shudder.

'Well believe me, it'd help us out a lot right now if they could natter. So is Mister Nelms in?'

The woman reached for a telephone, prodded a couple of numbers with slender, painted fingernails. Cradled the handset in the crook of her neck and resumed tapping at her keyboard. After thirty seconds she hung up.

'Going to voicemail,' she said. 'Might have popped out. He likes to pop out.'

'We can wait for him here,' said Beck.

'Ah,' the woman said, and stood. 'I'll take you down to his office. He has a habit of not answering his phone. And we get a lot of miserable rellies in here crying about their dead so-and-so and it's all a bit depressing. And anyway he has a coffee machine. Provided by the council, too.'

'How the other half live,' said Beck.

'Oh, he's a right one percenter,' the woman chuckled, and motioned for them to follow.

The bowels of the crematorium were typical of council properties, MacReady thought. Drab, functional, plastered with Health and Safety signs, although given what was going on in the bowels of the building he assumed the staff took a little more notice of the hand hygiene information than in most other places of work.

'Here you go,' the woman said, stopping outside a nondescript fire door. She rapped the wood below a black plastic sign: *Crematorium Manager*. Turned to MacReady and Beck, humming quietly and bobbing her head as they waited.

'Perhaps he has popped out,' MacReady said.

'Well well, he speaks,' the woman smiled at him, mock-surprised. She grabbed the door handle. 'Come on, I'll get you settled then I can go back to answering emails about setting fire to dead people.'

She pushed at the door; it rattled in its frame but didn't open.

The woman frowned. 'Mister Nelms?'

'He's probably locked it,' said Beck. 'No problem, we can wait in recep—'

'The doors don't have locks,' the woman replied, and yanked down the handle again. She pushed at the door with her shoulder;

it moved a centimetre or so then stopped. 'Mister Nelms, is everything all right in there?'

MacReady and Beck exchanged a look. He turned back to the woman. Saw confusion in her face.

'Can you give us some room?' Beck asked, hand gesturing for the woman to move aside. 'Will, help me out here.'

Beck placed her shoulder against the door beside MacReady. He pulled down the handle, felt it warm and slick from the woman's hand. Placed his mouth to the small gap between door and frame. 'Greg, it's DC MacReady. I spoke to you earlier at your mum's house?'

Nothing.

He glanced at Beck. Saw the nod.

Shoved his bodyweight into the door, heard Beck grunt alongside him, the door opening slowly, brushing against carpet, hinges straining, MacReady's thighs burning with the effort, the door like a concrete slab.

Nelms' office: empty.

MacReady stepped in, Beck alongside him. Coffee maker gurgling, blinds drawn, desktop computer on standby, filing cabinets closed, Nelms' coat slung over the back of a swivel chair.

'That's weird,' the woman's voice from behind them. 'He always hangs his jacket on the back of the door.'

And then she screamed.

They sat in silence for a long time, car thick with heat, figures in paper suits drifting in and out of the crematorium building in front of them. Harrison, talking with the receptionist, her features still pale and hollowed out, hands flitting about in exaggerated jerks as her mouth moved and head shook constantly. Adrenalised. Shock. A few feet away from her: Danny Fletcher, sitting on a low wall with elbows on knees and phone pressed to ear, shoulders slumped as he updated whoever needed to be updated.

'I know what you're thinking,' Beck said, 'and it's not your fault, Will.'

Nelms. Simple belt around coat hook around neck job. Lean forward, and away you go. And he was gone, had been gone for at least half an hour by the time they'd arrived, and they'd found him dangling, face mottled with purple and wet tongue swelling between lips, eyes straining and bloodshot and on nothing.

Of course, they'd unhooked him from the back of the door, worked on him, MacReady trying to resus the guy until he was just as purple from the effort and then it had been pointless and he'd sat back on the office carpet, breathing on the stink of Nelms' voided bowels and wondering how the fuck they were going to explain this to his mother without giving her a stroke.

He turned to Beck. 'We pushed him to it. We should've stayed with him at the house. Brought him in. Anything except leave him alone.'

'Nobody was to know that he'd do this.'

'You're right,' MacReady spat. 'Because we don't know anything. Do we? We haven't got the first fucking clue.'

'That's not true, Will,' said Beck. 'Look at all we've done. Look at all the things you've done.'

'And don't they look pleased about them all.' He gestured out through the windscreen, at Fletcher and Harrison. 'Nelms should be in custody now, Sarge. In a cell, constantly monitored, safe and ready for us to speak to him. The IPCC will be all over this now. It's a death after police contact.'

She nodded quietly; there was nothing she could say because MacReady was right. Instead she straightened in her seat. 'Heads up.'

MacReady looked, saw a morose Fletcher approaching the car. The DI leaned in as Beck lowered the window.

'This place is sealed for searching,' he said. 'So get over to Nelms' house. Now. Don't stop. Call when you're there.'

Fletcher paused and turned to the crem when the receptionist began crying, great sobs shuddering from somewhere deep within. Behind her, ambulance staff wheeled out a trolley, Nelms in a body bag on top. MacReady watched, thinking it was odd to see a corpse being shipped out rather than in.

Beck glanced at MacReady, back to Fletcher. 'What do we tell the mother?'

'You don't go near her,' the DI replied, and pushed himself away from the car. He jabbed a forefinger at them. 'If she has a clutcher and keels over I will go postal. You don't go in, you don't speak to anybody. But nobody leaves, and nobody approaches the house until I arrive. You do not say a word to her, am I absolutely clear?'

Beck started the engine as he walked away.

And they both heard him: 'I've had enough of dead fucking bodies for one day.'

Nelms' mother knew.

When they'd arrived, parked a short distance from the gate, sat waiting for Fletcher and whoever else he could magic from across the force – they were fast running out of bodies to deal with bodies – she'd appeared at the front door and, upon seeing them, when she'd suddenly realised why they were back, when it all became horribly real, she'd staggered down the driveway towards them, wailing and clawing at her eyes.

Nelms had told her before he did it. Quick phone call home, said his goodbye, said he was sorry, ended the call.

Ended him. And he hadn't told her why.

A neighbour heard the screams, came out, face flushed with anger at the noise polluting her leafy retreat and ready to complain. Beck had explained; the neighbour, shocked yet energised in that way MOPs tended to be when tasked with dealing with the extraordinary, had whisked Nelms' mother away with the promise of ringing relatives and comforting cups of tea until the FLO turned up to do the official hand-wringing and stirring-in of sugars.

They'd watched as CSI vans and Major Crime suits turned up in dribs and drabs, blocking the lane, busy busies, humping boxes and bags into the unkempt house as faces appeared in neighbouring windows. Fletcher and Harrison rolled up not long afterwards, a pair of scowls in a beat-up Peugeot, had nodded at MacReady and Beck to follow them inside as a pair of uniforms took up positions outside the gate.

'Stay out of the way,' Fletcher had said to MacReady, jabbing a finger at him.

The bourbons were still on the table in the lounge. Cups of tea, as cold and pale as the son of the woman who made them.

MacReady leaned back on the settee, hands in pockets. 'Naughty step.'

'Rather this than rooting through filthy cupboards,' said Beck. Her legs were crossed at the knee, one boot raised and circling constantly. 'Look at the place. I've been in cleaner junkie houses.'

He chuckled. Watched people flitting past the doorway, heard footsteps on stairs, on the ceiling above. 'Remember this one time, doing a warrant after I pinched a guy for selling amphet wraps in a pub. Did his house afterwards. His wife was there, hopping from foot to foot, pissed off that we were trampling through her place.' He turned to Beck. 'She started cleaning in front of us. Vacuum on, polishing the laminate where we'd been booting about, all frantic and goggle-eyed. When my old stripey stood still for a minute she started polishing his shoes.'

Beck smiled. 'Speed?'

'Christ, yeah,' he laughed. 'Off her box on it. Turned out she was cutting her husband's base amphet for herself. It was the cleanest place I'd ever been in. Spotless.'

'They could do with a bit of that here,' she said.

MacReady looked away. Thought of Nelms' mother, face twisted as she approached their car. 'I don't think it makes much difference anymore.'

He felt a hand on his arm. A light squeeze of Beck's fingers. 'Not your fault, Will. I'll keep saying it until it gets through that thick, stubborn skull of yours . . .'

Somebody called Fletcher. Loud, insistent from upstairs. MacReady saw him dash past the doorway, heard him thunder up to the first floor of the house.

MacReady stood.

'Will . . .' said Beck, and shook her head.

'Come on,' he urged.

She hesitated. Looked at the pathetic plate of biscuits. Back up at MacReady.

'Not like he can kick us off the team for taking an interest,' he shrugged. 'There isn't anybody else to replace us.'

Numerous photographs along the stairs and landing; MacReady saw a life lived through a lens, recognised the woman in each of them: Nelms' mother, smiling on a beach with feet hanging off the end of a lounger, at a restaurant and grinning as she lifted food to her mouth, at her wedding, the man with arm hooked through hers the spitting image of the body he'd unhooked from the back of a door not two hours ago. As he moved along the uneven floor he studied each one, wondered if the woman frozen within ever had an inkling that the son she brought into the world would leave it before she did.

Nelms' bedroom was boxy and smelled of damp, its walls lined with film posters MacReady assumed had been positioned to hide mildew stains; he could see them creeping from behind a one-sheet of *Raging Bull*, De Niro gloves aloft and glistening in black and white. In one corner sat a widescreen and fancy home cinema setup, behind it shelf upon shelf of DVDs and Blu-rays. It gave the impression of a man who spent considerable time alone in a world not of his making.

MacReady and Beck watched from the doorway: Fletcher, Harrison, a female CSI, one of the Major Crime stuffed shirts, hands in latex, rooting through drawers, cupboards, piles of clothing. Barely room to move inside.

'Anything?' MacReady asked. He bent down, grabbed some gloves from the CSI's case, snapped them on.

Fletcher turned at the sound of his voice. Gritted his teeth. 'Did you not understand?'

'We could help out,' said MacReady. 'It's a big old place –'

'Jesus,' the Major Crime officer said.

Fletcher waited a beat, eyeing MacReady and Beck. He swivelled to look at the Major Crime officer. In his hand was a jewellery box. Old-fashioned, cheap, something a grandmother or mother would give a child to play with. Glossy black with red lining. A worn Post-It note taped to the lid.

The word *Insurance* written on it.

MacReady stepped into the room. Ignored Beck's hand on his shoulder.

Shifted to get a better view. Squinted at the contents of the box.

Saw Fletcher lift out Dane Sillitoe's business card.

Saw what had been hidden underneath.

Heard Fletcher, incredulous: 'Please don't tell me they're what I think they are.'

Part 3

Things Fall Apart

Cardiff Airport

The shriek of jet engines in his ears, the buffeting blasts of warm air on his skin as they powered down. The sky cloudless: a beautiful day here for once. The compact airport going about its business, the sun reflecting off the viewing windows in the departure lounge.

Gonçalves hurried off the plane's steps to the apron, waved the private ambulance towards him. Watched as its reverse lights flickered on, Felix behind him, unlocking a hatch in the fuselage, barking at the pilot to help, to raise the ambulift so they could offload the children. Two airport officials hovering nearby, clipboards and pensive smiles as the first stretcher appeared at the hole in the Learjet's flank.

Bepeh. They needed to hurry.

'Doctor,' one of the officials nodded solemnly, the same as he always did, the same as all of them did wherever they landed. He'd see it in their stricken faces: these sick children, so terrible. So desperate for treatment they couldn't get in their own country. Then they'd catch Gonçalves' eye and lower their heads, press their lips together, reverent almost, as if marvelling at the selfless work he was doing, and he'd busy himself and think how next month it

was Bristol, a fortnight later Birmingham, then Exeter, Stansted, Leeds Bradford. Three or four months from now: Cardiff again. Alternating, rotating, ensuring questions were never raised about the number of patients arriving in one area.

Patients.

It was the first time he'd ever thought of them as such.

'Thank you,' he said, and took the clipboard being proffered to him. Pretended to scrutinise the paperwork. Signed where he always signed. Handed it back, willed them to go away. 'Matters are urgent. I trust my associate had all the papers in order?'

'Everything's fine. Visas, documents.' The official looked at the ambulance. 'He doesn't talk much, though, does he?'

Gonçalves frowned. Their driver was annoyingly garrulous, a cocky and ignorant boy, a *grosseiro* whose constant talk and sickly aftershave gave him headaches every time he came here.

He turned towards the ambulance. Saw the driver's door open. Didn't recognise the man who unfolded himself from the cab: rangy but taut and ripped to the muscle, shades atop stubbled head, acne-scarred cheeks framing wet and rubbery lips. Long arms hung from his black tee, the skin greened to the wrists with tattoo sleeves.

Gonçalves thought of the cigarillo-smoking brute who'd come to the clinic.

Felt a flutter of panic.

He glanced at Felix, momentarily widened his eyes. Saw his assistant pause as he lowered Bepeh to the tarmac, watching the driver advance towards them.

Gonçalves intercepted him at the side of the ambulance, out of earshot of the officials. Leaned in close. In English: 'Where is the boy?'

Dead eyes on the driver. A brooding stillness Gonçalves found unnerving, as if the man was not quite present: detached, silent, the antithesis of the boy who usually collected them and who he now, ironically, wished was here, his foul mouth and fouler aftershave more welcome than spending any time with this man would ever be.

'Not here.' It came from the side of the driver's mouth, a grunt, the accent clear, and Gonçalves knew it was the only explanation he was going to get. Knew, despite the feeling of unease he felt, that it was more than wise not to question things further. And then the driver brushed past him, so close Gonçalves smelled the stale body odour, and loped towards Felix, towards the open fuselage, hands up and ready to shift the first stretcher to the ground.

Ten long minutes to load the ambulance. Gonçalves waited in the rear with Bepeh, clutched his cold hand. Adjusted the ventilator. Only so much he could do, now. Only so much until they reached their destination. He raised the boy's head and placed the necklace around his neck, adjusted it so it lay straight, the gold bright against his greying skin. His chest heaved and struggled to work, the necklace flashing in sunlight that fell through the windows.

Felix groaned, shunted the last stretcher in through the doors, its frame folding beneath it, castors rattling against metal floor. The driver stood next to him, slack-jawed, tongue resting on a glistening bottom lip.

'We must leave,' Gonçalves said. He could hear the urgency in his voice, a slight shrillness that he was struggling to keep under control.

Felix glanced at the driver. Held his hands out in fists, rotated them as if gripping an imaginary steering wheel. Motioned for him to move. When the man walked away he turned back to Gonçalves. 'Be safe, Luis.'

A door opened and closed; he felt the ambulance rock as the man dumped himself into the driver's seat. 'Four hours,' Gonçalves said.

'We'll be here,' Felix nodded. 'Four hours. And then we go home.'

He slammed the double doors shut. Tapped the roof of the ambulance. Gonçalves held his eyes through the rear windows. Held Bepeh's hand as the driver accelerated away, the plane shrinking in the glass, the airport officials waving and shuffling off to fill in their forms and tick their boxes and carry on being clueless about what was going on under their pudgy noses.

Three armed police at the emergency gate alongside the terminal building. They pressed fingers to earpieces, heads cocked. Slid the bolt, yanked open a section of fence. Sunglasses and body armour and machine guns and quick nods which the driver acknowledged with a raised index finger.

Working together for the mercy mission.

Gonçalves watched from the rear, hunched over, a hand on Bepeh's sternum, the ambulance slowing to a rumble as it eased through the gap, eased over speed bumps and pitted concrete and past smiling, helpful British policemen and his lungs ached with the breath he'd been holding since Felix shut him inside.

And then they were through.

And Gonçalves exhaled.

'Easy,' said the driver, over one shoulder, and dropped his shades to his nose.

Then Bepeh stopped breathing.

'Hurry.'

No response. No increase in speed.

The driver sat shades forward, one hand draped over the steering wheel as he guided the ambulance away from the airport. Foot traffic everywhere, taxis lined in front of the departures building and dumping pale, excited faces onto the pavement. Orange-faced travellers snaking down the ramps outside arrivals, miserably tugging with them wheeled suitcases and tired children and the already-fading taste of a life Gonçalves could not wait to return to.

'I said hurry,' he yelled, and slapped at the side wall of the ambulance. There was a pulse, a faint pulse, and the boy had begun pulling air but the breaths were intermittent, spaced out and ragged. 'Or this one will not live.'

The driver slowed to allow a taxi to pull out.

'It not matter now,' he said. Broken, matter-of-fact English.

Gonçalves ground his teeth. Shifted off the folding seat, towards the front of the ambulance, bent at the waist, fists clenched.

At the door to the cab: 'Faster, cuzão, or I will make things very difficult for your people –'

He didn't have time to duck the fist. Barely saw it before it connected with the bridge of his nose. A flash of tattoo, of knuckles swinging towards him, then momentary blackness, his shoulder blades hitting the ambulance floor. Hands up to his nose; he heard the crunch of splintered bone between his eyes, felt warm liquid *gathering between his fingers. Gagged on the warm, coppery taste at the back of his mouth.*

Gonçalves rolled onto his side. Grabbed the base of a gurney, bloodied hand slipping on the aluminium. Pulled himself to a sitting position as the ambulance slowed to a stop.

Saw the driver climb out of his seat and push through the gap into the rear. Lift his shades onto the top of his head.

Crab-walk towards him, silver pistol in one hand.

He placed it on Gonçalves' forehead, the muzzle cold against his skin and Gonçalves swallowed, eyes crossed as he looked upwards at the trigger guard, at the long finger and dirty nail curled through it, at the arm extending away from him with the driver's distended lips sneering at the end of it.

'Know your place, yes?' the driver nodded.

Gonçalves recoiled as the muzzle was pushed into his forehead, the metal gouging skin. Forced himself upwards, onto his feet, thighs trembling.

'Please,' he said, breathing hard. 'We must hurry. We must . . .'

He flicked his eyes to the left.

To Bepeh. His hand hung limply from the stretcher.

The driver cocked his head. Followed Gonçalves' gaze.

Swung the pistol across to Bepeh.

'This thing?' he asked, incredulous.

'Please.' Gonçalves placed his hands together as if in prayer, implored the man in front of him. Pictured Teo and Thalia. 'He's just a child.'

The driver chuckled.

Dropped his sunglasses to his nose.

Shot Bepeh in the chest.

Gonçalves sunk to his knees, a high-pitched whine in his ears and for a moment he couldn't be sure if it was the gunshot ringing or the sound from his own mouth.

'Shut up, pas.'

The driver cracked him on the skull with the pistol's handle. Gonçalves crumpled. Watched from the floor as the driver ripped the necklace from Bepeh. Held it in the palm of one hand. Studied it, eyes barely visible behind sunglasses. Nodded to himself and shoved it in a pocket as he stepped towards the cab.

Not much time.

Not much time, Gonçalves knew, and he flopped over, onto all fours, a string of blood and mucus hanging from his nose, fighting the tiredness, the urge to lie down and let everything fade away, because it had all become clear to him, had crystallised in these last few minutes of madness: he wanted out. A long and miserable moan from deep within him. His hand, feeling for the edge of Bepeh's stretcher. The driver, revving the ambulance engine.

Gonçalves gripped the sides of the stretcher. Pulled it towards him, shoulders straining, eyes blurred with tears that fell for his family, for this boy, for this life he had allowed himself to fall into. His shaking fingers worked the restraints, unbuckling, threading nylon straps, trying not to look at the hole in Bepeh's sternum, seeing it in the corner of his eye anyway: a black dot, so small, but so much blood. Pooling in the cavity at his neck, trickling towards his armpits.

He pulled Bepeh off the stretcher, into his arms. Cradled his naked body. Felt the ambulance begin to move, looked up and saw the terminal building with its armed police and medical facilities shift further away. Checked the other children: no time. Checked over his shoulder, towards the cab, saw the driver's left hand on the wheel, smeared with red where he'd punched Gonçalves.

On his knees he shuffled towards the rear doors. Yanked on the handle. Bepeh wrapped in a blanket and limp underneath his arm.

Gonçalves pushed open the ambulance doors.

Jumped.

24

'I can't believe they lost him.'

Just after 5 p.m. on the dashboard clock, MacReady slumped low in the passenger seat, elbow propped on the door, head resting on his hand. One of several teams plotted up at various known haunts and waiting for Dane Sillitoe to show, although MacReady knew the likelihood of Dane showing up here was slim to none. He watched a BMW convertible pull out of Scott Sillitoe's business, head for Rover Way, the driver a woman with cropped copper hair and shades; Dane's mother, obviously done for the day and on her way home.

'Well, that wasn't our boy,' Beck said. She sipped on her petrol station coffee, grimaced. One of her arms dangled out of an open window; the car was sweltering. 'Unless he's taken to wearing a wig.'

It was pointless but MacReady jotted the number plate down in his notebook anyway, just for something to do. He tilted his head so he could see into the car park: Scott Sillitoe's hulking 4x4 the only vehicle left. 'Maybe that's how he gave the surveillance team the slip. All five of them.'

'It happens,' she offered. 'Just takes one to lose eyeball for a few seconds.'

He clenched a fist around the pen he was holding. 'Dane's not going to come here, though, is he? Word will have got around about Nelms. And we don't know who else Nelms called before topping himself, so we have to work on the assumption that he rang Dane. He'll know we're looking for him and would put obs on his old man. He's not the smartest but smart enough to slip the surveillance and work out we'd sit on this place.'

Beck was nodding in agreement. 'I know,' she said, and there was more than a hint of annoyance in her voice. 'But this is Fletcher's idea of giving us a bollocking and keeping us out of the way. It's what he does.'

'Well it's wrong and petty and a waste of resources.' MacReady stretched, arching his back against the seat, tensing his thighs. 'We could be doing things.'

'Such as?' Beck asked.

'Pinging his mobile for a location. Ringing it until the bastard answers. Things.'

'It's being done,' she replied. 'Fletcher requested the cell-site analysis as soon as the surveillance people called in about the total loss. It's all in hand.'

'*Teeth*, Sarge,' MacReady shook his head.

'I know.'

'Human teeth. *Kids*' teeth, by the looks of things. A dozen of them. In a fucking jewellery box with Dane Sillitoe's business card on top.'

'I know, I was there, all right?' Beck tipped the coffee onto the pavement. 'It's horrific.'

'So what are we talking about here?' MacReady scooted around to face her. 'Has Nelms been burning children's bodies in that crematorium of his?'

'We've shut the place down and searches are under way. Fletcher and Major Crime –'

'What for, though? Are we looking at more bodies now? Is Nelms involved in murdering kids? Is anyone checking MisPers or –'

'Christ, Will,' Beck said, hands palm upwards. 'Enough. Please. I know as little as you, except that it's being dealt with, OK?'

He chewed at the inside of his mouth, turned away from her and looked around the other units of the industrial estate: shutters coming down, people drifting off into the warm evening carrying rucksacks and work bags, a steady flow of cars and wagons accelerating towards the main drag. His clothes itched, his shirt soft and damp with two days of sweat, and he wasn't sure when he'd be pulling on a fresh one. No change of clothes in his locker. Everything at home. And he wasn't sure when he'd be going back there.

Beck yawned beside him, long and loud and it morphed into a moan as she rubbed at her eyes. 'Jesus this is boring,' she said. 'And being cooped up in here with you is driving me mad.'

He slid his notebook and pen into a pocket and looked at her. Looked back at the Viper Travel site. The lone vehicle in the car park. Scott Sillitoe, probably on his own inside.

'Let's go then,' he said, and opened his door.

Beck snapped her head to him. 'What are you doing?'

'Going to speak to Dane's daddy,' he flashed a smile, half out of the door, the heel of his shoe grinding on chipped tarmac. 'Find out what the score is.'

'Will,' Beck said, 'we've been told to sit tight until Fletcher releases some of the Major Crime people to come back us up.'

'We've been here over two hours, Sarge,' he said. 'And we may not have seen him go in, but he could have arrived before we did. He could be in there right now.'

She pointed at the passenger seat. 'All the more reason to sit. We wait until they shift people from the search at Dane's flat to here. Then we go in mob-handed.'

'And what if the old man drives off before they arrive? What if he takes pity on his boy and decides to squirrel him away in the boot?'

'He doesn't seem the type. So just sit down. Now, please.'

He raised his hands. 'Quick chat with him. No harm done. No pressure. He seemed straight up when I came here with Harrison. I doubt he wants to bring any more aggro to the door of his business so will probably help us out.'

'Will . . .'

MacReady hesitated, one foot on the road, a hand on the door. No traffic now. Everybody gone. He bent at the waist, looked back into the car. 'You said this is boring.'

'Obs are always bor—'

'So let's go put the arm on him,' MacReady said, and closed the door on her.

Beck watched him stride towards Scott Sillitoe's business, her mouth open.

'Fuck,' she muttered, and clambered out of the car.

Outside Cardiff Airport

Gonçalves watched from the treeline with nowhere to go.

High security fencing behind him. The open car park to his right. In front, a grassy slope leading up to the road. Up to the ambulance and its driver.

'What's going on, mate?'

A large man, but out of shape, belly hanging over garish three-quarter-length shorts, white football shirt hugging sunburned skin. He stood before the driver, arms wide, questioning; he'd dropped suitcases and left behind his open-mouthed female companion to lumber up the steps from the car park when Gonçalves jumped out of the ambulance with Bepeh, and it was a distraction Gonçalves was thankful for: it had allowed him to go to ground in the wooded area. To buy some time. To hope the British airport police with their guns and sunglasses would hear of the commotion now taking place at the roadside.

He no longer cared about being caught. The police could lock him away for twenty years as long as it meant he was no longer part of this. As long as they got Bepeh the medical attention he so desperately needed.

Gonçalves held him close. Placed two fingers to his throat: a pulse, but dangerously weak. Blood seeping through the blanket wrapped around his limp torso. The life draining out of him.

'Fight, boy,' he whispered. 'Fight.'

'I asked what's the problem, bruv, yeah?'

The large man. Pointing down the slope, towards the spot where Gonçalves hid. The driver ignoring him, standing at the lip of the slope, face expressionless, metal rim of his shades catching sunlight as he scanned the clutch of trees and bushes.

And still no sirens.

'Debs,' the large man called over one shoulder to the female. 'Ring the Old Bill, love, there's something not right with this cunt.'

Gonçalves had seen men like this before. Men, tall and burly, who bawled and barged their way through life, always needing to take control, to exert authority, their size lending them confidence yet blinding them to their lack of real ability, to the obvious danger they faced, until it was too late.

And it was too late now because the man stepped close to the driver, still not seeing the pistol hanging by his side, stepped close until they were nose to nose with the man's jaw jutting as he grunted something then the shot rang out and he staggered backwards a few paces, hand over his heart, a confused look on his face.

He dropped to the ground, sunburned legs twitching, a gurgle from his frothed lips.

A scream from the car park.

Gonçalves shrunk back into the foliage as the driver tromped down the slope.

Heard the woman's voice: Policepolicepleasepleaseplease-myhusbandohmygod . . .

He shifted further into the bushes. Slowly, quietly, dragging Bepeh. The driver coming towards them, silver pistol swinging at his thigh. The woman shrieking at somebody, asking for the police to come. His heartbeat loud in his ears, blood from his nose dripping onto the blanket, onto Bepeh's blood.

The driver stopped six feet away from them. Licked at those fat lips. Sunglasses shifting as he quick-panned across the bushes.

Gonçalves froze.

Watched the driver tilt his head one way, then the other. Peer through the undergrowth. Take a step closer. Almost on top of them now.

Gonçalves closed his eyes. Squeezed Bepeh.

Hunched over to protect him.

Heard sirens in the distance.

He looked, saw the driver check over his shoulder at the road. Turn back to the bushes. Lift the shades to the shaved dome of his head. Blink rapidly, as if making mental calculations.

Walk away.

Relief washed over Gonçalves.

And then Bepeh groaned in his arms.

The driver stopped. Spun around. Cocked his head. Walked back to the bushes and lifted the pistol. Parted the branches with the tip of the muzzle and met Gonçalves' wide eyes.

'No,' Gonçalves breathed, and raised a hand to ward him off.

Thought of Beatriz and Teo and Thalia.

Pictured small hands forming cookies in a sunlit kitchen.

The driver smiled and pulled the trigger.

The firearms officer took the slope slowly, MP5 raised and pointed at the overgrown corner of the security fence. His partner walking with him, ten feet away, covering from another angle. Behind and above them, at the roadside, the line of ARVs with officers leaning on bonnets and roofs, weapons drawn, sighted on the treeline. Force helicopter looping above the car park, the noise deafening.

Paramedics already at scene, treating the untreatable. The dead man's wife shivering and numb in the back of their wagon, uniform holding her hands and offering the usual empty words of comfort.

'See anything?' he transmitted, and stepped closer to the bushes.

'Negative,' his partner replied in his earpiece.

He nodded. Shifted the stock of the Heckler, tight into his shoulder. Finger on the trigger, sun warming his back.

Pushed through the undergrowth. Saw the man, cross-legged, slumped forward beneath a tree, a blanket bundled in his lap. Saw bullet holes in his shoulder, the left side of his chest, the top of his head.

'Great,' he said, a little louder than he intended.

'What you got?' His partner, crunching through foliage. Then he saw it. 'Jesus.'

The firearms officer leaned forward, gloved hand reaching for the dead man's chin. He tilted the head upwards, grimaced at the shattered nose, the dull eyes. Tilted it too far, until the man began to topple over.

His partner: 'Careful, you don't want to mess with the crime sce—'

The dead man slumped backwards into the long grass and they saw the boy.

The boy, head lolling backwards, draped over the dead man's lap, his dark brown eyes fixed and unblinking, his small frame washed and crusted with blood.

'What the fuck?' his partner blurted.

The firearms officer stared at the boy whose stomach was ruined and open and empty.

Wiped at his mouth with a gloved hand. Swallowed.

Said, 'Get on the blower. Tell them just what we've found here.'

25

'Mister Sillitoe.'

Scott Sillitoe turned in the doorway to the main office, bunch of keys in one hand, the door ajar. His eyes widened a fraction, just momentarily, but it told MacReady all he needed to know: the man knew why he was there.

'DC MacReady,' Sillitoe nodded. 'Just about to lock this place up.' Then the practised smile, all teeth and no mirth. He was done for the day: tieless, shirt unbuttoned at the neck, suit jacket draped over the briefcase at his heel. His eyes shifted over MacReady's shoulder as the front door opened; MacReady heard Beck's laboured breaths behind him. 'And this is . . .'

'This is Detective Sergeant Beck,' MacReady said. She appeared alongside him, a look of displeasure on her face.

Sillitoe dipped his head in acknowledgement. The jangle of keys as he dropped them into his trouser pocket. He gave a long sigh. 'I don't know where he is either.'

MacReady checked through the doorway into the darkened main office: empty seats, powered-down desktops, a solitary bulkhead light above a fire exit. 'I'll be honest with you here, Scott. I find that very hard to believe.'

Sillitoe raised his hands. Took a long, deep breath, paunch straining against his waistband. 'If I knew, I would tell you. Don't you think I would tell you?' He waved one hand about. 'Of course I would help you people out. It helps me out, I have a business to run, you can see that. I don't need police officers coming here every week looking for that bloody son of mine. If I knew where he was I'd tell you. After I'd throttled him first, of course.'

He laughed but it was forced and dissolved into a flush of red cheeks that MacReady found strange. He said nothing, let the silence hang for a moment, was glad Beck didn't feel the need to fill it with another question.

There was something off about Sillitoe. A stiffness in his posture, a tightness in his face, and his cheery efforts were betrayed by eyes that kept darting from MacReady to Beck to the window that looked out onto the car park.

'He's not answering his phone,' MacReady said.

'I know,' Sillitoe nodded. 'I've tried. Left messages. Rung family, friends. Nothing.'

'Does he have more than one mobile?'

'Not as far as I'm aware. But then, I don't keep tabs on what he spends his money on. He may well do. We don't discuss that sort of thing.' He patted a bulge in his pocket. 'You're talking to someone who likes his ten-year-old mobile brick to make calls.'

Another manufactured chuckle.

'Is there anybody else here?' Beck asked. She handed MacReady the job mobile, shifted to the row of plastic chairs, pulled out her notebook and pen as she sat down.

'Just me,' replied Sillitoe.

Beck scribbled. 'Your wife?'

'Left about ten minutes ago. I have a few errands to run before I make my way home. She's just as worried as I am about Dane. More worried, matter of fact.' Sillitoe gestured at Beck. 'You know what it's like, maternal instinct and all that.'

'Not really,' Beck replied without looking up.

'Do you know a man named Gregory Nelms, Scott?' asked MacReady.

'No,' Sillitoe replied. He checked his watch, gave a tiny shake of the head.

'What about Leon King?'

'Other than you mentioning him when you picked Dane up the first time, I've never heard of him.'

'You must have talked about things after Dane was released, surely?'

Sillitoe furrowed his brow. 'You seem to be labouring under the assumption that Dane and I are best buddies who share intimate secrets in pub corners. As you well know, he caused our family a lot of pain during his teens, and some of that hasn't healed. We don't talk much, even now. I gave him this job, he works, I have him close so I can keep an eye on him, but that's it. It seems to be doing the trick.' He looked away. Muttered, 'Or at least I thought it was.'

MacReady flicked his eyes at Beck, saw her knee jiggling, a sure sign she wasn't buying what Sillitoe was saying and wanted to butt in. He turned back to Sillitoe. 'Has Dane talked about the crematorium in Northwood?'

'Of course,' Sillitoe replied. He pulled at the collar of his shirt. 'We do regular business with them. Ferrying families about, moving the dead from hospitals to the crem, whatever's needed. Dane is there a couple of times a week. But then he's at other crematoriums too. So are my other drivers.'

MacReady leaned against the front door. 'Death is big business.'

'We do OK,' Sillitoe nodded. 'You've seen our fleet.'

'We've seen the motors your staff drive,' MacReady said. 'I think it's safe to say you're doing more than OK.'

Sillitoe shrugged. 'Death is big business,' he repeated.

Beck looked up from her notes. 'Do you mind if we take a look around?'

Sillitoe bent and picked up his briefcase and jacket. 'Again? Look, I don't want to be awkward, but shouldn't you guys have a warrant or something?'

It was MacReady's turn to smile. 'You did say you'd help us out.'

'Can you help us out, Scott?' asked Beck. 'We want to avoid as much hassle as you.'

Sillitoe paused for a few seconds, looking from one to the other. Nodding silently to himself. He glanced through the doorway into the main office. Back out to the car park. Checked that expensive-looking watch of his.

'Of course,' he said eventually, evidently frustrated; it came out as a weary sigh. He fished in his pocket, retrieved the bunch of keys and handed them to MacReady. 'But there's nothing here you didn't see on your last visit. So can you make it quick? It's been a long old day.'

'Hasn't it just,' said MacReady. He turned to Beck. 'Where first?'

She stood, shoving the notebook and pen into her jacket. 'Office?'

Sillitoe moved to one side and held open the office door as the job mobile vibrated in MacReady's hands. He checked the screen: Fletcher's number.

'Boss?' he answered.

'Where are you, Will?' Fletcher barked in his ear.

MacReady frowned. Fletcher's voice was ragged, urgent. He heard a siren in the background. Harrison cursing and yelling.

He looked at Beck, walking towards the office door. At Sillitoe, briefcase in hand, irritation in his eyes.

'Scott Sillitoe's place, as ordered,' he replied.

'Plotted up outside?'

MacReady paused. 'Not exactly.'

'Not exactly? What the fuck does that mean?'

'We're talking to him now,' MacReady swallowed. 'Inside.'

Static in his ear. The siren fading in and out. Sillitoe's eyes on him. Beck hovering in the doorway, a quizzical look on her face.

Then: 'Jesus Christ. I told you to stay outside. *Told* you.'

'Sorry, boss –'

'There's been a shooting at the airport. It's fucking carnage there. Three dead. One of them is just a kid, and the APG found him with his guts cut open and baggies of coke lying everywhere. It's drugs, Will. They're bringing drugs into the country by sewing kilos of the shit into their guts.'

MacReady pressed the mobile against his ear, his mouth dry.

'The shooter's driving one of Sillitoe's ambulances,' Fletcher shouted. 'We think he's on his way back there. We're en route, we've got ARVs, but we're ten minutes away. Just get out of there, Will. *Get the fuck out now.*'

The line went dead and MacReady looked at Beck.

'What?' she asked.

He shifted his eyes to Sillitoe.

Said: 'It's you.'

Sillitoe dropped his briefcase to the floor. Backed away from Beck. Eyes flicking between Beck and MacReady: both doors blocked, nowhere to go. He held up his hands as if to surrender.

'Will, what?' asked Beck.

And then Sillitoe's gaze drifted out to the car park.

'Shit,' he breathed. 'You took too long.'

MacReady turned. Saw the black Mercedes Sprinter van kick up gravel as it swung into the car park, *Private Ambulance* in white on its bonnet. Saw the driver's door swing open. Watched the man climb out of the cab, shades perched on his head, heavily tattooed arms dangling at his sides. Saw him look through the window at Sillitoe: hands in the air, pressed against the wall of the reception.

Saw the flicker of confusion, then the look of realisation on the driver's face.

The silver pistol in his right hand. The hand dark red with dried blood.

Beck cried out; MacReady swung around to see her hit the floor, Sillitoe unclenching the fist he'd used to gut-punch her before stepping over her as he ran into the office. MacReady spun back to the door, fumbling at the bunch of keys, the driver advancing towards the building, lifting his arm, the silver pistol clenched in his fingers.

A silver pistol just like the one used at the Garratt shooting.

'*Lock it, Will*,' Beck screamed from the carpet.

MacReady worked through the keys, frantically checking blue tape wrapped around each one – *side shutters, toilets (male), kitchen, garage shutters* – his fingers heavy and stupid and fumbling and then a loud crack, a firework in the car park and the UPVC frame above his head seemed to exhale sharply, to buckle and there was a dull thud behind him and he turned to see a bullet hole in the reception wall.

He cowered towards the floor.

Feeding them around the fob. A dozen keys, more. Hands shaking as he spun through them. And then: *entrance door*. The key. MacReady shoved it into the lock, turned it. Heard the click. Felt his heart drum against his shirt.

Heard another firework. Felt the door shake. Glanced up, saw the spider crack in the window, the small hole at its epicentre. Saw the cord hanging from the ceiling, pulled it. Ducked down as a plastic Venetian blind dropped to cover the window.

He turned to Beck.

Saw her running into the office after Sillitoe.

'Charlie!' he called, but she was gone.

The door rattled, the driver pulling at it from outside.

MacReady scooped up the job phone from the floor and ran.

Through the office, chairs spinning on castors, paperwork blowing from desks.

A door: *Staff Only*. Open, steps visible beyond.

'*Charlie*,' MacReady called again, and sprinted through the door. Took the steps three at a time. Lungs heaving already, back oily with sweat and sucking at his shirt. Behind him: banging noises at the front door of the building, loud and insistent as the driver repeatedly hurled his body at the entrance.

He reached the basement garage. Low light, limousines, blacked-out ambulances, tools and spare tyres and tuning equipment. The pungent stench of engine grease and old diesel spillages. A radio playing quietly, left on by workers long gone, the tune a soothing nineties ballad that did nothing to slow the thump in his chest.

'Sarge?' he breathed.

Beck's voice, barely audible: 'Over here.'

He ran towards it, scuttling low. Found her in an alcove. The wall of girly mag cutouts, of Page Three calendars. Breasts and filthy grins and coquettish looks towards camera. Beck on her haunches beneath them.

'Where is he?' MacReady asked.

She shook her head, breathing rapidly, licking at dry lips.

'You lost him?'

She rolled her eyes angrily. Jammed a hand over his mouth. Placed a finger up to her lips. Let the finger drift away. MacReady followed it, watched it drift downwards, towards the oil-stained floor, to the base of the titty wall.

To the thin strip of light, barely two millimetres thick, that ran the length of it.

MacReady couldn't believe it.

Beck nodded. Lifted the finger again. Lifted another: counting.

Two.

Three.

MacReady launched himself at the wall.

Felt his shoulder connect, was expecting brick but felt metal, the door swinging inwards, faster than he expected, ripping breasts and smiles away from the false wall and throwing him forward into a concealed room. He skittered across concrete, skin raking off the palms of his hands, rolled away to the side and up to his feet. Saw Beck rush in behind him.

The room was compact, brightly lit by a clutch of hundred watters. Breezeblock walls, no skim. Bare concrete floor, pitted and stained and sloping to its centre. A part-clogged drain there, dark and viscous.

Two stainless-steel gurneys, trolleys beside them, a smattering of dirty surgical tools laid on each.

Scott Sillitoe stood between the gurneys, pointing a snub-nosed black pistol at MacReady's chest. His eyes wide and glassy, skin ghostly beneath the harsh striplight.

'This is where you do it,' MacReady whispered. 'Isn't it?'

The pistol trembled in Sillitoe's hands. 'I don't do anything. I'm a businessman –'

'This is where you cut them open. Take out the drugs. They die here, don't they? And Nelms was burning the bodies for you.'

'I'm a businessman,' Sillitoe repeated.

'And death is big business, isn't that right?' said Beck. 'They're fucking *kids*, Scott. *Children*. We found their teeth. Dozens of teeth in Nelms' house. How long has this been going on?'

Sillitoe swallowed, face twitching. The pistol shaking in front of him as he swung it from MacReady to Beck. 'You don't understand *how* big this is. You just don't get it at all.'

MacReady stepped towards him. 'Dane's friend. Jermaine Tate. You got him involved.'

'Jermaine wanted to do it,' Sillitoe whispered. 'Wanted to go to Portugal, bring the stuff back –'

'He volunteered for this madness?'

'He was promised a lot of money for it. A *lot* of money. But he wanted more. Too much, after what he went through. And they wouldn't tolerate it. They killed him within a few hours of him stepping off the plane.'

'We found a torso in the dock, Scott,' Beck said. 'Another one, the same injuries.'

Sillitoe gave a sickly laugh. 'That was a fuck-up. Nelms, he failed to show for work, failed to do what he was supposed to do. They had to do it themselves, then they dumped what was left in the river. You got what was left and Nelms had a kicking for his troubles.'

'The so-called burglary,' MacReady shook his head.

Noticed the banging had stopped.

A squeal from the far end of the garage. MacReady didn't look away from Sillitoe. Knew it was the roller shutters inching their way towards the ceiling. Felt his stomach clench.

Sillitoe blinked. 'He knows the entrance code. He's in.'

'Who are *they*?' Beck asked.

'I'm just a working stiff,' Sillitoe said, voice flat, his eyes bright but not tracking very well. He was lost now, MacReady could see. 'Just like you two. And I've got myself involved in something I wish I could walk away from. But I can't. These people, they don't like loose ends. You saw what they did to Leon King. That was for fucking up with Nelms. King was supposed to kill him.'

'Who are they?' Beck asked again.

'This goes a lot further than you realise,' Sillitoe said. 'It's huge. Bigger than you can imagine. This is just one tiny part of –'

'One of my colleagues is dead because of this.' MacReady inched closer.

'Wrong place, wrong time,' Sillitoe said. 'And the fucker who did it is walking down the ramp as I speak. You need to believe me when I tell you: you have to get out of here.'

MacReady nodded at the pistol. Could see Beck out of the corner of his eye, moving around the other side of the room towards Sillitoe. 'Give me that, Scott. We don't have time. Give it to me and then come with us. We can protect you.'

Sillitoe backed away. Gave a bitter laugh.

'This isn't you,' MacReady said. 'You're a businessman, like you said. Not one of them. You could come onside, give evidence. Help us to stop this. Please.'

The roller shutters went silent. Sillitoe threw a look at the doorway. Back to MacReady, his eyes glittering. Footfalls, getting louder. 'He's coming.'

'The gun,' MacReady rasped, and kicked the door closed. He shifted one of the gurneys against it; next to useless, but it was all he could think of. He turned back to Sillitoe and said, 'Give it to me, plea—'

A blur in the corner of his eye: Beck, rushing Sillitoe. Hands grabbing for his forearms, grabbing for the pistol, a blur of blonde hair and the flash of Sillitoe's expensive watch.

'Wait,' was all he could say, and was about to raise his hands to ward her off, but stopped because there was an explosion in his ears, the gunshot deafening in the confined space of the room, and he shrank into a fearful crouch, hands over his ears and teeth grinding.

Beck continued to wrestle with Sillitoe for a few moments, but it was a strange dance, slow and awkward, as if neither of them had their hearts in it. Then, as if she'd remembered something odd, Beck let go with a mildly irritated expression.

Stepped back and looked down at the bright red bloom at her left hip.

'Ah, damn,' she said, and then her eyes fluttered closed and she keeled over.

'I'm sorry,' blurted Sillitoe, and dropped the pistol. He pushed himself away from Beck's prone body, pushed himself tight into the corner of the room, his face twisted in horror.

'*Charlie*,' MacReady shouted, and ran to her. Turned her over, saw the blood spreading along her trouser leg, her midriff. The pale yellow of her face, the shiver in her arms: shock already. He pressed against the wound, looked to Sillitoe for help but saw it was pointless; he was turned into the wall, sobbing, pleading, asking for his wife.

The door clanged open, the gurney wheeling across to the opposite wall at speed, and Sillitoe whimpered when it clattered against breezeblock.

MacReady swung his neck around.

Placed a hand onto the floor, close to Beck. Held it there, ready.

The driver appeared in the doorway.

Chest hitching. Wiping a bloodied hand against his mouth. He jerked his head from Sillitoe to MacReady to Beck on the floor, taking it in.

'Fucking idiot,' the driver said to Sillitoe, and MacReady noticed the heavy accent.

Noticed the silver pistol as he raised it at Sillitoe.

MacReady scooped up the pistol Sillitoe had dropped; it felt too light in his hand, somehow, not dangerous enough, not powerful enough, but he yanked it from the floor where it had come to rest near Beck's thigh and spun in a crouch towards the driver, extending his arm, the tiny black snub-nose arcing across the room and onto the centre mass of the driver's muscled chest.

MacReady closed his eyes and pulled the trigger.

Another roar in his ears. White noise after it. The thump of his heartbeat in his skull. Tightness in his elbow from the recoil. A sudden feeling of dread: that he'd missed, that he was fucking useless, that the driver was now standing over him and Beck, about to finish her. Finish him. Finish them all.

MacReady opened his eyes to a squint: the driver lay on his back, silver pistol hanging limply from one finger, blood bubbling from his mouth. Muttering something to himself, muttering it over and over as his legs twitched and trainers scraped concrete.

And in the distance, coming down the ramp, ARV officers sweeping the garage with MP5s drawn. The unmistakable outlines of Fletcher and Harrison behind them, framed in sunlight and running.

MacReady threw the gun aside, shifted around, back to Beck. Her eyes closed now, skin on her face so pale as to look blue. Murmuring quietly, making no sense, lips tinged with red, her guts mangled by the bullet. The blood, so much of it. Beck bleeding out right here, in a shitty garage in the shittiest part of the city.

'Come on, Sarge,' MacReady urged, and placed his hand to the entrance wound. Pressed. Leaned on her until she groaned.

Then another gunshot.

MacReady screamed, and instinctively hunched over Beck. Scrabbled around on the floor for Sillitoe's pistol. Hand patting concrete, unable to find it.

Looked up at Scott Sillitoe.

Saw the snub-nose in his hand, a hand that now dropped from the side of his head, limp and useless and with one finger wrapped around the trigger. A fan of blood and skull fragments on breezeblock behind his head.

His eyes, dull balls that rolled upwards into their sockets as he slid down the wall in the corner of the room.

MacReady watched Sillitoe spasm on the floor. Turned back to Beck.

'*Come on, Sarge,*' he urged, but her eyes were open now.

Unblinking.

26

Midnight.

The road slick with November rain, glistening beneath street lights. The Sat Nav on the dashboard guiding him in from the M4: a left off the M32 here, a straight on there, into the guts of the city, into St Paul's, an area he'd never visited before, had heard enough about to never want to visit. Years ago, the scene of riots, of gunfights in broad daylight, the Aggi crew taking on Yardies who were trying to gain a foothold on the Bristol drug trade. Quieter now, the street walkers and muggers gone, the notorious Black and White Café long demolished, the operation more streamlined and professional and low-key.

But bigger.

Bigger than the Cardiff operation. That operation also gone, now.

Gone, like Scott Sillitoe. Weeks ago, that late afternoon in the basement garage, but still raw, still waking MacReady on occasion, the nightmare the same every time. Gunshots. Smoke. Drab concrete and bright splashes of blood. Beck, squirming in agony amongst oil and dust. Nobody had mentioned her during the journey across the bridge into England. MacReady was done talking about it anyway – he'd been served disciplinary papers, endured repeat interviews with Professional Standards, with the IPCC. The investigation: ongoing.

He fed the steering wheel through clammy hands, guided the beat-up CID motor into the car park. The Wellington pub was closed for the night but he heard music playing over the thrum of rain. Beside him Fletcher was sitting with one elbow propped against the passenger window, chin resting on his hand. In the back: Harrison, arms splayed, spread across both seats, breathing quietly.

'Here'll do,' Fletcher said.

It was the first time he'd spoken since the call from Avon and Somerset Police.

MacReady switched off the engine. Checked out into the gloom: police tape and suits and technical staff around a tented sterile area, a sight he was sick of seeing. He drew in a deep breath. Climbed out into cold night air awash with the wax and wane of myriad blue lights. Traipsed after Fletcher. Harrison bringing up the rear, leather satchel over one shoulder.

Soaked by the time they reached the alleyway at the side of the pub. The uniform who lifted the police tape looked them up and down, gave a cursory examination of Fletcher's warrant card. Beckoned them into the cordon with a tilt of the head, jaw working a piece of gum. Behind him drizzle danced in a cone of light from the crime scene arcs.

'Danny?'

The man approaching them was ruddy-cheeked and smiling, thinning hair matted to his scalp with rainwater, a latex-covered hand lifting in a quick wave. Covering his shoes were paper booties, as soaked and filthy as the suit he wore.

Fletcher nodded. 'Sure is.' He pointed at the advancing male. 'DCI Edmunds?'

'Call me Andy, please.' Edmunds lifted his head a little, twitched his eyebrows at MacReady and Harrison. 'Hey, guys. Thanks for coming across. You want to get dressed and come look-see?'

'It's what we're here for, boss,' MacReady said.

'To make sure,' Edmunds smiled. Shrugged when there was no response. 'We heard what went on over there. Nasty business.'

Harrison opened the satchel. 'Just a bit.'

MacReady and Fletcher took turns to reach in and pull out kit: booties, gloves, paper hair nets, face masks. Slipped them on quietly in the thickening rain.

'You coming?' Fletcher asked Harrison.

A shake of the head, hand pulling a crumpled pack of Bensons from a pocket. 'Nah. I'm just the bag man. And I honestly couldn't give a shit if it's him or not.'

Into the inner cordon, fat drops of water falling from tar-black sky, MacReady listening to Edmunds and Fletcher make Job small talk as they walked, the alleyway a narrow channel of high, moss-covered redbrick walls and cracked, puddled tarmac. Its farthest end blocked off by the grimy rear wall of the pub, the scene a tableau of motionless silhouettes backlit by halogen lamps, the figures standing around and staring down into the tent as their breaths gathered in a cloud around them.

MacReady and his companions reached the small patch of waste ground at the dead end. Found beer crates and smashed bottles, mushed newspapers and countless fast-food cartons. The frame of a child's bicycle, tattered Sonic the Hedgehog decals on its rusting paintwork. The moss thicker here, enough to carpet most of the ground, the sun never reaching into this place.

The CSIs and detectives gave them room, downing tools and shifting aside. MacReady, Fletcher and Edmunds formed a line at the edge of the detritus. Quiet for a moment. Still. Staring through the tent flap at the pathetic scene in front of them.

'This your boy?' Edmunds asked.

MacReady tilted his head one way, then the other. Just to be sure. He nodded. 'That's him.'

A single hole in Dane Sillitoe's forehead. Shock on his face, fixed there, rainwater collected in the folds and creases of his skin, his eyes wide, one eyeball askew and bloodshot. That rag-doll look all dead bodies had: limbs at odd angles, seemingly thinner, as if sunk into their surroundings, as if they had partially deflated when life left them.

MacReady thought back to his first day on the team. Of Bob Garratt, lying on the patio in Hodges Square.

It seemed an age ago. A lifetime.

'Never thought I'd say this,' Edmunds muttered alongside him, 'but I preferred the old lot running the drugs here. These new guys, they're . . . brutal, to say the least.'

Fletcher gestured at Sillitoe's corpse. 'You have any ideas?'

Edmunds didn't look up. 'Heard the name Jozo Zecevic?'

Shrugs from MacReady and Fletcher.

'Bosnian,' Edmunds said after a moment. 'Businessman. Salt of the earth type, if you listen to his pals.'

'And if you don't listen to them?' asked MacReady.

'He's a fucking savage.' A tired smile from Edmunds. 'That's what we can get from the handful of people who aren't petrified of even mentioning his name, anyway. Ruthless pretty much sums him up. Drugs, toms, extortion, money laundering . . . Zecevic runs them all in Bristol. And beyond. We think he has fingers in a few cities. Cardiff included.'

'Not any more,' Fletcher said, but MacReady noted the uncertainty in his voice.

Edmunds tilted his head up at the sky, blinked into the downpour. Looked down, pulled his suit jacket tighter around his chest, shivered quietly. Nodded at the corpse. 'Well this sorry spectacle was our one link to Zecevic. And that's gone now.'

MacReady turned back to the waste patch. Mentally filed away the name: Jozo Zecevic. Took a final look at Dane Sillitoe.

Thought: *loose ends.*

27

A cold day, the chill reaching into his bones as he waited and watched the funeral from a distance. It felt right to stay on the margins, given the family blamed him for all that had happened.

The mourners milling and doing their thing beneath pale blue sky. The hugs and awkward smiles and promises of get-togethers that would never happen. Pockets of black clothing, suits and dresses and even a couple of tracksuits, the organ music drifting from the crematorium door and dying on the freezing air. Klaudia Solak, yet to spot him, but hovering on the fringes just as he was doing. The rest of the coming and goings at the crematorium a blur as MacReady clung to the shadow of a colossal conifer and waited.

He tensed as she walked towards him.

Soraya Tate. Slick in a suit jacket and pencil skirt, a slight bulge at her abdomen, her heels clickety-clicking on the pavement, eyes red-rimmed yet face loose and relaxed beneath a veiled beret. As if she had made peace with things. With losing her boyfriend, with his cremation today. And it was not just Leon King: there was Jermaine's fate, her brother's remains yet to be released to the family when they would have to repeat what they had done today. Tate's calm demeanour was all the more remarkable given the press intrusion; MacReady glanced across at the pack of journalists, at Solak again, her fingers brushing and swiping at an iPad, making notes and live-Tweeting her report.

'I saw you when we arrived,' Tate said to him. They were in the shade of a stand of trees on the edge of the main car park. The motorway whooshed and whispered behind them. The city went about its business in front: the constant stream of cars travelling down from the valleys, ferrying people to the big smoke for work, for business, for that shop you simply couldn't find in an ex-coal mining village built below the flanks of a slag heap.

MacReady nodded. 'I didn't know if I should come.'

'You shouldn't have. Leon wouldn't have wanted you here.'

'But *I* wanted to. I wanted to pay my respects. I felt it was . . . the right thing to do.'

Tate looked at him. Looked away to the ground. 'I wanted to tell you.'

MacReady nodded. Thought of the statements Marie and Nathan Brissett – after much cajoling and promises of safety – had provided. That they knew Jermaine was dead all along. Had known since the day he was murdered by the very people who had paid for him to fly to Portugal and have bags of cocaine fed into him. That the bruises and holes in the lounge were not the work of Brissett but of gang members sent to their home to beat them into silence, to shove loaded pistols into mouths, to threaten to rape Soraya and bury her next to her brother.

That they'd beaten Soraya until she agreed to lure King to the maisonette for his punishment.

'I know you did,' said MacReady. He had to stop himself reaching out and touching her arm. People watching them already. Enough for Tate to have to field questions once he was gone.

Tate looked him in the eyes. 'Your lot promised us. Is this over now?'

A National Crime Agency suit had rocked up at the MIR a couple of weeks back, had offered a robotic *thanks for all your hard work guys* before proceeding to shut everything down and transfer it to people who clearly thought they knew – and could do – better.

In truth MacReady didn't know if it was over. And he didn't want to lie to Tate. She'd endured so much already.

'We've done all we can,' he said.

'Is that enough?' she asked, worried.

MacReady turned to look at her. Held her gaze. 'That's all you ever can do, I think. Keep an eye on the small things, fight the small fights, and hope they make a difference.' He looked down at Tate's belly. The slight bump there. 'How far are you along?'

She rubbed at her midriff. 'Just over four months.'

'Such a tiny thing,' he said quietly, and struggled to keep the emotion from his voice.

Tate gave a soft smile. 'But such a good thing. My beautiful son.'

'A boy,' MacReady nodded, and returned the smile. Pictured the young boy they'd found at the airport. Lying on a trolley with Barnard hovering over his tiny frame and poking at what remained. Wondered what sort of life he'd had. The horrors he'd suffered.

Then he thought about Megan. He hadn't seen her since the night she told him she was pregnant. Had been ignoring and deleting her calls and texts and emails. Had spent the last few weeks crashing at cheap hotels, and when the money grew tighter than tight on floors in the nick, on settees that were offered to him. Even Beck's spare room, his Sergeant deep into her recuperation, hobbling about on crutches yet still capable of demanding tea and coffee by the bucketload while she fidgeted and fussed and tormented him – *you useless numbnuts* – about letting her get shot.

And then yesterday the letter.

Lying on top of his in-tray when he'd wandered back to the CID office after lunch. He'd picked it up, nonplussed. Opened it. Had checked around the room when he'd found Megan's handwriting inside the folded paper, her pleas for him to read on. Her apologies, her explanation, which was that MacReady was wrong but right – in a way – and that she would never do anything to hurt him, that there was never anything physical with Stuart. That she had come to a business arrangement with him, paying his brother – MacReady had flashed back to that night where Kirsty had talked of Stuart winning on the bookies – what little money she had saved so he could give them what MacReady couldn't ... MacReady had finished reading and swallowed, staring out of the window with eyes stinging as he thought of her, of his brother, of Solak. Of the godawful mess they were in. His head, reeling with it all. Not knowing what to believe anymore.

Tate looked up at him, watching with narrowed eyes.

MacReady smiled, a tired twitch of his mouth. Nodded slowly, almost to himself.

'Thank you, Soraya,' he said.

She was confused by the tone in his voice.

'I've got to get back,' she said.

Tate hesitated for a moment then walked away, joined the crowd of people outside the crematorium chapel. MacReady watched her go, watched her mingle and offer thin smiles and thank people for their condolences.

Said to himself: 'So have I.'

Dusk as he pulled to the kerb and switched off the engine, the temperature in the gloaming low enough to catch at the back of his throat as he climbed out of the car.

At least, that was what he told himself was the cause.

He hadn't called ahead. Thought it best not to. Thought it best to catch each other cold as the night air which now crept into his collar and made him shiver. No opportunity to talk themselves out of it. No chance for him to bottle it, at least.

Lights on behind blinds and curtains. Her car in the driveway.

MacReady paused at the front door. Took three or four deep breaths, the freezing air metallic on his tongue. Rang the doorbell.

Remembered his conversation with Soraya Tata.

Such a tiny thing . . . But such a good thing.

The door opened and Megan filled his vision.

'Will?' she breathed, hand flying to her mouth.

'Hey, Meg,' he said softly. 'I think we should talk now.'

Acknowledgments

I would like to thank Karolina Sutton at Curtis Brown: a very fine person to have in your corner, and without whose ongoing support, tenacity and hard work this novel would never have seen the light of day. Also Lucy Morris for fielding my numerous inane calls, questions and emails – you deserve a medal.

At Bonnier and Zaffre, massive thanks to Joel Richardson, Kate Parkin, Mark Smith, Emily Burns and the entire team – their energy and enthusiasm is infectious. It has been a pleasure to work together and exciting to see the new venture take flight. Plus: you do an awesome free bar.

Also: David Watson, whose patience and sound guidance helped make the edits painless and the novel leaner and meaner; Molly Powell and everyone at whitefox for those tiny but oh-so-important tweaks to add the final polish; Caroline Ross and Teddy Kiendl for the encouragement, copious bottles of wine and free lodging when the novel was in its embryonic stage; top Hull man Nick Quantrill for his advice and wise words upon reading the first draft; Tony Platt and Liz McNally for support they probably didn't even know they were giving; for the canine stuff – and *that* anecdote – Emma Viant, a fine dog handler and credit to the Job; Helen Higgins and Nigel Hodge, experts in their respective fields and – despite the interruption of a small fire and evacuation of the building – incredibly helpful with the forensic side of things; in perpetuity, the creative writing faculty at the University of South Wales, where all these shenanigans began.

My parents, my sister, my nephew: I love you, and miss you. Get on a plane.

My beautiful wife and children: got there in the end. This is for you guys.